AUTHOR	CLASS
LINDGREN, *Torgny*	F

TITLE Bathsheba   *204596 599*

BATHSHEBA

TORGNY LINDGREN

BATHSHEBA

Translated from the Swedish by
Tom Geddes

COLLINS HARVILL
8 Grafton Street, London W1
1988

William Collins Sons & Co. Ltd
London · Glasgow · Sydney · Auckland
Toronto · Johannesburg

BRITISH LIBRARY CATALOGUING IN PUBLICATION DATA

Lindgren, Torgny
Bathsheba
I. Title II. Bat seba. *English*
839.7'374   PT9876.22.1445

ISBN 0-00-271053-6

First published in Sweden under the title
Bat Seba by P. A. Norstedt & Soners Forlag, Stockholm in 1984

First published in Great Britain
in 1988 by Collins Harvill

© Torgny Lindgren 1984
Copyright in the English translation
© Tom Geddes 1988

Photoset in Ehrhardt by
Goodfellow & Egan, Cambridge

Printed and bound in Great Britain by
T. J. Press (Padstow) Ltd, Padstow, Cornwall

To my children
This story was the first I heard
in my life. Now I have
told it to you.

TORGNY LINDGREN

Shaphan was attendant to King David. He was small in stature but broad across the shoulders and he was a speedy runner; his hair was long, and he played the lyre for the King.

They stood together on the roof of the royal palace. At the very instant the King's gaze fell on Bathsheba, Shaphan too caught sight of her. His eyes were well practised in the art of moving in the same capricious yet calculating way as the King's tiny squinting eyes.

She had come out into the garden behind the houses of the Cherethites and Pelethites. She had bathed and now she was drying herself with a large linen cloth, and her hair was flowing loose. Even Shaphan, who did not yet know the nature of lust, saw at once that she was terrifyingly beautiful. The King's head stretched forward, heavy with desire, as if he were trying to reach her fragrance and and catch the soft sounds of her limbs as they brushed against each other. His breathing was deep and laboured.

The distance of a bowshot, thought Shaphan, without really knowing why. Prepare yourself in readiness, my daughter: forget your family and your home, so that the King may take his pleasure in your beauty. For he is your lord and before him you shall kneel.

'Has she got wings?' said the King. 'Is her head encircled with light?'

'No,' replied Shaphan, who was used to the King asking questions that were not at all obvious or natural to an ordinary person. 'She does not have wings. She is just as you see her in every particular.'

I

'Bring her to me,' said the King. He remained standing in the same position, bent forward, peering intently.

'What shall I say to her?' Shaphan asked.

But the King did not reply; he merely shook his head impatiently, which meant: say whatever you like, say that the King was overcome and faint with the sickness of love when he saw her, say that the King will have her whipped and stoned and burned if she does not come, tell her the truth!

Shaphan took two men from the bodyguard with him. He knew that women despise boys. If she had a man with her in the house, he would perhaps have to have that man slain; if she had a man with her whom she loved, they would definitely have to slay him. The King is like a child, he thought affectionately. He is brimming over with emotions. His heart contains too much warmth and love. He is over thirty years older than I am, and yet I feel sometimes as if he were my child.

This headlong pursuit of holiness.

Bathsheba combed her hair, placed a yellow jasmine blossom at her temple, fastened a gold chain round her neck and dressed herself in a veil and red linen cloak. Shaphan and the two guards waited at the door. She let them wait; she let King David wait.

Finally she came. She turned to the men, whose powerful shoulders were covered with gilded armour, whose swords hung like male organs against their thighs.

'Am I pretty?' she asked, anxiously and without guile.

'You are stunningly beautiful,' Shaphan replied in his absurdly squeaky child's voice.

The King was sitting on the little ivory stool when they came to him with Bathsheba. The leather thongs of the seat creaked as he moved.

He gazed at her for a long time, not merely with desire but also in awe or perhaps in appraisal, just as he had observed the Philistines before the battle of Keilah. She had taken off her veil and wrapped it round her right hand.

2

'What is your name?' he said at last.

'She is called Bathsheba,' said Shaphan officiously. 'Her husband is Uriah, the mighty warrior. The Hittite.'

The King signalled to the guards to leave; he wanted to be alone with her. Shaphan stopped two paces behind Bathsheba: he could see that she was trembling.

'Are you dumb?' the King asked.

'She is not used to talking,' said Shaphan. 'She is a shy and respectable woman.'

'What do you command me to say?' Bathsheba asked.

She raised her head cautiously and looked at him. His coarse, curly hair hung down over his shoulders; he sat leaning forward with his elbows resting on his knees, holding his head out just as birds of prey do – indeed, he resembled a bird of prey.

'Say that it is an unimaginable honour for you to meet the King,' said Shaphan.

'It is infinitely wonderful for me to be face to face with my lord the King,' she said. Her voice was deep, almost a little gruff; the strange lilting tone indicated that she was born in the mountain region to the south, or that her mother came from the south.

'How old are you?' asked the King, and his voice sounded oddly strained and stifled.

'I am nineteen,' Bathsheba replied. 'Uriah bought me from my father Eliam when I was thirteen. He did not know then how pretty I would be.'

'Can you dance?' the King asked.

She tried to meet the look in his half-closed eyes but the slits of his eyes were too narrow; he seemed to be jealously sparing with his gaze, as if it were of inestimable value.

'I dance for Uriah,' she said. 'He drinks wine and I dance.'

'You shall dance for me,' said the King in a thick and husky voice.

So Shaphan fetched his lyre, and took up position against the pillar beside the King's stool. He supported the instrument against his hip, held the triangular frame with his left hand, and beat a slow rhythm on the strings. The music flowed forth from his right hand like a blend of holy oil and the trilling of birds. As he played, he watched the King, the poor, sensitive King. It was clearly apparent that something had happened to him, something had affected him, he was like an animal caught in a trap. Shaphan felt an almost irrepressible desire to go to him and stroke his hair and cradle his head to his breast. The tenderness of his affection felt as if it would choke him.

No, she was no dancer. She moved slowly, almost clumsily, her feet dragging on the cedarwood floor, raised her arms time and again and ran her fingers through her thick, glossy hair, as if she could make it perform the light, soaring dance that she herself was incapable of achieving. Her belly and hips seemed chastely immobile.

But as Shaphan increased the tempo with his right hand and his fingers began plucking more quickly on the plaited camel-gut strings, she at last let her cloak drop to the floor with a swishing sound that seemed to echo from the King's throat and half-open mouth. Shaphan who was the only person able to see the King's eyes and interpret his look, saw him staring intently first at her face and then at her groin, his attention alternating between these two poles: the face covered in a deep blush and the groin in glossy black hair. In the heat and passion of his emotions he seemed to be trying to find a connecting link between the face and the groin, the spirit and the flesh, a means of uniting and fusing them.

Suddenly, with a vehemence caused perhaps by his fear of exploding under the terrible internal pressure, the King shouted at Bathsheba to stop dancing. She stopped at once, panting, with the look of an ashamed yet expectant child, and she lifted her breasts with the palms of her hands, breasts that really needed no lifting.

The King's voice still sounded flat, strained and anguished as he said, 'Have you carried out your sacrifices?'

'Yes, my lord, O King,' she said. 'I believe so.'

Any man that touches anything unclean, thought Shaphan, himself becomes unclean; he shall wash his clothes and bathe himself in water and remain unclean until the evening.

Unclean?

So the King ordered Shaphan as a special precaution to see that two young doves were sacrificed to the Lord; the Lord lived in a tent in the palace garden. He was to buy the doves from the blind bird-breeder at the house of the Phoenicians, and himself take them to the priests. A woman's pudenda can never ever be clean enough.

When they were alone he commanded her to come to him. He bent forward and took hold of her knees and pushed his head in between her helpless thighs as if he were seeking refreshment or warmth or simply protection and security. Thus they remained for a while immobile. She thought that that was perhaps all the King desired, he perhaps had need of nothing more, but then she felt him pressing her backwards with his heavy torso, and she endeavoured to avoid falling by leaning forward quickly. She wanted above all to prevent the King from falling in that contorted and ignominious position. But she was too light, their fall was inevitable, and as they fell he freed his head and turned round quickly so that when they finally hit the floor they were lying side by side, he with his head on her anxiously outstretched arm and she with her eyes and mouth caught up and covered by his rough curly hair. She heard him stripping off his clothes wildly and impatiently, muttering over and over again in his ardour the name of the Lord. The cloth ripped and tore, and already she could smell the odour of his sweat.

At that moment Shaphan returned. He had intended calling to the King that the doves had been bought and that the priests had received them. But now he halted at the door, half hidden by a pillar. I did not manage it in time, he thought. I did not run fast enough, the priests have not yet sacrificed the doves.

Then the King came to her, fast and merciless as if she were yet another enemy to be conquered. He was so heavy and embraced her so hard that she felt the bones bending and almost breaking within her body. When he entered her he cried out in pain, just as if it were he who had been pierced. She strove to submit and bear it; she wanted the King to be able to carry out what he had determined to do, she was merely the object of his unbridled love. That was the nature of love: to be the object of another's love.

She stretched out her hands and pressed them against his hairless, tautly quivering buttocks, exploring the movements of his body with the palms of her hands. King David loves me, she thought, that is why he is doing this. Because he is doing this with me, he loves me.

Finally his mouth opened in a terrible, almost unbearable scream. He screamed as he would scream over a fallen enemy, over a giant or a people with a strange god or a city full of gold and pearls. Then he rolled himself off her, heavy, limp and exhausted.

She heard him immediately begin to speak with the Lord. The sound was a melancholy monotone lament, reminiscent of the songs she had heard from within the tent where the Lord dwelled. A grey but glistening drop of saliva hung in his beard.

When at last he stopped, she said, 'You have been speaking with the Lord?'

'I am always speaking with the Lord,' he replied. 'He is the only one who understands me.'

'What is the nature of the Lord?' Bathsheba asked.

'He is like me,' said King David.

Like me.

And Bathsheba thought of how he had almost crushed her and of his uncontrolled lust.

6

'The Lord is good,' the King said didactically. 'His love is boundless.'

He is like me? thought Bathsheba. What will he do with Uriah? What will happen to me?

'I still do not understand Him,' she said. 'Even if His love is boundless. Love, too, is incomprehensible.'

'Yes,' said King David. 'Even love is incomprehensible. Love is insecurity and uncertainty. The most appalling uncertainty.'

'And that is the nature of the Lord?' said Bathsheba.

'Yes,' said the King. 'That is the nature of the Lord.'

And with his lips against her hair he sang, whispered, murmured one of the songs with which he was wont to entertain the Lord and Shaphan:

O Lord, thou has searched me, and known me.
Thou knowest my downsitting and mine uprising,
thou understandest my thought afar off.
Thou compassest my path and my lying down,
and art acquainted with all my ways.
Thou hast beset me behind and before,
and laid thy hand upon me.
Such knowledge is too wonderful for me;
it is high, I cannot attain unto it.

Shaphan looked upon them. They lay tightly clasped to each other, whispering; he heard their voices but not their words, The King had, only moments before, descended from the heights of his emotions, and now he lay completely still with his lips to the woman's ear. Shaphan would have liked to be lying there in Bathsheba's place. He thought of the unutterable sense of security he would have felt if he had been able to rest his head on the King's arm or had been allowed to offer his own frail and slender arm for the King's heavy head. It was strange that he, a mere boy, could feel like a father to the King, when at the same time he could think of the King as being like a father to himself.

Now King David turned his head and caught sight of him.

7

His eyelids narrowed so that not even Shaphan could see his eyes, not even he, and a violent spasm contorted his face. I must play for him! Shaphan thought. The King's whole demeanour was now completely impossible to interpret: he had withdrawn into his own inscrutability.

'Shaphan!' he cried. 'How long have you been standing there behind that pillar?'

'I have been standing here the whole time,' said Shaphan, his voice trembling with fervour and involvement. 'I saw it all!'

Then the King raised himself up on one elbow and shouted for the guards in a peculiarly alien and strained voice. And as they immediately came running in he screamed at them: 'Take that boy away! Carry him out to the yard and run him through! And gouge out his eyes!'

And the only thought that came into Shaphan's head was:

This too is possible, love is as uncertain as the wind, uncertainty is the only thing there is. It besets me behind and before, it opens the eyes of the blind.

And he turned towards the King. He put his soul in his hands and held it out to him. He could not leave the King without expressing something of all that filled his heart. But he could not get out a single word, not even a whimper.

And Bathsheba said nothing.

After a while, King David rose. He did not look at her; he turned his broad, slightly crooked back towards her as he adjusted his clothes. His movements were slow and careful, as if to show how imperturbable and free of passion he was. His ruddy, bushy hair rested on his shoulders.

Only moments ago they had become almost one flesh; it was his sweat that had moistened and cooled her skin and it was a hair from his beard that had caught between her lips. But now, suddenly, his body seemed so remote that she would not have been able to reach him with even the most anguished cry. He looked as strange to her as a statue carved by a Phoenecian sculptor. She could now scarcely even recognize that he was a human being.

As Bathsheba also rose to gather up her clothes and dress, she imitated, without knowing why, the King's way of moving: she bent her back as if it were weighed down by a kingdom, she moved her feet as if every step demanded a fateful decision, and she raised her arms tentatively and sluggishly, as if they were covered with copper armour.

Suddenly, quite suddenly, the nauseating thought raced through her mind that the King had taken possession of her and that it was he himself now moving inside her body, that she had let herself be filled by him as if she had been an empty, unused vessel. A painful cramp gripped her stomach, and when the King abruptly turned and looked upon her, she bowed her head as if in self-defence, and began with nervously tensed fingers to smooth her loose and tangled hair.

She must not loose control of herself, must not vomit on King David's floor, his cedarwood floor.

But Bathsheba returned to Uriah's house, accompanied by the men with the mighty swords. The King's seed oozed stickily down the inside of her thighs. She thought of the prisoners and the slaves and the conquered warriors with bowed heads, all those whom she had seen being led up the steps to the King's house. Captured, conquered: that was how she felt. The vanquished have no further desires, she thought, no aspirations and no purpose; the vanquished are free of hopes and dreams, forsaken and free. Free to be prisoners.

If she herself did not want to remain in this situation for ever, then she would have to conquer King David.

The rain fell every evening; it was spring, in the month of *abib*. Joab, his men and his mighty warriors were laying siege to Rabbah, the royal city of the Ammonites. Uriah was one of the thirty-seven mighty warriors. The King of Rabbah, Hanun, had shamed the servants David had sent to his coronation. Uriah had been among them. Hanun had accused them of being spies and had shaved off half of their beards, and cut off the lower half of their garments. Therefore the Lord had commanded David to conquer the land of Ammon and to destroy the children of Ammon. Now Joab and the army were camped outside the city walls. They had laid waste and pillaged the land around Heshbon and Medeba in accordance with God's will, they had slain 10,000 men and sent 3,000 slaves to Jerusalem, the city of the Lord, and soon they would storm the walls and crush the city and destroy the Ammonites' god, Moloch, so that he would never again be able to claim that he was the same god as the Lord, whose real name was Yahweh.

'Uriah?' said King David. 'The mighty warrior? The Hittite? Send for him! Send a message to him where he is encamped with the army before Rabbah! Tell his commander Joab that it is the Lord's will that Uriah should come at once to the King in Zion!'

Then he ordered Shebaniah, the trumpeter detailed for holy duties, to go down to Uriah's house, to Bathsheba.

'You shall guard her,' he said. 'You shall watch over her as if you were a shepherd and she were the most precious ewe in all Israel!'

Shebaniah was already out of the room, had already turned round to start running down the stairs, when the King called after him: 'She is not to leave her house. She belongs to me. I have conquered her: she is my prisoner. She is irreplaceable!'

As he heard Shebaniah's footsteps receding, a feeling of emptiness welled up inside him, and he wished he had been in the young trumpeter's place, that he had had to run down to her house and guard her, free of all demands but that of obedience; to see her making herself ready for the night, to carry a cup of water to her bed, to render her captivity manifest by making his bed on her threshold, to hear her trusting breath as she finally fell asleep.

She is the first woman, he thought. She is descended direct from Creation, she has not been deformed by all the births and deaths through which the human race has gone, she has come down direct from the Creator's hand.

Have I perhaps created Bathsheba myself? he thought. Did she perhaps come into existence at the very moment my glance fell upon her? Was it the strength and desire in the light of my eye which gave her substance and formed her out of the air? Is she just a cloud, which will pass and soon disappear?

And he thought of his wives, the fifty-two wives, and all the concubines in the women's house, Abigail of Carmel and

Maachah and Haggith and Eglah and all the others – the smell of their bodies, their murmuring and occasionally shrill voices, their clumsiness and their heavy flesh.

The thought of Ahinoam of Jezreel brought a momentary feeling of sadness. She had borne him Amnon, his first son. She had assisted his other wives when they had given birth to all his other sons. She had never complained if he forgot for a while that she even existed. Her black, glossy hair had turned grey, her left hand had become stiff and almost useless from an unknown disease caught from another of the wives. Only when she helped to deliver one of the others did the hand become briefly usable again. She had lost three of her strong, white teeth, and her upper lip was covered in thick black down. Melancholy and sorrow are like love, he thought. Ahinoam and Bathsheba. The first and the last, security and transience, truth and illusion, satisfaction and hunger.

He felt that he had to speak to someone, and the only one he could speak to was the Lord.

The Cherethites and Pelethites, with their mighty spears and their heavy copper shields borne on straps across their shoulders, followed him out. They thought he was on his way to the women's house to fulfil his kingly duties. They were in the habit of amusing themselves with the slave girls in the great hall on the first floor while they waited for him. The Aramaic slave girls used to dance for them.

But he went not to the women's house but to the tabernacle of the Lord. It suddenly seemed to the guards that he looked rather frail; they gave one another disappointed and meaningful glances. There was nothing to entertain them at the tabernacle of the Lord, except possibly the chance to chance for a while with dice or with the beggars who sat or lay on the gravel outside the forecourt of the tabernacle. If necessary they could even get the beggars to dance.

David spoke with the Lord in the innermost room of the tabernacle, the one that was divided off by a tapestry in red and blue and white, the holy of holies where the ark of the covenant lay. The Lord sat invisible and unfathomable on the seat of mercy beneath the cherubs' wings; the seat of mercy was set upon the ark. Diagonally beneath Him the Lord could see the seven-branched golden candlestick and the Shewbread table with its oilcakes and round cakes and thin unleavened bread.

There too lay the invisible fragrant bread that only the Lord could see and smell, the Shewbread of Shewbread, which the priests, imitating ordinary bakers, kneaded with ritualistic sweeping movements, and with which they performed a baking ceremony at the altar for burnt offerings. Feigned bread, mock bread, imaginary bread, bread baked with nothing but religious ritual.

The smell of the morning's incense offerings and the midday burnt offering was still strong. David had never managed to get used to the heavy sweetness of the smoke; he only knew that the Lord demanded these soporific fumes every day.

He went down on his knees before the ark of the covenant, raised his hands and his eyes towards the seat of mercy, and listened for a moment for the breath and silence of the Lord. Then he began to converse with the Lord, using sentences which he and perhaps the Lord too had long known by heart. He spoke low and carefully, as if to himself, and slowly as if the words were groping their way along a narrow bridge over an abyss. His upturned face was calm and expressionless, almost as it used to be when Shaphan had played for him.

'Lord, rebuke me not in Thy wrath,' he said, 'neither chasten me in Thy hot displeasure. For Thine arrows stick fast in me, and Thine hand presseth me sore. There is no soundness in my flesh because of Thine anger; neither is there any rest in my bones because of my sin. For mine iniquities are gone over mine head: as an heavy burden they are too heavy for me. My wounds stink and are corrupt because of my foolishness. I am troubled; I am bowed down greatly; I go mourning all the day long.

'For my loins are filled with a loathsome disease.

'I am feeble and sore broken. I have roared by reason of the disquietness of my heart. Lord, all my desire is before Thee. My heart panteth, my strength faileth me; as for the light of mine eyes, it also is gone from me.'

He knew that the Lord esteemed, indeed was even greedy for, humility and lamentation. The Lord liked to see man as he really was. As he spoke he lowered his voice to a whispering sibilance rather than speech; he did not want the Lord to hear how strong and demanding his spirit actually was. The lamps of the seven branches of the candlestick illumined him from the side so that half his face lay in shadow, highlighting the sharp, bold, manly, but reverentially submissive aspects of his figure. That was the way he wanted the Lord to see him.

'To Thee, O Lord, I lift up my soul,' he continued. 'In Thee I put my trust; Thou art my God: do not destroy me! Do not let mine enemies rejoice in my defeat! Return, O Lord, deliver my soul: oh, save me for Thy mercies' sake. For in death there is no remembrance of Thee: in the grave who shall give Thee thanks?'

He did not hesitate to speak thus to the Lord: 'In the grave who shall give Thee thanks? Be not silent to me as Thou art to those who are already buried!'

Now his face was no longer calm. Even in the pale, slanting light of the lamps it was apparent that the skin on his high cheekbones was quivering and that weighty thoughts were furrowing his brow. He must come to the point, he had completed the necessary measure of eloquence, he would have to be completely honest, yes, even contradict himself – the Lord wanted to know the truth. And now his voice could be heard no longer, but his words would be audible even though unvoiced.

'Bathsheba,' he said. 'I have already possessed her and I wish to own her for ever. Lord, with mine inner eye I can see Uriah making love to her, and it is not to be endured. The bones in my body are powerless. I have sunk into a deep pit which has no bottom. Why didst Thou place Bathsheba within my sight? Why didst Thou pierce her with the light of mine eye? Why hast Thou punished me with such suffering? Why hast Thou cast me far down into the murky darkness to which only the black goat goes? Let me remain free, let me remain King. I can see Uriah, O Lord: he takes her nipples between his lips, he sucks at the damp sweetness of her groin, his rough hands and fingers press into her flesh. It is insufferable, he devours her as a wolf devours conies! When he returns from the destruction of Ammon he will bed her again and again, he will drool over her and assault her frantically as if he would kill her! That is how men are when the battle is done! O Lord, love is terrible, it is more deceitful than evil itself, it is created by the Corrupter and the angels of the bottomless pit, it gushes forth like the waters of the flood!'

The King was no longer using his voice at all, he had forgotten that he had a voice, and yet he was shouting; the pain distorted his face and he was shouting what for him was the self-evident truth: 'Lord! What shall I do with Uriah? Why dost Thou command me to kill Uriah? Uriah must die, I hear Thy voice inside me; I am to have him slain, I am to proffer him as a sacrifice and call for Thy blessing on him! Thou shalt deliver me, O Lord!'

His face became calm again, the violent tension seemed to loose its grip on him, he no longer heard the voice that called within him, and he ended his conversing before the seat of mercy in a quiet and dignified manner, his voice once more regally cool and moderated.

'O Lord, empty and transient are we mortals, we move through life like fleeting dream images. My hope lies in Thee: I am a stranger whom Thou hast taken into Thy care. Thou givest me joy in my heart, a greater joy than that of others when Thou givest them grain and wine in abundance. I will both lay me down in peace, and sleep: for Thou, Lord, only, makest me dwell in safety.'

*   *   *

15

Shebaniah made his bed at Bathsheba's threshold with two goatskins from the tabernacle of the Lord. She did not speak to him: she realised that the King had sent him. When she had returned to her house she had suddenly begun to tremble with weakness, perhaps even fever. All she wanted to do was to lie down on the flagstone floor as if there were an earthquake; she was shaking just as if the earth was moving beneath her. But she supressed the panting of her lungs and the feeling of weariness in her limbs, and, with an effort that caused her heart to ache and her eyes to dim, she performed her toilet in an outwardly calm and normal manner, combed her hair and made herself ready for the night.

That is the kind of woman I am, she thought. I cannot simply get straight into bed.

When Shebaniah saw that she had lain down on the bed and pulled the cover over herself, he went to the water jug behind the door and filled a little clay cup with fresh water to set on the floor at the head of her bed. When he came up to her he saw that her body was convulsed with silent sobs and that her face was hidden under the bedcover just as a dead person's face might be covered. He stood there irresolutely with the cup in his hand: He ought to do something, there must surely be something the King would expect him to do. It should obviously be his duty to warn her against violent emotions and harrowing thoughts and feelings. She had not heard him come; she lay alone, forlorn and helpless under the bedcover.

After hesitating at some length about the right course of action, he bent over her and raised the cover from her face. He had expected her cheeks to be suffused with tears and her mouth to be contorted with sobbing. But her skin merely glistened with a slight perspiration and she met his gaze with wide, surprised, dry eyes. She seemed to want him to say something.

'I know how it is,' Shebaniah said uncertainly. 'I too am a chosen one. My parents handed me over to the priests on the

16

same day that the ark of the Lord was taken to Jerusalem from the house of Obed-edom. My parents selected me as a thank offering.'

'Chosen one?' said Bathsheba, hesitantly.

'We chosen ones must understand one another,' said Shebaniah. 'I sound the trumpet at the entrance to the tabernacle of the Lord and before God's seat of mercy. When my hair has reached its full length and my throat is completely covered by beard, I shall be set apart for my life's work in the tabernacle of the Lord. They will anoint my right ear lobe and the thumb of my right hand and the big toe on my right foot with blood from a ram, and ordain me as a priest.

'If I am not chosen before then for something else,' he added.

He had a vague presentiment that the duty the King had now given him might lead to selection for some other purpose.

'Chosen one?' Bathsheba repeated. Then she asked, 'Why are you here?'

'The King has sent me.'

She looked at him. His beard was still sparse and downy, his forehead smooth and shiny, and his eyes as large and trusting as those of a child. His nose was small and pointed; his sleek, dark brown, almost black hair was combed to the sides, covering his ears. He smiled at her anxiously, appealingly, questioningly, his deep red lips pouting slightly. His clothes exuded a faint, musty odour of incense and spirituality.

'But why did he send you?' she asked. 'A trumpeter of the Lord?'

'It is my duty to guard whatever is holy,' he said.

'Holy?' said Bathsheba doubtfully, almost to herself. 'What is holy here in Uriah's house?'

'You.'

'Am I holy?'

'You are chosen,' said Shebaniah. 'It is in the King's power to choose what shall be holy. And even that which is not holy at

17

the moment of being chosen is gradually transformed by its association with the kingly, and becomes holy.'

She felt her body relaxing as Shebaniah looked at her and talked to her. She was no longer panting and sniffling. Perhaps it was in his goodness that King David had sent him to her.

'Is King David holy?' she asked.

'Yes,' Shebaniah replied. 'He is the Lord's Anointed. The prophet Samuel from Raamah chose him on the instruction of the Lord. The holiest of all living creatures is the Lord God, but next after him in holiness comes the King.'

'And I?' said Bathsheba. 'How can I, a simple woman, be holy?'

'Anything can be holy. The copper vessel in the tabernacle of the Lord, and the trumpet that I blow, and the King's sons, and the priests sandals. Everything depends on being chosen. Everything that is chosen is holy. And that which is chosen to be the highest is the holiest of all.'

When he spoke excitedly the corners of his mouth became moist. He was pleased at being able to teach Bathsheba.

'Anything that is chosen to be sacrificed is also holy.'

'Give me the water,' she said.

He handed her the cup and she drank, supporting herself on her left elbow. Then she gave him back the empty cup and lay down again and was silent. Shebaniah saw from her face that she still had much to ask and that there were still traces of fear and confusion. Why was she frightened? Was it because she found herself in King David's power? We are all in somebody's power!

One can also be chosen to live through the life of another.

Or was it holiness that frightened her?

'The Lord is exalted over all people,' Shebaniah went on, trying to think of something more to say. 'His glory reaches beyond the heavens. Yes, who is like the Lord God, He who sits so high and sees so deep, who indeed either in heaven or on earth? He who raises up mankind out of the dust, and lifts up the beggar from the dunghill and sets him among princes?'

When Bathsheba uttered the question that she had been keeping back the whole time, her voice was trembling and uncertain. 'What will he do to Uriah?'

'Who?'

'The King. King David.'

Shebaniah did not reply immediately. He would have to think about what the King's will might be in this particular case. He realized that Bathsheba required him to answer on the King's behalf.

'Do you love Uriah?' he asked.

'Love?'

'I know of no other word for that difficult question.'

'I belong to him,' said Bathsheba.

'You did belong to him,' Shebaniah corrected.

'Perhaps I have been in love with the knowledge that I belonged to him,' she said hesitantly. 'That in any event I belonged to someone.'

And then Shebaniah answered her question truthfully: 'Either he will act with mercy,' he said, 'in which case he will raise him to be a leader among the Aramites. Or he may act with wisdom. Then he will return you to Uriah and forget you. Or he may act cunningly and shrewdly. Then he will have him slain.'

Bathsheba's hands had turned white and cold; she pulled them down under the covers to warm them against her thighs, and felt the muscles contract with the cold.

'And how do you think he will act?' she asked, her voice beginning to shake suddenly as if she were shivering. A chill went through her when she realized it was for her own sake she was asking, and not for Uriah's.

'I do not know how he will act,' Shebaniah replied cautiously. 'One can know nothing for certain. But holiness has made King David very cunning and shrewd.'

He could not think of any more compassionate way to say it.

'Holiness is an incomprehensible quality,' said Bathsheba,

her teeth chattering. 'It seems its consequences and effects can result in anything at all!'

'The products and manifestations of holiness can never be foreseen,' said Shebaniah.

'But why is life itself not holy?' Bathsheba asked suddenly and almost desperately. 'If copper vessels and anointing oils and priests' sandals can be holy, man's life should also be holy! The holy spirit which is in man!'

She went on, 'Even if you violated me as warriors violate the women of the vanquished, I would not be able to take your life!'

Shebaniah felt a warm glow of pride when she mentioned that possibility: that he might violate her.

Then he considered the strange question about the sanctity of life. He had never asked himself this question, he had never heard it asked, so he hesitated a moment before answering.

'Holiness is cruel and inhuman,' he said at last, 'slow and yet relentless. It is blind, it pays no regard to human beings and their fleeting lives. It is like the bird-catcher's snare or the plague.'

'So nothing is sacred for holiness?' asked Bathsheba, in a tone of subdued resignation.

'That is so,' said Shebaniah.

They were silent. There seemed nothing more to say. Shebaniah stood with the empty cup in his hand. Bathsheba looked past him with wide-open eyes, as if she were trying to capture with her gaze the remote incomprehensibility of which they had been speaking. Finally she put one last question to him: 'How, then, has King David become so holy?'

And Shebaniah had an answer even for this:

'Being chosen, and priestly unction and blessing have made him holy. And the potent warmth of the hands of Samuel the prophet. But above all, of course, it is his own strength and power that have made him holy. Strength and power beget and engender holiness. Every heroic feat he has accomplished, every war he has won, every city he has laid waste, every people he has annihilated, each of these things has made him more holy!'

Now Shebaniah paused in profound thought. 'That is why,' he continued, 'we men lust after power. Power makes us holy before God and before mankind.'

Yes, that is what he said: 'We men.'

'Until ultimately a man has no equal on earth, and above him there remains only the Lord of the heavenly hosts.'

Then they talked for a while about the nature of sleep, of which they now had need as they lay there with drowsy eyes. Shebaniah told her she should sleep for the sake of her beauty: if she were to lose Uriah she could not afford to lose her beauty too. And Bathsheba did not notice the depressing remark about Uriah because the mention of her beauty was so comforting and uplifting to hear.

And that very night Bathsheba knew that she was pregnant. She felt the King's seed rising and swelling in her body; in her dreams her breasts grew into giant pumpkins; and she felt the unborn, newly-conceived son sucking as he rested against her arm and ribs and the damp, warm skin of her belly.

And when morning came, even before the morning watch, she sent Shebaniah up to the King's house with the message: Bathsheba is with child, she shall bear a son.

When his communion with the Lord was over, King David returned to the royal palace. He sat with his sons Amnon and Absalom, who would soon be men, and Mephibosheth with the club foot, and ate a roasted lamb. During the whole meal he uttered not a single word.

The King had been a shepherd: in his childhood he had watched over his father's sheep, all thousand of his father Jesse's sheep on the hills between Tekoah and Bethlehem. He still slept outside on some nights to keep alive in himself the tender and generous spirit of the shepherd. Behind the royal palace a section of the field had been kept for that purpose. He slept under a cover of goatskin on the bare earth, watched over by twelve Cherethites. After every such shepherd night, Asaph the Levite, leader of the temple choir, would have to be summoned, since only he could convince David the shepherd that he really was King David. Although David had been the lowliest of Jesse's sons, the eighth and last, the Lord had chosen him and raised him up; he was the King of Zion, he had himself conquered the mountain and royal castle of Zion. The black night in which he had slept like an animal on the ground was over, and he was again the Anointed One, he was risen from the pit of death.

There was a special song for this awakening, composed by the King himself; the temple choristers would sing and read it with their arms outstretched towards the pale pink brightening sky:

> The King shall joy in Thy strength, O Lord;
> And in Thy salvation how greatly shall he rejoice!
> Thou hast given him his heart's desire
> And hast not withholden the request of his lips.
> For Thou preventest him with the blessings of goodness:
> Thou settest a crown of pure gold on his head.
> He asked life of Thee, and Thou gavest it him,
> Even length of days for ever and ever.
> His glory is great in Thy salvation:
> Honour and majesty has Thou laid upon him.
> For Thou has made him most blessed for ever:
> Thou hast made him exceeding glad with Thy countenance.
> For the King trusteth in the Lord,
> And through the mercy of the most High he shall not be moved.

It was thus that he spent that first night after the first meeting with Bathsheba, out of doors with only a thin covering between himself and the darkness of the heavens. The ground was still damp from the rain. When he was awakened in the morning by the trumpet blasts from the forecourt of the tabernacle of the

Lord and saw the temple choristers coming towards him from the portal of the royal palace, he found that his thoughts had clarified and grown more profound, as if they had been refined by sleep. He now knew at once what he should do about Uriah.

But first he sent for his scribe.

The scribe had been found in Jerusalem when David had conquered the city. He knew the holy signs for four different languages, and wrote with a stylus on clay tablets. The object of writing was to reduce the transience of words.

What was written remained the property of the speaker. It was hidden in a compartment in the floor, and was never put to use. It existed, which was enough.

Sometimes the King made his scribe write down a song that he had composed. The clay tablet was then dispatched with a servant to the temple choir so that the words were preserved in the tabernacle of the Lord, before the face of the Almighty.

With the scribe the King was compelled to speak slowly, every word had to be the result of a decision, and that perhaps was the scribe's true role – to check and restrain the flow of thoughts, to open the words one by one so that the speaker was forced to look into them, just as the mussel fisherman peers into the opened shell of the mussel.

The object and significance of writing was the act of writing itself.

The scribe had had his tongue cut out, a simple security measure by his former owner. King David saw a deeper meaning in this excision: the scribe should be completely pure in his capacity of writer. Words should never be able to come from his lips, but only from his hand.

Scribe, write this about Shaphan:

Shaphan is dead.

I, King David, loved him as dearly as my own life, his heart was joined to mine own heart. He was like an apple tree among the trees of the desert.

He shall be buried in Hebron. Three hundred men and 100 mourning women shall accompany him; they shall tear their clothes to rags and lament for three days, and I shall myself walk behind the bier; I shall wail and whimper like an abandoned child. We shall make his grave under the tamarisk tree, next to the mighty heroes of Hebron.

My God, my God, why didst Thou not let Shaphan live!

He dwelt with me as once did I, in my youth, with King Saul. He played for me when my heart was heavy, as I used to play for King Saul when Thine evil spirits possessed him, O Lord.

Why didst Thou not hold out Thine almighty hand over Shaphan and save him? Twice King Saul tried to kill me as I played my harp, twice he chased me with his spear to pierce my heart and pin me to the wall, but I dogged as I played, and played as I fled; I well remember how agonizingly difficult it was.

But Shaphan did not flee, he did not dodge, he went to his death with open eyes. Open eyes, which were then gouged out.

Thou didst spare me but sent Shaphan to the realm of death.

Was it for Bathsheba's sake he had to die?

It was for Bathsheba's sake he had to die.

Scribe, this you must write down forcefully: Bathsheba is the guilty one – she brought about Shaphan's death.

His death rests upon her slender shoulders. She will never be able to cast off her guilt; she will remain guilty her whole life long. She sinned by letting herself be seen at the very moment of her selection.

Shaphan saw her loosened hair, her dove-like breasts, her funny little navel, her dancing feet with their shining soles, her thighs, which are like bottles of wine, he saw the unclean slits and openings in her body. Because he saw all that and saw that it was holy, he had to die.

Who shall play for me now when Thou sendest Thine evil spirits to me, O Lord?

Shaphan had four brothers, older than himself, who are now fighting at Rabbah under Joab. A message shall be sent to them so that they can lament his death and sacrifice an immaculate she-goat for his sake, as a sin offering.

Now is his name Rephaim, which is: he who does not exist. Or: he who in his likeness to a shadow scarcely exists.

Blind, bloodstained and non-existent.

The Lord placed his life in His sling and hurled him towards the setting sun, to the land in the west. To the empty, hollow nowhere, the deepest chamber, the subterranean cave, the blackest darkness; to murky chaos, the abyss of destruction, the land of forgetfulness; to eternal sickness and disintegration.

It was in King Hadadezer's city, Berothai, that I, King David, first saw Shaphan. He was seven years old. He was standing at the door of his father's pillaged house, that was how I found him. Inside lay his sisters and his mother and father whom my soldiers had slain; his brothers had been taken prisoner. His face was covered in tears. His twin sister Achsah also lay slain within. I bent down to him – and to this very day I do not know why he had been spared – took his little head in my hands and comforted him, saying: 'It is God who has done this.'

And he raised his eyes towards me and asked, in such a childlike, trembling and fearful manner that my heart began to throb and ache: 'What is the nature of God?'

And I answered him: 'He is mighty. He is mightier than life and death together. He is so powerful that we may not even express His real name.'

'Is God then not his name?'

'No,' I replied. His true name is not God. But that is what we call Him.'

Alas, O God, how wretched and terrified and beautiful he was. He was like Bathsheba: he was like a sparrow caught in the bird-catcher's trap, his eyes were as wide and open and innocent as Bathsheba's. His cloak hung in tatters from his shoulders. The sweat of his fear smelled like a woman's – yes, he smelled like Bathsheba.

He was not yet circumcised, since his father was a Canaanite, so I had him circumcised. It was I who gave him his name, Shaphan. And I sacrificed a year-old lamb for his sake, just as if I had been a midwife. And then I brought him here, to my city, the city of David; then, truly, I owned him.

All he brought with him was a rattle, a moulded copper rattle that his first father had made for him.

Scribe, write this: His rattle shall be buried with him beneath the tamarisk tree.

It lies beneath his pillow in the little chamber in front of the hall of the Cherethites and the Pelethites, it lies in a box of embossed silver, a box which I gave him.

Now I can speak no longer.

I weep. My soul is clothed in mourning for my servant Shaphan. Let not the flood of bitterness and grief drown me, O Lord. I have eaten gall and drunk vinegar for my thirst. The chariots of God are ten thousand as He advances. But Shaphan's own lyre, the little harp, that we shall save, that can still give pleasure. Do not forsake me, O Lord: do not remove me from Thy sight, let me rest in Thy hands and not in the sling of Thy fierce wrath. *Selah.*

Uriah rode through Gilead towards Jerusalem. He was not a
natural horseman, but Joab had given him one of the Egyptian
steeds. The King had summoned him: he could not delay. His
heavy legs thumped against the horse's flanks as he jolted up
and down in the saddle, hunched forward over the withers. The
horse was weary and its head drooped and swayed in front of
him, its pointed ears flopping sideways like an ass's ears. Uriah
squinted towards the silvery light. He had just crossed the River
Jordan at one of the fords outside Bethabara, and was now
riding uphill out of the valley. He could still feel the freshness of
the water on his feet. Before him he could see the mountains.

He was alone, and was avoiding the villages and towns. His
sword lay in front of him across his thighs, and his short spear
and shield were held by leather thongs across his back. He ate
his meals on horseback, with difficulty, swaying unsteadily. His
supply of food hung in a leather bag against the horse's withers:
dry roasted meat and raisin cakes.

He did not know why the King had sent for him. He was not
one of the greatest warriors, he would never be a captain.
Perhaps he was to be put in command of the royal palace guard
or of the prison guard in Zion; perhaps he was to be rewarded
for some great and beneficial feat that he had performed without
realizing it; perhaps he was to be disciplined, punished for some
evil or treacherous act he had unknowingly committed.

He had been one of King David's followers ever since he had
become King of Hebron, for those seven years and the countless
years in Jerusalem since then. He had taken part in the slaughter

of the 360 men at Gibeon. He had fought at the King's side against the Jebusites. He had been one of the first to storm into the conquered city of Zion. He had sat with the King in the valley of Rephaim and had listened to the sound of the Lord's footsteps in the tops of the mulberry trees. Yes, they had sat in the warm darkness and heard God go out before them into battle – their God, who on that occasion had without the slightest doubt justified the appellation 'Almighty'. They had heard Him walking in the treetops over the strong and impenetrable branches; had it not been for the darkness they would have been able to see the soles of the His feet. And he had been present when David and Joab conquered the Philistines at Baal-Perazim. And he had assisted the King and Joab when the defeated Moabites were taken prisoner and subdued at Kir-Moab. He knew better than anyone else in the army the secret of the power of numbers. He was the most reliable when separating the wheat from the the chaff: the vanquished were measured with a line – the King cast them to the ground, and with two lines measured those to be put to death and with one full line those who were to live.

King David.

Uriah thought about him, anxiously and affectionately. Over the years the King had become even stranger, increasingly remote. He himself no longer took part in his wars; he sent out his army and his warriors to attack cities and peoples, but he stayed in Jerusalem. Wars no longer seemed to give him any pleasure: they were mere necessities. He composed songs, begat children, and communed with the Lord God. It was said that he was of Philistine blood, that the blood of the enemy ran in his veins – where else would he have got his red hair and fair complexion? He had always alternated between gentleness and cruelty, love and hate, the music of the lyre and the trumpet of war. Sometimes his mercy knew no bounds; sometimes his bloodlust was unquenchable. Perhaps his dubious origins were the cause of his vacillating character: he bore his own enemy within himself. Some of the odd numbers could be very fateful. That too might explain his insatiable desire for justice. He was aware of the dual nature of all existence, he knew that good and evil were indivisible, but that they nevertheless must be separated, that truth and lies were always intertwined like the weaver's thread, but that they must be unravelled for the sake of the divine order. He knew that the love of justice, which the Lord had set in man's breast, was partly a desire for goodness, partly a desire for evil, but always separately, never simultaneously, that the love of justice was from the beginning a horror and loathing of this indivisible duality.

Of one thing Uriah was certain: whatever King David had in store for him, it could be nothing but justice.

There had at times been a muttering and a murmuring in the army, especially among the men from Judah and among the officers, that the King, too, should be subject to justice: such as the occasion when he had Ish-Bosheth's murderers executed and their hands and feet chopped off, and had them hung up at the pool in Hebron – after all, Ish-Bosheth had been King Saul's heir, and the men who had eliminated him had thought that they were serving King David in the best way possible – or when he took Jonathan's lame and club-footed son Mephibosheth into his house. Or when he had all the Philistines' good, useful gods burned to ashes; or when he had 1,500 horses hamstrung after conquering King Hadadezer – horses which might even have been holy! But nobody had ever attempted to carry out that most unthinkable of all acts of justice, since to touch the man anointed by the Lord demanded a degree of courage and madness that none of the mighty warriors had yet managed to summon. All the individual acts of justice had merged and become indistinguishable; they had fused together into one all-embracing and inviolate, even divine, justice.

Nevertheless, it occurred to Uriah's tired and sluggish mind that his commission might be to dispatch the King with the sword of justice: even that was not unthinkable. He would carry out whatever had been assigned him; life was but a discharging of duties. Uriah's profession had always consisted of fighting, plundering, capturing, and then discarding what had been won, leaving it for others, giving it to the beggars, casting it into the river, and moving on, ruthless and indifferent. He would never resist his lot.

He also thought of Bathsheba, his body thought of her; if the King permitted, he would sleep with Bathsheba.

Of all holy numbers, two is the holiest of all: it is the number of love, of creation, of woman's breasts and of the loins.

When he reached the first ridge he raised his head and looked upon the world. The sunlight streamed like rain through the transparent trees, and in the olive grove ahead of him he could see the movements of a group of women in flame-red garments. The mountains were united with the heavens in a shimmering haze that reminded him of the sea – he had once glimpsed the sea from a hill in Japho. The awe-inspiring, incomprehensible beauty of existence filled his heart.

Even the number thirty-seven is awe-inspiring and beautiful. Three times thirty-seven is 111. Twelve times thirty-seven in 444. Twenty-seven times thirty-seven is 999.

Lord, our Lord, how glorious is Thy name!

He straightened himself and moved his heavy sword a little further up his thigh. The sun glinted on his scarred, fire-scorched, ruddy face; his gaze turned towards Jerusalem, the city of David. He had no particular expectations. The head of his horse drooped and swayed in front of him, he felt ill at ease and apprehensive, he was full of hope.

Women need a well to gather round.

So the King had a well dug and constructed of stone in front of the palace, on the hill that led to the tabernacle of the Lord. It was a well without water, an artificial well; the real water ran in the subterranean channel from the spring of Gihon to Zion, and the Gihon water was carried in barrels to the houses, a task for slaves and servants. The women's water, the mock water from an empty well, was carried in light clay pitchers with leather thongs; it was water that did not exist.

The women gathered at David's well when the day began to cool. It would always be so, throughout all eternity.

When Uriah reached the well, he stopped. It was expected of all travellers from afar that they should stop for a moment by the closed circle of whispering and gossiping women as if waiting to be offered a cup of fresh water, and sometimes they really were given a cup of mock water to pretend to drink.

But as Uriah came up, the women fell silent and turned away from him. They bent their heads towards the well; they wanted nothing at all to do with him, not even to look at him. He could see that Bathsheba was not there; despite the fact that there were more than a hundred women, he saw that she was missing, and he realised that they knew something about Bathsheba that he did not know. All the women who were not undergoing their monthly purge were gathered at the well.

The women were forbidden to drink water from David's well during their monthly cleansing.

The Cherethites keeping watch on the roof had seen him

coming, and now one of the unarmed doorkeepers came running up and took hold of the horse's bridle and led him to the palace steps. Uriah climbed down from his horse, ponderously and clumsily. He had to catch hold of one of the straps beneath the horse's belly to stop himself falling, and he swayed as if he were giddy: his legs had gone numb from sitting so long in the saddle. He stamped his heavy feet on the gravel to set the blood flowing again or perhaps to reassure himself that he could still stand upright like a man. Then he went in to the King.

In the hall outside King David's room he met Mephibosheth, the club-footed, the grandson of King Saul, the royal cripple who had to eat every day at the King's table.

'What mood is he in today?' whispered Uriah.

'He is cheerful,' Mephibosheth whispered in reply. 'He has eaten a ram's heart and drunk a cup of wine, he has spoken with his scribe, and now he is sitting at the window, waiting for you.'

And Uriah went in to the King and fell to his knees before him and pressed his rough forehead to the polished cedarwood floor. He was filled with a confusion of feelings: the soldier's haughty pride and the loyal subject's foolish sense of self-contempt.

'Get up,' said the King. 'You need not crawl on the floor like an infant.'

His tone of voice implied: Even by crawling in the dust no one can escape the fate decreed by the Lord.

'I wished only to greet you as one ought to greet one's king,' said Uriah, rising with difficulty.

And the King pointed to a stool on which Uriah could sit.

'I see that you are playing your flute, O Lord,' said Uriah.

'I am not playing,' said the King. 'I am simply holding it in my hand. Then I hear the tunes within myself.'

'My hearing is not what it used to be,' said Uriah, as if wanting to explain to the King why he never heard any tunes within himself.

'And how are my men faring at Rabbah?' the King asked. He

asked in an uninterested tone: he already knew as much as he wanted to know about the siege.

'A siege is a siege,' Uriah answered.

'Yes,' said the King, 'a siege is a siege.'

And Uriah thought of Bathsheba, who had not been down at the well. What does he want of me? he thought.

'And Joab?' asked the King. 'What is Joab doing? How does he intend to go about it?'

He knew all there was to know about Joab.

'He is waiting,' said Uriah. 'Joab is very skilled at waiting. There is none among all the generals who can wait as he can.'

'Yes,' said David. 'I know him.'

And he went on: 'He is my nephew, we have the same blood in our veins, if blood can be the same. It is impatient but cautious blood, it flows restlessly but is also constantly waiting.'

'We often wonder what it is that Joab is waiting for,' said Uriah.

'What do you yourself think?' asked the King.

Uriah hesitated for a moment with his answer. But then he declared vehemently, almost accusingly: 'I believe he is waiting for the great madness. He is waiting until one of the men is seized by madness and attacks the city walls, alone, ahead of all the others.'

'Yes?' said the King.

'An outburst of crazed impatience can have very beneficial results,' said Uriah. 'An intense mad rage on the part of a single soldier can be as powerful and devastating as an attack with a thousand horses and chariots.'

'So that is what you believe,' said the King thoughtfully. 'That Joab is waiting for an outburst of holy madness.'

'It need not be holy,' Uriah murmured, as if to say that normal human madness could be quite adequate.

'All madness comes from the Lord,' said King David didactically. 'The Lord send His spirits to us. It is the spirits which make us mad. Even holiness is a form of madness.'

Uriah had nothing to say about holiness. And he asked himself again: Why has he sent for me?

'Without holy madness no wars would be won,' the King continued. 'Without holy madness wars would hardly even begin.'

'Why have you called me here to Jerusalem?' asked Uriah.

But the King did not reply. He raised the little cedarwood flute to his lips and blew a single, shrill, drawn-out note, as if trying with this absurdly diminutive wooden pipe to mimic the mighty call of a battle-trumpet. The smell of burning entrails and meat and birds' feathers wafted in through the window from the tabernacle of the Lord below.

And Uriah repeated his question: 'Why have you called me here to the city of David?'

'Why do you ask that question?' said David. And he added, 'The word "why" sounds strangely weak and childish from the lips of a soldier.'

'You taught me it yourself,' said Uriah. 'I have heard you sing it to the Lord thy God: "Why art thou cast down, O my soul? And why art thou disquieted in me?" '

'A mighty warrior such as you,' said the King, 'a mighty warrior such as you should never ask questions. It was by not asking questions that you once became one of my mighty men. If you start to wonder and question, you will soon be an ordinary man among all the others, and will fall like thousands of others, and your mouth will be sealed with the only conclusive answer there is, the only answer which refutes all questions. A mighty warrior such as you, Uriah, obeys orders without hesitation. If there were not all this hesitation in men's hearts, the world would be full of mighty warriors.'

King David spoke fervently, the words flowing fast: he wanted to lead Uriah quickly away from that insistent 'why'.

'What am I to do in Jerusalem?' asked Uriah with a sigh.

'Haven't you a woman?' enquired the King. 'There's no lack of whores in King David's city. And no shortage of wine in Jerusalem.'

34

'I have Bathsheba,' said Uriah, his tone almost defiant. 'I have Bathsheba.'

And immediately, at the very instant he mentioned her name, something strange happened to the King's face: it was contorted by a sudden spasm or contraction of the skin, a spasm that began under his right eye, just above his cheekbone. Her name seemed to prick his skin like a needle just at the point where the cheekbone meets the corner of the eye.

And then they both knew everything, David and Uriah; There was no longer any secret between them. That one twitch on the King's naked face had revealed the whole truth. Her name was not just a name: it was a confession. Yet it was a secret confession. It had to remain secret, or they might both be seized by holy madness.

Bathsheba.

The Lord shall set every man's sword against his fellow, thought Uriah, feeling suddenly very tired.

'It will soon be time for the army to storm Rabbah,' said the King. 'Joab will soon have waited long enough. The besieged and surrounded people are waiting impatiently for their liberation.'

But Uriah said nothing. It was strange that King David had suddenly mentioned the encircled Ammonites, the enemy: Uriah had always thought about the siege only from the outside.

'So you must use the little time you have now to enjoy yourself,' said the King, 'take your pleasure in wine and indulge yourself with women during the short stay that is granted you here in the city of David, in Jerusalem. Soon you will again be drawing your sword, Uriah.'

And Uriah understood that this was an order to go, and he rose and stood for a moment looking at the King: he did not kneel, he did not even bow, he tried to catch the King's eye but it was impossible. King David was watching him, but without revealing his own eyes, which remained hidden beneath the narrow slits of his eyelids. Whereupon Uriah left. He turned and went without further ado, he turned his broad back to the King and went, just as if the King had been a mere man, as if they were both ordinary men and nothing more.

Then he roamed around aimlessly in Jerusalem, from Zion to the threshing place of Araunah. He did not go home to Bathsheba; no, that was the one place to which he really could not go. And when evening came he went back up to the castle, and bought a sacrificial lamb outside the tabernacle, a lamb of the kind used for women's purification. And he carried the lamb to Ophel, the sheer rock between Zion and Gihon, and there he slaughtered it with his knife, he sacrificed it to himself in his loneliness, and he borrowed fire from a camel driver who had pitched his tent in a cleft behind the rock, and roasted the lamb and ate it. When darkness fell he went back up to Zion and spent the night with the servants outside the great portal, the servants who had to be on hand during the night in case the King happened to wake and wish for something. They all recognized him and offered him blankets to sleep on and cushions to rest his head against and goatskin rugs to cover his breast. But he lay on his cloak, without a pillow and with his enormous clasped hands as his only protection against the cold of the night, and the servants whispered to one another in astonishment at how deeply he slept and how secure and unperturbed he seemed. They had never before had one of the King's mighty warriors sleep with them outside the gate.

At dawn he ate with them. They all ate broth from a huge iron cauldron that was carried out to them, a broth of grain and meat and bread boiled to a mush. But he spoke to nobody, he ate his broth with slurps and grunts, and the servants kept their distance from him. They were proud and pleased that he had wanted to sleep with them, and they were frightened of him.

Then he sat down on the ground in front of the steps; he sat with his hands clasped in front of his shins, now and then resting his head on his knees as if he had not slept enough after all.

Before him were the flat, square houses in the old city of the Jebusites and the olive groves of Kidron and the dense, blue-shimmering cedars of Gihon; he saw it all and yet he saw it not.

Uriah's thoughts about Bathsheba were very simple. All his thoughts were simple.

Her little house-god has no pudenda. Her little god of fig-tree wood has neither vulva or phallus.

She belongs to me, I own her.

There is a gentle sibilance in her nostrils when she sleeps.

She cleans out my ears with the nail of her index finger; my own fingers are too thick.

She also has another name; Naomi, which is: the exquisite one.

A great and real god must have a sex organ.

She is probably infertile. Or perhaps I have never managed to penetrate deep enough inside her.

She likes to sing a little song about the dove that was swallowed by the raven.

I own her. She belongs to me.

But I am usually able to penetrate very deep into them.

A god who has neither vulva nor phallus is a powerless god; at most it can only be a homeless spirit of the desert.

I often tickle her on the inside of her thighs.

The smell between her legs is like a bumblebee's nest. I would give my life for her.

At noon, when the call came from the King, Uriah finally got up. He was heavy and sluggish and stiff from an inner chill; his whole body ached with impatience and uncertainty.

King David had had a meal set out for them in the inner room: doves, quails, roast suckling lamb, bread that the servants warmed in their hands, boiled trout, fried Hagab locusts, grapes, figs, dates. And wine, white and red, sweet and dry.

They do not speak to each other, they just lie down at the table.

37

First David and then Uriah, and the cup-bearer fills their cups with wine, the dry white wine to begin with, and they drink quickly, almost defiantly, as if drinking were a difficult and exhausting skill. And David hands Uriah a dove, which Uriah crushes between his teeth. They eat the fowl first, then the lamb, then the bread and fish, followed by fruit and finally locusts. With the fruit and the locusts they drink sweet wine, drinking cup after cup in complete silence throughout. They dare not utter a word, for one of them might mention Bathsheba's name. They both seem obsessed by thirst and hunger.

When Uriah feels his face beginning to go numb and stiff from the wine, he tries to rub it back to life again with his free right hand, running his fingers over the scars and wrinkles and rough patches, and David follows his example. To the servants it looks as if the two men are trying to reassure themselves that their faces are still there, as if they were afraid that their features would dissolve and disappear.

Then David loosens his sandals, unties the straps, takes the sandals by the heels and throws them to the servants. And Uriah does the same.

Thereupon David points unsurely yet commandingly at Uriah's weapons, the shield at his left elbow, the spear that he had laid behind him, and the sword still hanging at his side. And Uriah loosens his belt and hands the sword to the servants, gives them the shield and the spear too, and watches hazily without demur as his weapons are carried off. One servant carries his spear, another his shield, and another his sword. And now he is weaponless.

When the dancers come in, both David and Uriah are half asleep, and it is only with difficulty that they manage to prop up their nodding heads for a short while longer. Despite all their efforts neither of them can really see the dancers properly – they see their movements but not their bodies. And soon the cups fall from their fingers and they are asleep, first Uriah and then David, and the servants carry out the messy remains of the food, and the cup-bearer sends the dancers back to the women's house and covers David with a blanket, a camel-hair blanket adorned with a glitter of stars.

When they wake up, the light has gone: it may already be night. It is David who wakes first. He lies for a while staring into the painful darkness, then throws off the blanket and sits up. The damp evening air is streaming in through the window above him. He calls for the servants: an oil lamp and a fire bowl.

As the servants set down the big copper bowl of glowing coals between them, Uriah wakes too, the light from the oil lamp penetrating his eyes like burning brands.

And he sits up and turns his lowered head to one side and sees David beyond the fire and the lamp.

Now at last they will talk to each other. Their tongues are stiff and swollen, their heads ache like abscesses, their lips are rough, as if encrusted with scabs. Now that every word and sound and syllable requires an effort as great as climbing over a massive wall, now they will finally talk to each other.

'Why have you brought me here?' Uriah asks with a sigh, and the sound of his own voice thunders in his ears like the noise of Assyrian chariots.

'I have a mission for you,' David replies, and his voice is surprisingly clear and gentle.

'A mission?'

'Yes. A mission that will make your name immortal.'

'My lord King, I am unworthy.'

'You shall lead the assault on Rabbah. You shall give the sign to attack, you shall lead the army. Without you the siege will last for ever.'

There is a gently persuasive, almost anxiously tender tone in David's voice.

'But Joab?' says Uriah. 'Joab?'

'You are the one Joab is waiting for. It is your return that Joab has been awaiting all along.'

And Uriah thinks: Bathsheba. Somewhere there is a point where all these things meet and coalesce: my mission, Bathsheba, King David, Joab, the assault on Rabbah.

'I am not the right man,' he says. 'I am no leader of armies. I am strong and dangerous, but I am also tardy and slow.'

'That is so,' David replies. 'You are slow. We must set you in motion.'

'I can carry a message,' says Uriah. 'More I cannot do. I can take a message to Joab and the army.'

'More than that,' says David. 'You are the message. You yourself will be the message.'

When Uriah tries to shake his head, he is close to being overcome by pain. It feels as if a spear has been driven into the back of his neck, his cheeks and forehead are dripping with sweat, a fried locust is wedged between his molars.

'But I am just an ordinary man.'

He says this defensively, as if he cannot imagine how his tough, firm flesh could be transformed into anything as fleeting and light as a message.

'I am just an ordinary man.'

'I have chosen you. Yes, more than that: the Lord Himself has chosen you.

'The Lord?'

'Yes. The Lord has chosen you.'

And Uriah realizes that what David is saying must have a dreadful meaning, something inevitable and final, and his right hand reaches in vain for his sword.

'No,' says David. 'You cannot have your sword. Not yet.'

'I am not chosen,' says Uriah.

'You are chosen,' David repeats.

'No,' says Uriah. 'I am condemned.'

And David is silent.

'I am to be sacrificed,' Uriah shouts. 'That is what it means – I am to be sacrificed!'

'No one but the Lord can distinguish between being sacrificed and being chosen,' says David.

And for the first and only time he opens his eyelids fully and lets Uriah see his eyes: Believe me, I know of what I speak.

And Uriah thinks: All this is Bathsheba's fault. Yes, she is the guilty one. Bathsheba.

And then he says, and he says it more to himself than to David: 'What then is the nature of the Lord? What is the nature of the Lord my God?'

And David replies: 'He is an implacable and merciless god, he is a desert god, in the desert he came to us, he is a destructive god, a god of fire and wind, he still has sand in his hair.'

Then Uriah is overcome with a feeling of sickness and pain, and the sumptuously rich, undigested meal threatens to force its way back up; he is scarcely able to lean forward over the fire bowl on his hands and knees before, with a single torrent of vomiting, he floods the glowing coals with sour wine and bile and humiliation. But David merely watches him calmly and sympathetically – who can look at a person in distress without feeling compassion? Then he commands the servants to bring in a new fire bowl to replace the one that has been polluted and extinguished.

And King David had Uriah castrated, he had him circumcised right back to the pelvic bone. That was the sign that Uriah had been chosen.

Then he had his wounds bound, and the prophet Nathan anointed his hands and breast, he anointed him over the sixth and seventh ribs where the heart is, and he laid his hands upon his head to stop the flow of blood.

And King David girt Uriah with his sword and set his shield upon his arm and spear in his hand. And twelve men of the Cherethites and Pelethites carried Uriah to the army encampment at Rabbah; they carried him as King David had commanded.

And they had to bind him with leather straps and copper shackles, for he was filled with holy madness.

For King David had sacrificed Uriah's manhood for the sake of Bathsheba and at the command of the Lord.

And when they came to Rabbah they carried him to Joab and set him down on the ground before him. And they said: 'Behold, the King has sent him.'

Then Joab loosed his fetters, and Uriah screamed unceasingly with pain and frenzy. He had lost everything, but he still remembered Bathsheba who was the embodiment of love and who had robbed him of all life's possibilities and thus of life itself. And when, maimed and sanctified, Uriah realized that he was free, he took up his sword and hurled himself in a state of holy madness towards the gate of the city of Rabbah, the great bronze gate on the northern side, and slew ten men of the guard.

But when then soldiers of the children of Ammon saw Uriah attacking the city in holy madness, they made a sortie and smote him to death.

And Joab had Uriah the Hittite buried outside the gates of Rabbah. Uriah's grave is there to this day.

When Bathsheba moved into David's house, she brought nothing with her but the little house-god of fig-tree wood. And David took the house-god in his hands and examined it, and saw that it was a sexless and harmless god: it had no vulva and no phallus. So he allowed her to keep it.

'Life is an unceasing pursuit of God,' he told her. 'Without God there is not a single prize of any value or significance.'

'I was given it by my father when I was born,' said Bathsheba. 'It has always stood by my bed.'

And she pressed it to her breast, as if the god needed warmth and protection, as if the god were dependent on her help and love.

And David could not help laughing when he saw them, the woman and the god, their defencelessness and impotence, their touching, confused and meaningless clinging to each other.

They were standing in the upper hall, at the head of the staircase. The guards who had accompanied Bathsheba were waiting on the top step.

'God does not allow himself to be given form by human hands,' he said, with laughter still bubbling in his throat. 'God cannot be captured in a piece of wood.'

'I like him,' Bathsheba said simply. 'He is enough of a god for me.'

'Poor woman,' said David. 'You do not know what you are saying.'

'I hardly ever use him,' said Bathsheba in self-justification. 'But I have become accustomed to having him standing by my bed.'

'Well,' said David, 'he can neither harm you nor help you. He has no phallus.

'He does not need one,' Bathsheba replied. 'His godly strength is contained within himself.'

And King David was obliged to instruct her.

'Man is made in God's image,' he said. 'God is like man. Without fertility both God and man would be doomed to destruction. The phallus is the means of combatting death. The phallus can regenerate life in the cycle of the seasons. The phallus is the staff which causes life to spring forth from the soulless rock. Without the phallus the universe would relapse into the chaos that reigned before Creation.'

'When I got him,' said Bathsheba apologetically, 'he had a phallus. It was an enormous phallus that reached up to his chin. It was actually far too big. The weight of it made him keep falling forward. If he was not propped up with a twig, all he could do was lie prostrate.'

'Yes,' said David. 'Such men do exist.'

'So,' Bathsheba continued, 'I borrowed by father's knife. I borrowed the knife one evening when my father was asleep, and I cut off the horrible phallus. And I rubbed and polished the place where it had been with a piece of stone. Since then it has always stood on its feet easily.'

But this was more than King David could bear to hear.

'Sacrilege!' he cried. 'Do you not understand, woman, that you desecrated him? You cut off his strength! You robbed him of his holy weapon! You castrated your own god!'

'I cannot remember exactly now,' Bathsheba said to excuse herself. 'It may not have been my intention to rob him of the whole of his phallus. But the dagger slipped in my hand.'

'Whatever is holy must never be violated!' said the King. 'That which is holy must never be cut by as much as a hair's breadth! That which is holy must not even be polished with a piece of stone!'

'But it is only an image, carved from the branch of the fig tree,' Bathsheba reminded him.

'Even so,' said the King.

'And if it had still possessed its phallus, I would not have been allowed to bring it with me into your house. You would have had it burned and its ashes buried in the Valley of Hinnom.'

And now King David calmed down again.

'Yes,' he said. 'Yes, you are right. No genuine idols may come into my house, my house shall be pure and righteous, my house shall be the home of the truth. In my house all idols and fig-tree carvings must be divested of their power. Thou shalt have no other gods before me.'

Bathsheba would not be living in the women's house. And she would no longer be meeting the other women at King David's well in the evenings.

No, she was to live in one of the rooms behind the King's room. It had been kept for some, as yet unknown, venerable, even holy purpose. Musical instruments had been stored there previously. It was situated next to Mephibosheth's room, to which he was always carried after the royal meals.

In fact he had to be carried there by the servants almost every evening, since King David regarded it as his duty to provide him with such a rich profusion of food that he could not possibly move on his own shapeless feet; he was usually unable even to crawl, but had to be carried sleeping to his room, where there was nothing but a wide leather-covered bed. And around the bed was a channel in which all the nightly excretions from his body could collect.

Mephibosheth was the son of Jonathan, Jonathan was the son of King Saul. King David and Jonathan had been very close to each other; their friendship had had a warmth of an almost painful kind, for one of them would succeed Saul, the Lord's Anointed, and they could not be certain which. Both had lived in fear of the slaughter that one of them might have to perform: to slay a dear friend was harder than anything else ever could be. So David felt great relief when both Saul and Jonathan were slain simultaneously on Mount Gilboa. It was the Philistines who slew them. He commanded that the people's mourning should continue till the month of *ethanim*, and that everyone, men and women alike, should sing a lament for Jonathan every evening.

> Ye mountains of Gilboa, where Jonathan lies slain,
> let there be no dew, neither let there be rain, upon you.
> I am distressed for thee, my brother Jonathan:
> very pleasant hast thou been unto me:
> thy love to me was wonderful,
> passing the love of women.
> Man's love is as lasting as the water and the air:
> thy love was like the thunder of the storm.

Mephibosheth was a cripple. He had been a cripple since his childhood: it was his nurse who had made him so.

She was of the family of the Danites, the same family as Samson – he who slew a thousand men with the jawbone of an ass. She was four ells tall and had the strength of three men. When Saul and Jonathan had been slain on Mount Gilboa she had fled with Mephibosheth from the Philistines. She thought he would become king. Mephibosheth was then five years old. She lifted him up in her hands and held him high above her head as she ran. He was the grandson of the King, and she raised him towards the heavens so that even in flight he would retain his dignity and nobility. But as she reached Jezreel, the plain below Gilboa, her left foot hit a stone and she fell forward, and Mephibosheth was thrown out of her hands and his feet crushed in the fall. Both feet were crushed and never grew into feet in the proper meaning of the word: they became fleshy, formless lumps without movement or direction, and Mephibosheth had to use two sticks to walk with. The sticks were carved from mulberry wood, with serpent heads at the bottom and the claws of birds of prey at the top.

Bathsheba's room, then, was next to his.

When David had captured Jerusalem from the Jebusites and became king there, he had asked: 'Is there anyone still alive of Saul's family, anyone who might need my charity, anyone whom I can love instead of Jonathan?' And they had answered: 'Mephibosheth.'

Yes, charity. Mephibosheth.

Love?

Then King David had ordered Mephibosheth to be brought to him, and commanded that he should eat and drink at his table every evening, and that it should remain so as long as they both might live. Never should Mephibosheth go to bed hungry or thirsty – particularly not thirsty; every evening they would celebrate together the memory of Jonathan, and also of Saul. They would eat, drink and be merry and every day sing a new song to the glory of the Lord.

Mephibosheth lived at that time on a little farm in the Valley of Kidron. The farm was all he had been able to keep of the legacy of his fathers: King David had robbed him of all the rest. He lived quietly and peacefully and happily with his wives and his cattle and his children and his club feet. But now he was forced to eat at David's table every evening. Only occasionally was he able to pay a fleeting visit to his farm and his wife and his children: eating and drinking took all his time and energy, and very soon the wine robbed him of his procreative powers so that he no longer desired his wives. It was as if his sex organ had been cut off, and he said once to Bathsheba: 'Every meal is a sacrificial meal, and it is I who am the sacrifice.'

At the time when he and Bathsheba were getting to know one another, when they were in fact becoming as close as brother and sister, King David had handed back to Mephibosheth all the land that had once belonged to King Saul. Mephibosheth had immediately become the biggest landowner in the country after the King, but these immense landed properties gave him little joy since he never saw them. All he had were reports of his huge herds of cattle grazing in many places throughout the land.

And he said to Bathsheba: 'My properties exist only in my mind: they are imaginary flocks and imaginary cattle. And my wives are imaginary wives.'

Mephibosheth and Bathsheba had met for the first time during the evening of Bathsheba's first day of living in the house. They could hear the clattering of servants on the stairs outside, carrying or dragging pots and bowls and pitchers from the kitchen to the King's room, and on that first meeting Mephibosheth had said to her: 'He is very dear to me.'

'Who?' asked Bathsheba.

'The King. King David.'

There was a little hall outside their rooms, which was where they had met. Mephibosheth was sitting on a small stool, supporting his heavy, bloated body on his crutches.

'Why is he dear to you?' Bathsheba asked.

'I do not know,' said Mephibosheth. 'I cannot explain it. But he is extremely dear to me.'

'How do you know that he is dear to you?'

'When I hear his voice, tears fill my eyes. When he goes off to battle, I cannot sleep and my heart pounds like the running hooves of a wild boar. When I hear him telling of the exploits of his youth, I feel I am just an unworthy parasite on life, an intestinal worm at the King's table. And when he touches me with his hand I become as hot as a stone when it is licked by fire.'

'When he touches you with his hand?'

'Yes. And when I get drunk for his sake and at his command, I am transformed into a dove, a dove which is sacrificed as a flight offering.'

'And if he carries me to my bed himself – yes, he really does sometimes take me in his powerful arms and carry me – then I am once again a little child sleeping in the arms of God.'

Bathsheba looked at him: his eyes were yellow and purulent, his face consisted of heavy pouches of flesh; around his neck was a chain of gold which was hardly visible, embedded as it was in the folds of flesh. His hands were blue-veined and blunted and seemed to have no knuckles, his breath was laboured and panting, and on his feet he wore two rough leather bags.

Poor Mephibosheth! she thought. So he is capable of love. He is able to feel love. But how could anyone love him? That repulsive bloated body, that oppressive spirit?

And she felt compassion for him, she took pity on him, and her compassion grew and spread its warmth within her, and she thought: I cannot help loving him.

'They say you live as a prisoner,' she said. 'That the King keeps you locked up in his house.'

'Who says that?'

'Uriah has said so.'

'Uriah?'

'And the women at the King's well say so.'

'I am free,' said Mephibosheth. 'I can come when I wish. And I can go when I wish.'

'But you must eat at the King's table,' said Bathsheba.

'Yes,' said Mephibosheth, 'that is dreadful. That is frightful. Every day, every morning when I awake, I think to myself, I cannot go on any longer. But then comes the midday heat. And then the hunger.'

'Your wives and your children,' said Bathsheba. 'You ought to return to them.'

'I have not the strength to do so.'

'You can summon the strength when King David goes out to battle. When he himself goes to Rabbah.'

'He never goes to battle any more. He has handed over the business of war to Joab.'

'He may be forced to at some time,' said Bathsheba.

'May he never again be compelled to undergo the dangers of war,' said Mephibosheth. 'I pray to the Lord every day that the King shall never again leave Jerusalem.'

'But if he does,' Bathsheba persisted, 'then you may be granted the strength you need to leave him.'

'If I ever feel that strength coming to me, I shall fight it with all my strength,' said Mephibosheth. 'I have nothing but my weakness to give the King. If I lose my weakness, what else have I to offer him?'

And Bathsheba sought an answer, but found none.

'If I lose my weakness, he may no longer want me. If I were afflicted with the strength to get me back to my house in the Valley of Kidron, then I would have to use that strength to take my own life.

'My grandfather, King Saul, threw himself on his sword when he saw that the battle was lost.'

And he went on in a murmur: 'I cannot and may not ever fail him. He needs me. Therefore I need him.'

Bathsheba laid her arm upon his shoulders, combed her fingers through his thinning wisps of hair, and led him into the King's room, to his meal. And that very same evening she saw King David take the sleeping but still drunkenly mumbling Mephibosheth in his arms and carry him gently to his bed. His step may have faltered, but he nevertheless bore him safely and unhesitatingly. The dancers and the servants stood aside to let him pass and bowed right down to the floor as if it were a holy act he was performing, as if the swollen stinking body in his arms were a blessed sacrificial lamb.

And then he also came in to her and lay with her. He lay with her until she whimpered to him that she could take no more, that, blissful as it was, she could bear no more of this impassioned lovemaking, this suffocating struggle.

So, while the sexless god watched them in wonder and astonishment, he rearranged his clothes and let her comb her sweat-drenched tangled hair. Then he called the servants with the palanquin, and commanded them to carry him down to the women's house.

David was now fifty-two years old.

Bathsheba was nineteen.

A king must have a prophet.

King David's prophet was Nathan.

He had come the same day that David had conquered Jerusalem.

It had happened one evening. David had been on his way from Ophel up to the castle of the Jebusites. He was very tired, and was bleeding from a deep wound in the neck. Nathan had run to catch him up and pushed his way through to him, and the men around the King had let him push through because they though he was a Canaanite, a Jebusite who wanted to beg for some kind of favour or mercy. And he was unarmed, and his cloak was soiled and torn as if he had suffered in some way from the battle just ended.

On reaching the King he had shouted: 'King David, I am your prophet, the Lord has sent me! The Lord will protect His people henceforth and unto eternity. Those who put their faith in the Lord are like the Mountain of Zion which never wavers, they shall endure unto eternity!'

He spoke with mouth agape; his face seemed to consist almost entirely of mouth, nothing but a resonant mouth. His long, thin neck jutted forward, his voice was shrill and excited. He bore a strong resemblance to a trumpet.

'Are you circumcised?' David asked.

'I was born without a foreskin,' Nathan shouted. 'The Lord circumcised me in my mother's womb.'

Yes, even that was possible; Men could be born with all kinds of signs on their bodies, they could be born as hairy as devils, they could be born covered with gold dust, they could be born already dead with a beatific smile on their faces – and so, of course, they could also be born circumcised.

'And He has really sent you?'

'Yes, He has really sent me.'

Then the King had asked nothing further. He asked neither about Nathan's origins nor earlier life nor forebears. He could not admit, 'Yes, the Lord has sent you,' and at the same time ask: 'Where do you come from?'

His ragged cloak was woven of coarse hair – it was a cloak of mourning; he had a leather belt around his waist, his chest was covered by a goatskin. He was dressed as if he lived in the desert. Even in the King's house he went about dressed as if the palace were a desert. The mark of God, a cross, was branded into his forehead. On a leather thong around his neck hung a little drum, a copper vessel covered with calfskin.

King David already had a prophet; his name was Gad. Gad had followed him ever since he had fled from King Saul the first time. But Nathan soon became the foremost of the two: after all, Gad had joined him merely of his own free will, whereas Nathan had been sent, indeed cast at him, by the Lord.

Long afterwards Bathsheba's son, one of the sons, the Son, would ask her: 'Nathan? What does he do? What is his function? What is his purpose?'

And she would reply in as simple and clear, as artless and childlike a way as she could:

'To give himself up to seizures, to go into a state of ecstasy, to surrender himself again and again to the Lord, to take leave of his own self.

'And to dance, staggering and falling, tearing off his clothes and throwing himself to the ground – yes, he really is circumcised – to lie unconscious and thus to reveal the presence of God, to make those around him feel the power of holiness and God's immeasurable and terrible strength, to let himself be filled continuously with the Spirit of the Lord.

'It is the Holy Spirit that does all this to him. Nathan does not do it himself but allows it to be done. He simply puts himself in readiness – the Spirit is not God Himself but a power or substance which God sends to him.

'Sometimes to speak in his own, Nathan's name, sometimes in God's name. When he speaks in the name of God, he is like the scribe: he writes down with his lips and tongue the words which are spoken to him, he does not choose the words, he merely forms them and causes them to be seen or heard.

'To play on the little drum of calfskin and copper, making bloody scratches on his breast with the three-edged stone knife, to let himself be thrown through the air by the Spirit of God.'

'Really thrown?'

'Yes, thrown.

'Before any of you were born, before you were born, at the time when I was carrying the first of your little brothers and sisters in my womb, Nathan once became very angry. He could not bear the fact that your father the King called me his queen. Only heathens have queens, he said. And his anger, together with the Spirit of God, his anger, heated by the fire of the Spirit of God, cast him through the air a distance of two days' journey to the west, almost to the sea. He flew like a gigantic fish hawk through the air, and only returned three days later, on foot, ragged and wretched, starving, thirsty and dejected. But free of his anger.

'Oh, my child, you should have seen him!

'And it is also his task to bless or curse all that needs to be blessed or cursed.

'To stand with his hand over his mouth and his face to the wall from sunrise to sunset in order to be able in the evening to interpret dreams, foretell the weather or find places where objects or people have disappeared or been lost.

'To cast lots to discover the truth: truth is the will of God.

55

'To lead back runaway camels, asses and flocks of sheep.

'To know everything and to communicate something of what he knows.

'To call down fire from heaven when fire is required.

'In extreme need to call back the dead to life.'

'The dead?'

'Yes, really dead.'

'From the realm of death?'

'Yes, from the realm of death.

'Once one of the small boys in the temple died. He was only as big as you are now, my son. He was the boy who looked after the holy golden serpent which was used for purifying and sanctifying the King's wine. Nobody knew where he had hidden the little serpent, and we looked for it unceasingly and fearfully for two days. The King did not dare drink any of the wine. The boy had taken his knowledge of the hiding place with him into the realm of death. Even Nathan searched desperately. But then Nathan awoke the little boy from the dead – there was no other way. His name was Zadok, the son of Adiel, and when he returned from the dead he was able to tell us bemusedly where the serpent was hidden.'

'Where was it hidden?'

'It lay buried beneath the threshold of one of the storehouses. No one could understand why he had hidden it there. Then Nathan let him die, as he desired.'

Bathsheba knew all this about Nathan, the prophet. She knew this much after just a few years; perhaps she knew even more but did not want to tell. Nathan, too, was dear to her heart.

Without a prophet a king is not complete. The prophet brings him that glow of justice which renders him perfect.

David had Nathan. Nathan was an instrument filled with the Holy Spirit, a trumpet of the Lord.

When Bathsheba had moved into David's house, and several months had passed and everyone could clearly see that she bore the King's child beneath her breast – indeed, she did not conceal the fact but tied up her dress with a pearl-embroidered belt to accentuate the bulge of her stomach – then Nathan went to the King and said:

'Two women lived near each other: one was rich, the other poor. The rich woman had herds of animals grazing on the mountain pastures of Ephraim and on the plains of Ghor. She had an abundance of goats and camels and sheep and asses.

'The poor woman had one lamb, one single lamb, a lamb which the priests had rejected as too small to be sacrificed, and the woman had taken it to herself and anointed it with strengthening ointments and laid honey on its tongue and suckled it at her breast.

'Yes, the lamb was like a son to her. It slept in her arms at night, and by day it went along bleating at her side, with its head pressed against her right hip. And the lamb grew and became the finest and liveliest and most attractive lamb in the Valley of the Jordan.

'And they were very fond of each other, the lamb and the mother.

'And then a traveller came to the rich woman, a robber and a murderer who was sore troubled by his sins, and he asked the rich woman for a lamb which he could offer up as a sacrifice for his sins.

'"If you do not give me a lamb, I will kill you, too," he said.

'So tormented was he by his sins, so pressing was his need for a sacrificial lamb.

'And she sent her servants to the poor woman, servants with spears and swords and whips, and they took her lamb from her, that poor woman's beautiful suckling lamb, her beloved son, and the rich woman gave it to the robber to be sacrificed.'

'That woman must be put to death!' shouted David.

'Which of them?'

'The rich woman! She who gave away the poor mother's only lamb!'

'You are that woman,' said Nathan.

'No,' said David. 'Not even in a parable can I be a woman.'

But Nathan persisted, 'The woman is none other than you!'

'Your words are not always very apt,' said David. 'They often go wide of the mark.'

'There are depths and mysteries in my parables that you do not understand. No parables are necessary for that which is obvious and self-evident.'

'The most serious fault in your parables is that they have to be interpreted,' said David. 'A good parable should contain its own explanation.'

'A parable must be able to be interpreted in many ways,' replied Nathan. 'It must be like deep water which changes colour and appearance with the light.'

'Muddy waters,' said the King scornfully.

'The images of a parable,' Nathan continued, 'should be laid one on top of another like cloths on a weaver's shelf. When you hold up one image to the light you must remember that a new image lies waiting in the darkness: Beneath every pattern another pattern lies hidden.'

'I find such parables meaningless,' said the King. 'All I demand of a parable is clear instruction.'

'One must be humble and open and alert to be receptive to a parable in the depth of one's heart,' said Nathan.

'Humble and open?' said the King.

'A good parable contains an infinite number of pieces of clear instruction – yes, even countless pieces of clear instruction that contradict and exclude one another.'

'A parable like that is self-destructive,' said the King.

'Yes,' said Nathan. 'That can be the case. But if it is true and it has the source in the Lord, it will gradually arise anew in the heart of a man who can listen.'

'The Lord does not involve Himself with parables,' said the King impatiently. 'The Lord's thoughts are the clearest and simplest there are.'

'There you are mistaken, my lord King,' said Nathan, his voice becoming shrill with fervour. 'You do not know the Lord. You do not know Him as I do! You are only His Anointed One, not His shackled slave!

'You are not filled day and night with His voice,' he cried. 'I say to you: He is a God of parables, everything He creates is a parable. Man is a parable, the sea is a parable, birds and fish are parables, locusts are parables, wine is a parable, bread is a parable, the kingdom of death is a parable, your love for Bathsheba is a parable! There is nothing, nothing on earth and nothing in the heavens, which He has not fashioned as a parable!'

But now the King just sat in silence, twisting the little flute in his hands, not wanting to anger the prophet further. If he let the conversation continue, Nathan would finally go into a prophetic fit of madness, he would fall to the floor and foam at the mouth, and the whole thing would end in an agonizing frenzy.

After a while the King said, 'Can you not help me to understand your parable? The one about the rich woman and the poor woman, she who gave her only lamb as a sacrifice?'

And the prophet answered now in a very calm and controlled manner, his voice dull and forced, for he hated explaining and interpreting his parables: 'Uriah owned nothing on earth except Bathsheba. She was his little lamb, she lay against his breast, she was his only joy.'

At those words a wave of painful envy shot through the King's heart. She had lain against his breast, she had subdued him, she had slept in his embrace.

'But you took the little lamb away from him,' the prophet continued. 'You stole Bathsheba from him. You who have been given a kingdom by God! You who cannot measure or weigh your riches! You who already own fifty-two wives!'

'I have never counted my wives,' said David.

'No,' said Nathan. 'But they have counted themselves. They say, "There are already fifty-two of us."'

59

'Already,' said David. 'There will never be more of them. Bathsheba is my last wife. Bathsheba is the final wife.'

'And you violated Uriah,' Nathan continued. 'You violated him and had him put to the sword.'

'I had no choice,' said David.

'The Lord does not ask whether you had a choice,' said Nathan. 'The Lord does not say: David did it out of necessity. No, the Lord sees only your deeds, nothing that might by chance have preceded your deeds. According to your deeds he will punish you.'

'I bear no guilt,' said David, and his voice was very clear and full of falseness. And he continued, 'All the guilt lies with Bathsheba. By her very existence she has brought this guilt upon herself. She and no one else has Uriah's blood on her hands.'

'And you think the Lord will not punish a weak and defenceless woman?'

'The Lord is merciful towards the weak,' said David. 'He will spare Bathsheba because of her helplessness.'

'Do you really think the Lord will let Himself be led astray by your cunning?' said Nathan. 'Do you think he will let Himself be deceived by your excuses?'

David sat in silence for a long time. Then he sighed and said, 'No, at the bottom of my heart I do not believe that. But I would not be the person I am if I did not try. I am always looking for excuses. That is the way the Lord has made me – resourceful, cunning and wily. He fashioned me as a man of excuses and expedience.'

'He will punish you.'

'Yes, He will punish me.'

'He will never remove His sword from your house. "I shall take your wives from you and give them to another," says the Lord. "And I shall fill your house with suffering and pain, yes, I shall let sorrows and misfortunes breed and multiply like serpents in your house."'

'Yes,' said David. 'In truth I expect nothing else.'

'"And the child," says the Lord, "the child which Bathsheba carries in her womb, the first-born son. I shall let him be born and see the light of day, but then I shall demand his life and his spirit, I shall take him back out of King David's hands."'

'A sacrificial offering for my sins,' said David.

'Yes, a sacrificial offering. But you yourself will not die,' said Nathan.

'No,' said David, 'I shall not die. No, I shall not die.'

They had nothing more to say to each other. Nathan lifted his cow-hair cloak, which was trailing on the floor, turned and departed, and King David put the little cedarwood flute to his lips and let his fingers move over the holes. But he did not play.

Bathsheba had seen the prophet go in to the King. When he came out of the King's room she was waiting for him. She was alone; only the two guards on the door were standing there with their long spears, but they appeared almost non-existent in their immobility, hardly seeming even to breathe.

'What have you said to him?' whispered Bathsheba anxiously.

'I have told him the truth,' said Nathan.

'The truth?'

'Yes, the truth.'

'And what is the truth?'

'That he has Uriah's blood on his hands. That he had your husband killed.'

'We all have someone's blood on our hands,' said Bathsheba, and it sounded almost as if it were herself she was excusing. 'And after all he is a king.'

'Even a king should be just,' the prophet explained, in a gentle voice as if he were talking to a child.

And Bathsheba pondered his words.

'I think,' she said at last, 'I think that the kingly and the human are irreconcilable. A true king cannot also be a human being. And anyone who chooses to be merely human cannot rule over other human beings.'

'We are all human,' said Nathan. 'Some are chosen. It is as simple as that.'

'Can the chosen ones defend themselves against being chosen?'

'Everyone wants to be chosen,' Nathan replied. 'Everyone is eager to be chosen and anointed. That is how God has made us. We rush forward headlong, blinded by our desire to be held by His hand.'

'The King too?'

'Yes, David too.'

'If God has created him thus, then God bears the guilt,' said Bathsheba, speaking very softly and carefully.

'God has also created us to be punished,' the prophet explained. 'If mankind did not exist, God's scourge would whistle through empty space.'

'Uriah's suffering is over,' Bathsheba whispered. 'He is tormented no more. I had almost forgotten him.'

'And you have been stolen by David. You are stolen property. You are a treasure he stole from an innocent victim.'

'Can God not feel compassion?'

'God is a creator. If it is absolutely necessary He will create compassion.'

Bathsheba stood for a long time in silence. Then she cried out, not seeming to notice that the guards and perhaps even the King could hear her, 'Stolen property! Treasure! I am a living person! The Spirit of God is in me too! I rushed headlong towards the hand that held me!'

But now the prophet said nothing, smiling at her indulgently and reassuringly. His smile seemed to say: there is such a thing as innocent blindness, and pure-hearted impetuosity. You shall not be punished; no, you shall not be punished. Only the guilty one is guilty.

And he laid his thin, bony hand on her stomach, examining and blessing it, and he could feel the child moving within.

'Life is mysterious, even incomprehensible,' he said softly and intimately. 'The way God creates life from life, one human being from another.'

'Sometimes he twitches suddenly in my belly,' said Bath-sheba. 'As if he had awoken from a strange dream.'

The prophet bent down and pressed his cheek and his hard, pointed ear against her body. And a moment later he exclaimed in amazement, almost happily, 'I can hear his heart beating! It is fluttering like a little bird in a cage!'

'Yes,' was Bathsheba's hesitant and anxious answer. 'Exactly like a frightened, caged bird. A wild bird that has been stolen from its nest.'

And before the prophet departed, he laid his hands on her in blessing so that the Lord would protect her and the child, especially the child, against evil spirits and against Lilith, the child-stealer, the female devil that lived in the desert and had to slake her thirst every day with the blood of an infant.

Something always happens to all of us, thought Bathsheba. We are afflicted with illness or hatred or love. We are taken away or abandoned or killed. We are always at risk from something.

Yes, that is the nature of life.

The women's house was like a stable. There were three women to a room. The children lived everywhere – with their mothers, and in the separate children's room, and in the narrow spaces between the rooms, and in the long passageways – the countless children who had not yet been chosen to live in the King's house or serve in the temple, and the girls who had not yet been sent away to be wives. There was also a room for the King in the women's house, a room where he could lie with his wives, and a separate room for births. Every month there were three, or seven, or some other holy number of births.

But Bathsheba would not give birth to her child in that room. No, it was to take place in her room in the palace; she was the chosen ewe who would lamb in the shepherd's house.

And the women who gathered around the King's well could never satisfy their thirst for talking about it:

'King David has commanded twelve bulls to be sacrificed. As soon as the pains begin twelve bulls are to be slaughtered as a sacrifice to the Lord.'

'A servant always walks in front of her, bending down to support her belly.'

'She carries her house-god between her breasts, and the King does not know of it.'

'It will be a boy: Nathan has said so, the King has commanded that it shall be so, Bathsheba knows it will be so.'

'Nathan has already anointed him, he has anointed him in her womb. He shall be a prince of peace.'

'The King is going to divide the kingdom between himself

and the Son, King David is going to return to Hebron or to Bethlehem.'

'His name is already decided: he is to be called the Blessed One.'

'The child is going to die.'

'Who says it will die?'

'Nathan has said so. The prophet.'

'Will it really die?'

'It will never be given a name, it will not live to see the day of its circumcision. The Lord has said this to Nathan, and Nathan has said it to the King.'

'Why must it die?'

'Bathsheba was not clean. It is Bathsheba's fault.'

'In what way was she unclean?'

'She still belonged to Uriah: no one else could own her, and so she was unclean when the King lay with her.'

'Not all children who are conceived in an unclean state have to die.'

'No, not normal children, not children who are merely children, not children who will just grow into ordinary human beings. But a chosen child must be conceived in a state of cleanness and be born in a state of cleanness.'

'Is that really true?'

'Yes, it is true.'

'If he were to live and if he were to grow up and if he were to become king, then he would contaminate his whole people with his uncleanness.'

'Must the King always be clean?'

'Yes. Always.'

'How can he avoid being unclean?'

'By always being King.'

And Bathsheba asked Mephibosheth: 'What is it like to give birth?'

'I do not know,' sighed Mephibosheth. 'How could I know?'

'You have many sons. And daughters.'

'My wives bore them for me – I was never there. They brought the children to me afterwards and I blessed them. Even if I had no blessing to give.'

Bathsheba smiled to herself. Conversation with Mephibosheth had its own bitter humour.

'Do you think it is hard?'

'If it were dreadfully hard,' said Mephibosheth, 'then the Lord would have imposed it not on the woman but on the man.'

'Can it be like being pierced with a sword?'

'Yes,' he replied. 'I imagine it could be like having a sword through one's body.'

And now Bathsheba smiled openly. No one would ever want to pierce the lamentable Mephibosheth with a sword.

'Yet almost all women are strong enough to give birth,' she said. 'Only the infertile are too weak to bear children.'

'It is your first child?' he asked.

'Yes. He will be my first-born son.'

'Birth is a miracle,' said Mephibosheth. 'But it is an unclean and shameful miracle. God cherishes mankind, but he abhors our way of giving birth. That is why giving birth is carried out in seclusion.

'And that is why I know nothing about it.'

But Ahinoam, she who has always been midwife to her fellow-wives, she who herself has borne seven sons and a countless number of daughters, she who was the first to give birth in David's house, Ahinoam from Jezreel, she whose withered hand comes back to life at every birth, she knows everything.

She it is who will help Bathsheba to give birth.

'You who are to give birth shall kneel with your legs wide apart and the palms of your hands pressed to the floor, your face held aloft so that the Lord can see you. Your hair shall be tied back so that it does not cover your eyes and fall into your mouth and become defiled with foaming spittle and chewed up. You shall have a piece of wood between your teeth, a piece of acacia wood, and you shall take off your earrings, so that when blinded with pain you do not grip them with your fingers and tear your ears, and your back shall be covered with a soft cloak for the sweat, a sweat-cloth. And you shall writhe and bear down and undergo agony, you shall arch your back like the fallow deer when it answers the call of nature, and you shall cry to God in your distress, you shall beat your forehead against the floor until it bleeds and press your hands against your belly. And when your torment and your agony almost force you to relinquish your spirit, then you shall give birth to your offspring, then the midwife shall take hold of the child's head and pull it out of your body, and you shall be delivered.'

So Bathsheba gives birth to her child in her own room in the palace, on the floor. And when the child is almost fully born, Ahinoam, standing behind her, cries 'Fear not, it is a boy!'

But when the son is born, Ahinoam sees that all is not yet over: something is attached to his heel, something resembling a bird's claw, the claw of a dove or the claws of Mephibosheth's crutches. She shouts at Bathsheba not to lie down, she cannot rest yet, she must give birth to something more.

And Bathseba strains, she summons her last vestiges of energy, and gives birth rapidly and almost painlessly to a little girl, a child no bigger than Ahinoam's withered hand, a shrivelled yet fully formed baby girl holding on to her brother. She is dead, but her fingers are pressed into her brother's flesh below the ankle. Ahinoam has to use both hands to separate the two.

She quickly throws the bird-like girl to one of the servants, indicating with her eyes and a jerk of her head that the baby girl should be taken away, that it should be secreted in one of the rubbish bins. No one should ever know that it had existed, neither David nor Bathsheba, it is not really a child, it is just part of the uncleanness, just a piece of the afterbirth.

But Ahinoam knows what the baby girl means: the boy-child

will die. It is the child-stealer Lilith who has sent her; she has stamped the new-born child with the claw-mark of death.

His breathing makes a strange whistling sound. And he will not suck at Bathsheba's breast.

Nathan anoints his forehead and wheezing chest with oil, but it does not seem to help. And David thinks: Of course, it is he who has condemned the child.

Mephibosheth has three rams sacrificed for him, but he continues to decline.

Shebaniah plays the five sacred notes for him, but he seems not to hear them.

Perhaps Bathsheba's milk is infected by the spirits of sickness, perhaps the King should send for a wet-nurse in her stead, perhaps her milk is burning or corrosive as the desert women's milk can sometimes be.

It is Ahinoam who says this – after all, she has to say something.

So David tests her milk. He lies down at her side with his shoulder in her armpit as if he were a suckling child, and he takes her breast and presses his lips to the nipple and sucks. He sucks with such a force that Bathsheba feels a surge of pain right down to her finger-tips and the soles of her feet. He fills his mouth with milk and tastes it as if it were wine. He presses it against his palate and swallows it carefully in small gulps. He sips and sups with his tongue as if he were the most know-ledgeable expert on mother's milk in the whole of Israel.

No, the milk could not be better, he has never tasted a more delightful drink. It is as mellow as date wine, or honey mixed with sheep's milk. Before he gets up he fills his mouth once again till his cheeks puff out and shine like the skin of an over-filled wine bottle. And afterwards Ahinoam has to bind up Bathsheba's bleeding breasts.

But Bathsheba knows all along that he will die. Even while he still lives she is trying to forget him.

68

How does she know that?

She saw it in Ahinoam's eyes when she had wrapped him and placed him in her arms for the first time.

She knew it from the preoccupied way Nathan anointed him with oil.

She hears it now from the silence of the new-born child. A child who intends to live screams in fear and apprehension.

She senses it from his breath, which is cool and smells of the earth.

She knows it in her heart.

And as early as the third day her breasts dry up.

But David goes out to the little field behind the palace, tears his clothes to shreds and strews earth in his hair and lies down upon the ground. And he refuses to eat the food that Bathsheba sends out to him. For days on end he prays constantly for his son's life, and at night he sleeps without blanket or goatskin, and drinks only enough water to prevent himself dying of thirst.

But when the child eventually dies, it dies in Ahinoam's arms while Bathsheba is asleep. She does nothing but eat and sleep: she wants to be strong again as soon as possible. Then David gets up and puts on a magnificent cloak and orders a sumptuous repast for himself and Mephibosheth and the two young men, Amnon and Absalom. Having made his sacrifices and offered his prayers in the tabernacle of the Lord, he gives orders that the dead child shall be circumcised on the eighth day after his birth, that he shall be called the Blessed One, and that he shall be taken to Bethlehem and buried among his forefathers. His eyes do not need to be closed, since he has never opened them.

King David now had a new boy to play for him on the lyre: Shebaniah, the trumpeter who had guarded Bathsheba one night. It was Shaphan's lyre that he played. And the King was very fond of him.

Bathsheba, Mephibosheth and Shebaniah. Thus it was.

The city of Rabbah had withstood the Israelites' siege for over a year now. The encircled Ammonites had beaten back Joab and his army six times. On one occasion they had also overcome the lone Uriah.

But now the water was drying up in the wells, the cattle were being stricken with mysterious diseases, the animals were losing the strength in their legs – the besiegers had perhaps sent infected rats into the city – fires were breaking out, and the women had stopped giving birth.

King David had had the ark of the Lord sent to the army, and it stood now on the hill outside the western city gate. From there the Lord could see into Rabbah.

Then Joab ordered the army to attack the city walls from the north. The archers and slingsmen went first, followed by the men with battering-rams and ladders, and they advanced into the city. They needed to kill only seventy men – indeed, they only had the chance to kill seventy men. They captured the water cisterns and the only well that still provided water.

And Joab sent a message to King David that he must come immediately if he wanted to be the one to capture Rabbah, and that the Ammonites were, to all intents and purposes, already conquered.

But the King had not been to battle for six years, and he hesitated. He sometimes had strange pains in his left thigh, the flesh on his arms was not as firm as it had been, his belly had begun to grow fatter, the gold rings on his sword hand had become stuck behind the knuckles – even if he dipped his hands in cold water he could not loosen his rings.

And he sent the messengers back: 'Yes, I am coming. I shall bring the people with me and come, but you must wait a little longer. I must prepare myself for battle, we must not be too hasty.'

And Joab moved the army encampment into the city, inside the walls of Rabbah. From time to time he permitted his men to attack one house or another to take prisoners and booty. The men began to get impatient, and he let them empty the Ammonites' wine stores. But he waited.

Joab had never done anything else but wage war. He was now fifty, and he had brought to their conclusion all the wars that the King had started or decided on. He could use all weapons equally well: the sword and the spear and the sling and the bow and the club and the battle-axe. He was considered invincible with the sword in close combat. The short fast stab slanting up from below was his speciality.

Yet perhaps his voice was his most fearful weapon: however big his army, all his men could always hear every word he said to them. He could shout from the palace steps and be heard as far away as the threshing place of Araunah. He had once killed an ass by shouting its name in its ear and bursting its skull, and he could sing loud enough to drown out completely the sound of the trumpets. He was the son of King David's sister, Zeruiah. He was taller and stronger than the King. No other man could wear his shoulder plates. He had a dark complexion and his hair was long and black; in battle he wore it in a long plait down his back.

74

And the people of Rabbah sent their elders to Joab to negotiate with him, but he refused. He would not listen to them, would not talk with them.

And the women came of their own accord to the army encampment. They begged for their husbands' lives, they brought their virgin daughters. But Joab was immovable.

When he realized that the people of Rabbah would die of hunger and thirst, he sent out cartloads of bread and meat and had them set up in the squares. He had his men fetch flocks of sheep from the Valley of Jabbok. A city without people, a city full of the dead, cannot be conquered. For the King's sake he must keep the people alive.

When the wind dropped in the evenings the air was heavy with the fermenting odours of death and decay.

And the men of Rabbah came to him with their weapons, they came with spears and bows and swords loaded on carts pulled by emaciated oxen. But Joab forbade them to surrender their weapons: they were not to render themselves subject. If they were weaponless they were already conquered, and then King David could not conquer them.

But the men left the carts behind them, and Joab was forced to go out with his army and distribute the weapons among the Ammonites, leaving a spear, a sword, a sling and a bow in every house.

When the King of Rabbah, King Hanun, sent him his crown, which was of pure gold, adorned on top with an amethyst as blue as the sky, and so heavy that one man could hardly carry it before him – and borne now by two of the healthiest Ammonites between them – Joab refused to receive it. He loaded it on an ass and sent it back. Only when a king is vanquished shall he give up his crown; only at the top of the steps to the kingdom of death can a king relinquish his crown.

Such a man was Joab: he was not tempted by the crown.

If the people of Jerusalem had ever made him choose between the crown and the army, he would have chosen the army. That was the only love he knew: the love for armed men in their thousands.

Now he trained his men in the art of conquering rats, rats that were well on the way to taking over the city, by putting out bait for them and impaling them on their spears and setting traps of plaited root fibres. They were black rats with yellow underbellies. The rats must be prevented from destroying Rabbah and thus carrying out what was reserved solely and exclusively for King David.

And every day he sent a message to the King: 'You must come, my men cannot endure much more. This is the hardest battle campaign of my life. The Ammonites will soon be unconquerable. Only you can save me from this terrible situation.'

Scribe: do you know the strange sign that is used to form the word queen?

The King has many wives, but only one queen. I am Queen Bathsheba.

Bathsheba, the Queen.

He has commanded me to be Queen; he himself has said it.

I shall henceforth always wear this full-length robe.

The King has asked my advice. He asked, 'Shall I go out to the besieged city of Rabbah and take it?'

And I answered, 'Why do you ask me?'

'Whom should I ask?'

'You could go to Jehoshaphat, the Chancellor. Or Hushai, the one who sees the Lord in his dreams. Or to Seraiah, your scribe – he could write an answer for you. Or to Nathan. Or Mephibosheth.'

'They would only tell me their own will. They would not be able to advise me to do what I myself want.'

'And what do you want?'

'I do not know for sure. That is why I am asking you.'

But I could not give him any answer; I was overcome by a terrible weariness when he put his question to me. Never before has anyone asked me for guidance.

This full-length robe is a sign. It is a garment of office.

What is a queen? The King says simply: 'She is what she is.'

Mephibosheth says: 'She is a mother to the people.'

And Shebaniah, the poor boy who knows everything, his answer is: 'She is a chosen person. God ordains: He knows

77

where all things and all people have their rightful places. He makes someone queen, he writes her name in the genealogy of heaven and earth. A woman who is pierced by the spear of God's love becomes a queen.'

So says Shebaniah.

I believe that God's love is no different from man's love. A desire to conquer, nothing more.

Are you really writing down every word?

When my son was dead, he who is called the Blessed One, Ahinoam came to comfort me. She wept. She wept, but I did not. And she bathed my forehead and placed a cushion beneath my back and stroked my cheek with her frail yet rough hand, and wept the whole time. And I asked, 'Why are you weeping?'

'I am mourning for King David's son,' she replied.

'It is I who should mourn him,' I said.

'He was so soft and still and pretty,' said Ahinoam. 'I grieved for him even before he died. I mourned him while he still lived.'

'But, Ahinoam, you have seen hundreds of children die.'

'Yes. But not one was like him.'

'I could see from Nathan's face that he would die,' I said. 'Nathan never said so, but his detachment and his silence were an indication that God would quite certainly kill him.'

'Yes, the signs indicated that he would not live.'

'But I shall soon have a new son,' I said. 'A son who will not just be called the Blessed One but will also be so.'

Then Ahinoam began all at once to scream, I know not why. Her voice became as shrill as a professional mourner's, and she cried out: 'Why does God go among us like an angel of death! A child-stealer! What is the nature of God?'

And I tried to calm and console her. But I had no answer to her cries. Then Mephibosheth replied in my stead, standing in the doorway supported on his crutches, the carved claws on the crutches below his cheeks making him look like an owl, his fetid breath reaching right over to my bed; 'He is as He is. He exists in all the ways that can possibly be imagined, He has all the qualities that there are and that we can conceive. He is bloodthirsty and loving and vengeful and forgiving and abominable and beautiful. He deserves all our anger and hatred and all our love.'

And he continued: 'The questions "does He exist" and "what is His nature" can never be divorced. He has in His unfathomability moulded these two questions into one. By his very inscrutability He shows us that He exists. He is as He is because we do not know what His nature is. And so that we shall know that He is. God is the only one who could annul the existence of God.'

'But Mephibosheth!' I cried. 'How can you know all this?'

'I have thought it out myself,' he said. 'The Lord Himself has made me think it.'

And Ahinoam said, 'I have always found it dreadfully difficult to love God. I think it is a task that men and warriors should undertake, to love God.'

But she was shouting and weeping no longer. Before she left me she said, 'Yes, you shall have another son, you shall have many sons, God wants us to have sons.'

I believe my house-god is a god too. The world is full of gods. There is a god for every person. We do not have to be precise on the question of God.

Uncertainty is not an unbearable affliction.

I think it is possible to torment oneself to death with cries and questions.

What I am saying now, I am not saying for always. Perhaps, scribe, you will have to erase these words later on.

Are you really writing everything? I find it strange, not to say disquieting, that someone is writing down my words.

I am speaking slowly like this so that you can inscribe each word, the form of each word separately, though all words are dependent on each other.

My body has forgotten the Blessed One, it feels no pain from him. My breasts are like a virgin's again, and my navel has sunk back into my flesh.

I think that I am carrying a newborn son in my body. I shall never give birth to anything but sons.

Bearing children is complying with God's will and carrying out His work. In every human being there are other beings latent. Even Mephibosheth has produced new beings. I believe that God is life and humankind. If there were no death, life would not be necessary.

If I say anything that is too childish you must not write it down. If my thoughts are not queenlike you must not write them down: you can just pretend to write.

The King often sleeps with me. He seldom goes to the women's house now, and he never sleeps out in the open. And I know that they are saying in the house, it is as if he were the Queen's suckling child.

He says that my nose whistles when I sleep.

I often clean out his ears with my little finger; his own fingers are too thick.

'The one who shall reign after me.' The King often says that: 'The one who shall reign after me.'

Or simply: 'The one.'

I do not know who will reign after him, and he seems not to know it himself. That is why he so often talks about the one whose identity shall reign after him.

The King is incapable of living in uncertainty. Uncertainty is for him an unbearable affliction.

He is afraid that a prophet will choose a shepherd boy. That a man of God in a prophetic frenzy will find an ordinary boy of no particular family and be moved by love for him and choose him and anoint him with holy oil and proclaim him king.

'Rather Shebaniah in that case,' he says. But he does not mean it. Shebaniah seems to bear the mark of a chosen one on his forehead, but he is chosen in a different way.

And I say to the King: 'You yourself were just such a shepherd boy.'

But he replies: 'A person such as I is born only once in every thousand. In me the godly is united with the human in a natural way. Ordinary people are begotten and born by chance. But I was chosen in my mother's womb.'

'And the one who shall reign after you must also be chosen in that way?'

'Without being chosen no man can rule over other men. All power is based on being chosen.'

'Can you not leave that to uncertainty?' I ask. 'To the Lord?'

But this he cannot do, he believes that the Lord has left it to him.

'The choosing is in my seed,' he says. 'My seed has a strangely sweet smell, have you not noticed that, Bathsheba? It has an aroma of smoke. I believe it is the quality of being chosen that has this fragrance.'

And I do not want to tell him that Uriah's seed had the same smell.

So I am silent.

'But I have so many sons,' he says. 'Not even Ahinoam knows their number. How can I then know who is the chosen one?'

But I know that he is thinking: Amnon or Absalom.

He has already chosen those two.

Amnon is the son of Ahinoam; he is the eldest son. When he was born, the King was still living in Hebron and waging war against King Saul.

Amnon is like the King. He is broad across the shoulders and his eyes are hidden beneath his eyebrows, behind his eyelids. He already has six wives; he has them in his own women's house by the washing ponds. They are women the King has given him. He also receives wine from the King. He is a wine drinker, and if his wine runs out he comes here to the palace and demands to rule the kingdom jointly with the King.

Then the King gives him wine.

Absalom is the son of Maacah, King Talmai's daughter whom David bought in Geshur. His hair is long and black and curly, and is combed every morning by two servants. He is tall and handsome – he is one of the most handsome men I have seen – and he is always practising with sword or spear or bow and arrow. He worships God as God used to be worshipped here in Jerusalem before David came. His name indicates that he belongs to the God of Jerusalem. He himself says that Shalem, who was the previous god of the King's city, is the same as the Lord. I do not know.

Amnon or Absalom. One of the two.

But neither of them is the son of a queen.

I wish that the son I am carrying in my womb would grow up quickly – yes, that he could achieve in one year the growth that takes others twenty years.

And King David says, 'If I am unable to choose between them, then I commit a sin. Indecision is a king's greatest sin.'

But I say, 'Can indecision not also be a sign from the Lord? Perhaps it is to be neither Amnon nor Absalom who is to succeed you?

'You must have patience,' I say.

But uncertainty torments him like a continuously bleeding wound; it makes him whimper and cry like a baby.

I believe that uncertainty is the Lord.

Why do you look at me so wonderingly, scribe?

You are to write, nothing more.

Absalom has given me a dove in a cage. The cage stands on the table by my bed. It is a turtle-dove. I have named it Korban, meaning that which is presented. I often converse with it. Absalom bought it from the blind bird breeder at the house of the Phoenicians. He sent Mephibosheth to me with it. The King says that it is strange for him to have given me a bird. I do not know.

I feel a strange burning and tenderness in my heart when the King asks my advice, I am astonished and happy and filled with fear.

But finally I placed my mouth by his ear, I pushed aside the locks of hair and pressed my lips to his ear and whispered very fast but clearly and unhesitatingly: 'Yes, you must take Rabbah! You must delay no longer! You are the King! You shall bring out the children of Ammon as captives and put them to the axe, you shall slay their king, Hanun, and destroy their god, Moloch! You must conquer your indecision.'

Well, let me see now what I have said and what you have written.

The men who still remained in Jerusalem followed David to Rabbah. Many of them had injuries from past wars. They rode on mules or supported themselves on crutches as they walked. The youngest men were there too, those who had stayed at home to tend the sheep and guard the city walls and carry on business and trade while Joab and the army fought the Ammonites. They were in high spirits, proud and expectant. As they passed the women who had gathered at the Gihon gate they held their weapons aloft, their swords and spears and slings. No one could fail to see that they were on their way to their first battle.

On the King's orders they had all sacrificed a kid or a dove to the Lord. The King himself had sacrificed a bull. For the last three days they had drunk nothing but water and ewes' milk, they were taking no wine with them, and they had not been with a woman for seven days. They were clean.

The King rode at the head. He had a red woollen cloak over his shoulders. Behind him came Amnon and Absalom on their mules.

It took them three days to reach Rabbah. They followed the same path as Uriah on his last journey: it was already called Uriah's Way. They spent the first night outside Jericho and the second at a spring in one of the valleys of Gilead.

Bathsheba and Mephibosheth and Shebaniah stood at a window on the northern side of the palace as the men walked, rode, marched and limped off. Shebaniah had his trumpet in his hand, but in his excitement he forgot to blow the rousing flourish he had been practising beforehand. Mephibosheth sighed and moaned as he always did, which could mean anything at all. And Bathsheba fought against the tears that were welling up, regretting having in her confusion and vanity exhorted the King to undertake this uncertain and dreadful campaign, and when he turned and raised his hand in greeting, she was surprised by a violent cramp in her belly. It was the little baby giving a sign of life for the first time. It seemed to her as if he were stretching out inside her, as if he were kicking down against her groin with his feet and grasping for her heart with his hands.

When the Ammonites in Rabbah saw them coming, as they caught the first glimpse of King David's red cloak like a fiery flame against their age-old skies, when they saw how many of them there were and that it really was the King and his sons, King Hanun ordered the city gates to be opened. No swords were to be raised, all resistance was pointless and forbidden, no stones were to be thrown, and no one should hold his shield before him, no one should challenge King David with his shield. The time had come for submission and liberation.

And King David and his men took possession of Rabbah.

The Ammonites stood with bowed and bared heads, some on their knees. None of the men, the men still alive, dared to raise their eyes to the conquerors; many were incapable, from exhaustion or mourning, of emerging from their houses. Bodies of animals, butchered and half-eaten despite their emaciated state, lay on the streets, and the whole city stank of putrefaction and death.

The only creatures to flee were the rats.

The women stood close together in small groups, with their arms round one another as if they thought they could protect and defend each other.

In front of the houses lay children who had died of hunger and thirst, most of them lying on their stomachs with their little faces to the ground, as if even they had cast themselves down in submission.

And here and there old men and women sat in doorways: they had rent their clothes to shreds and gouged bloody weals on their bodies.

King David rode at the head of his men, his eyes fixed on King Hanun's palace. That was his goal, but he could not help also seeing the unarmed and subdued men, the rats, the women, the old people, the dead bodies.

Behind him came his two sons, Absalom with his sword lying across the saddle in front of him, sitting erect and dignified, his youthful expressionless face turned to the sun, and Amnon, hunched and indifferent, tired from the ride, thirsty, longing to be back home in Jerusalem – he would not have been there but for the King's command.

But when David saw the devastation and suffering in Rabbah, when he saw the reality of everything, when the stench and the lamentations penetrated his consciousness, he thought: Joab could have completed this just as well as I.

And when he caught sight of a young woman who resembled Bathsheba, standing in one of the doorways and holding a basket-work bird cage in her hands, alone and deserted, her face half turned away as if trying to refuse to see what she was being forced to see, he suddenly felt a suffocating pain in his chest and throat. She even had her hair tied and plaited just like Bathsheba. His face and eyes became burning hot and his breath laboured and gasping; he wished that the men of Rabbah had raised their weapons against him. He who fights needs an opponent and an enemy, or he may be vanquished by consideration and pity.

But the Ammonites had hidden or buried their weapons, the weapons that Joab had forced them to keep.

And he could not help turning to look once more on the woman in the doorway.

Then he could control his cheeks and lips and eyes no longer.

She was still standing quite still with the turtle-dove held in front of her. He began to wail and groan in as much anguish as the conquered people.

And so David wept unceasingly as he and his men took possession of Rabbah.

Moloch was a royal god. Although his image was carved in a block of stone in front of the royal palace in Rabbah, his mouth wide open as if he were making a proclamation to the people, and his belly swollen and heavy, he was in reality an invisible god, who dwelled within the King. When a new king was chosen from among the Ammonites, the god Moloch moved into his body and remained there for as long as the King lived and retained his power. Perhaps God was simply power.

But when the King died or was overthrown Moloch forsook him, and dwelt in the great void while waiting for another king to arise. The Ammonites could not remember ever having had another god. They prayed to him gladly, they sacrificed animals and offered bread to him, they had even given him their children. But when their need of him was greatest, he was often no longer present.

So these were King Hanun's words to David when they finally met on the steps of the palace: 'My God has forsaken me.'

But David did not reply: He thought only: Perhaps he has forsaken you. But it could equally well be that you have forsaken him. When your old father died I sent my men to you to console you, Uriah among them. But you accused them of being spies and enemies. You had half their beards shaved off and cut off their garments to reveal their private parts, and they could not fulfil the commission I had given them – to spy out Rabbah. You shaved and dishonoured them: You were godless even then. First one is forsaken by God, then one is visited by God's justice.

King Hanun was wearing only a tunic without a girdle; the

great royal crown lay at his feet; he had daubed his face with ashes and scratched bloody weals on his cheeks to show that he was nothing but an ordinary mortal.

Behind David stood Amnon and Absalom, Amnon holding David's ass by the bridle.

I wish I did not have to look at him, thought David. But he was indeed a king.

And he commanded Absalom and Amnon to fetch a cart so that they could carry the royal crown home with them to Jerusalem.

'You have brought about your own downfall,' he said to Hanun. 'Your arrogance and your godlessness have plunged you into ruin.'

'I obeyed God all the time He was with me,' Hanun replied. 'But when He forsook me I could no longer obey Him.'

And David thought of Moloch, whose image was engraved on the block of stone behind him.

'I do not know him,' he said. 'He is a false idol.'

One ought to be spared having to face an ordinary mortal, someone who is so obviously and plainly an ordinary mortal, he thought. All this poor creature needs is pity. But if God does not have mercy upon him, how can I be expected to?

'I wish you had thrown yourself upon your sword before I came,' he said, 'Then you would have avoided this humiliation. King Saul, our King Saul, threw himself on his sword when he saw that he was vanquished.'

'Everything must be completed,' said Hanun, speaking very softly and slowly, with neither bitterness nor defiance in his voice. 'One must never leave anything unfinished, says the Lord.'

'It is not you who had to complete this,' said David. 'It has fallen to my lot.'

And he saw that Hanun's lips were moving continuously; even as he stood in silence his lips moved and his larynx was working.

'What are you saying?' David asked. 'I can see that you are speaking but I can hear nothing.'

'I am speaking to God,' Hanun replied.

'Why are you speaking to him? Has he not forsaken you?'

'I am asking Him why he has forsaken me,' said Hanun. 'I am asking Him to have mercy upon us.'

'If you had not cut the garments of my men to shreds and exposed their private parts, you would not need to ask for mercy. You might just as well pray to the mountains to fall upon you and to the hills to hide you.'

Now Joab and his men came. They had been waiting behind the palace, one of them even sitting up on the roof keeping watch and calling out to tell the others the progress of David's entry into Rabbah.

But Joab did not go forward to the King; he stood at a distance of ten paces and looked at the two kings, the conqueror and the conquered, and felt almost as if he had entered the tabernacle of the Lord and disturbed two priests in the middle of some dread and holy ceremony.

'I did not know that your men's private parts were holy,' said Hanun. 'I only wanted to frighten them.'

But a tremor in his voice revealed that he was not telling the truth. All men know that a man's private parts are holy.

'You knew,' said David. 'No one can fail to recognize what is holy. Everything that is holy gives off a special aura.'

And now Hanun was silent.

But then he asked, and he put the question despite already knowing the answer: 'Have you never been vanquished?'

'I have fled. But never really been vanquished. One is only really vanquished once. Just as you are now.'

'It would have been easier to endure if I had been able to keep my god,' said Hanun.

'The Lord has always protected me,' said David.

'And my son will not reign after me.'

'Had you already decided who would reign after you?' David asked, a note of inquisitive envy in his voice.

'I have seventy-two sons,' Hanun replied. 'One of them.'

'The Lord will choose one of my sons,' said David. 'I have left it to uncertainty. I have left it to the Lord.'

'But if the Lord should withhold his hand from you?'

'That is not the nature of the Lord. The Lord is always present. You can see that He is with me now. Whatever I do, I can never free myself from Him – He is all around me. As long as we live He is with us. He watches over us constantly, He is our Protector day and night.'

'It is when one is forsaken by God that one really needs Him,' Hanun sighed.

'One can never be forsaken by a real god. The only God.'

'When one is forsaken by Him, one realizes how real He is.'

'He must be a victorious god. The gods of defeat are mere idols.'

'God is not responsible for my misfortune. He has merely withdrawn. With His power and His glory.'

And David thought: For how long shall my glory be turned into ignominy? This hour of victory is causing me nothing but pain.

And he thought: I thank the Lord that Bathsheba is not here.

The cart which Amnon and Absalom had fetched had two copper-rimmed wooden wheels and a leather pannier, and was pulled by an ass. It was Absalom alone who lifted the crown and set it in the cart, taking it in his arms and pressing it momentarily to his breast. It was, after all, a royal crown. Amnon had taken hold of the King's ass again with one hand, and with the other was absent-mindedly patting the hind quarters of the ass harnessed to the cart.

Hanun looked at Absalom. His eyes were calm and steady, not bitter or malignant. Perhaps there was a trace of pity in them, the pity he felt for himself radiating out from his eyes and falling upon Absalom.

'You know what has to happen,' said David.

'Is your realm of death the same as ours?' asked Hanun.

'The realm of death is not a realm in the usual sense of the word,' David replied. 'There are no kings in the realm of death. All are transformed into shadows.'

'And there is no god?'

'No, no God.'

All this was quite unbearable. King David felt that his body was rigid with cold, though the heat of the midday sun was streaming down upon them. He could see in this vanquished, destitute king something that he knew was also in himself, but he could not say what it was: a sense of abandonment and apprehensive trust or impassioned indifference. No, he could not put into words what it was, he knew only that they were, in some mysterious way, reflections of each other; he himself with his majestic red cloak over his shoulders and the other man divested of all his regalia. But nevertheless, or perhaps even because of that, still a king.

The situation was quite simply too ambiguous and disturbing, much too pregnant with meaning. It was unbearable.

'Down on your knees!' he cried. 'And bow your head!'

At that very moment his ass, the anointed royal ass, brayed loudly with hunger, boredom and weariness, and he gave a start as if he had been woken suddenly from a deep sleep. The braying of the ass seemed to wake and save him: it was as if reality had cried out to him from the ass's mouth. He took two quick steps back, away from King Hanun, who had humbly and obediently fallen to his knees and bowed his head, and looked around him, and at last saw Joab and his men standing by the stone image of the god Moloch. And he saw Absalom and the cart with the crown, and Amnon standing leaning against the ass with his head resting on its hind quarters as if they were a woman's hips. He lifted his shoulders and sucked air into his lungs as if he had forgotten to breathe for the whole duration of his conversation with Hanun, and he stood up on his toes and shook his limbs and raised his arms and rubbed his stiff neck with his clasped hands. Yes, it really was as if he had awoken from a mysterious and ill-omened dream. He stroked the ass's rough muzzle gently, as if he wanted to thank the animal, and took from a bag beneath his cloak a piece of dried salted partridge breast. He had learned that when he was a shepherd in Bethlehem: never leave home without taking a piece of dried meat with you.

And very quickly, almost as if he were reading out one of the holy texts he had long known by heart, he gave Joab and his men the necessary orders – what was to be done with the body of the slain Hanun, what should happen to the women and children, how the men should be put to death, what could be done with the few remaining animals, how the gold and silver should be collected up.

Then he turned round, as if Hanun had already been executed, and left the palace. He had conquered Rabbah, he had done what had to be done.

On the way back he looked over to the door where the woman had stood, the one who resembled Bathsheba. But she was no longer there; perhaps she was already someone's booty.

He led the ass by the bridle, and behind him came Absalom and Amnon, Absalom with the ass and the cart and the crown. All his men were now setting about the looting of the city, but he seemed not to notice it.

David and his sons, David gnawing on a partridge breast – and the only one who really had the look of a conquerer was Absalom.

Bathsheba lay awake, unable to sleep, the first night after David and his men had left Jerusalem. As soon as she felt sleep coming, frightful pictures rose up before her eyes: David with blood streaming from a wound in his chest, David with mutilated genitals, David with his throat cut.

Her love for David had put an armed guard at the portals of sleep.

Early in the morning she woke the servants sleeping outside her room and ordered a carriage to be got ready for her and Mephibosheth, and a mule to be saddled for Shebaniah.

And they set off at dawn, just as the sheep were stirring and beginning to graze, and followed Uriah's Way. Mephibosheth was still asleep; the servants had borne him to the carriage. It was a covered carriage, which King David had received as a gift from King Talmai, the father of Absalom's mother. Shebaniah sat stiff and straight on the mule: he had had almost no practice in the art of riding, and had only ridden a few times before, in play, within Jerusalem. He had borrowed a sword from Hosah, who guarded the wine in the stores. It was a dagger-like copper sword, its hilt shaped like a male organ. But a sword nevertheless.

They stopped for the night beyond the River Jordan, in Gilead, Bathsheba and Mephibosheth sleeping in the carriage, Shebaniah beneath an oak tree.

Bathsheba had thought that they would reach Rabbah at the start of the battle, that she would still be in time to stop David before anything dreadful and irrevocable had befallen him. But when they reached the last hill before the walls and the city lay before them, they saw neither his retinue nor the army, nor any sign of battle. The sun had just passed its midday zenith, the city gates stood wide open, and from within could be heard only isolated cries and wailing – no battle trumpets and no exhortatory battle cries. Here and there smoke rising from the fires shimmered translucently in the sunlight, and on the roofs occasional clusters of black-clothed women and children could be seen.

Shebaniah was now riding ahead of the carriage, his upturned sword propped against the saddle. They made their way slowly down towards the city. Bathsheba felt uncertain and confused: perhaps this was not the Rabbah of the Ammonites but some other unknown city, perhaps they had taken the wrong direction when they crossed the River Jordan at the ford. After all, Uriah's Way was still so new and in many places difficult to recognize.

But when they came through the gates, and no guards attempted to prevent them, and there was no sign of anyone on duty at all, they realized immediately that the battle, if there had been one, was already over: they saw the dead bodies, rats running hither and thither, women sobbing. And they could smell the stench of rotting flesh. But of David's and Joab's army there was no sign.

Bathsheba, who had expected to meet a throng of men madly hacking and cutting each other to death, was filled both with a sense of dismay and astonished relief. And she said to Mephibosheth, who sat leaning heavily on the cushions next to her, 'Perhaps they have already moved on?'

'I know nothing of how cities are conquered,' he groaned. 'Do not ask me.'

Mephibosheth had been dragged out on this journey to Rabbah without warning, and could not understand why.

'Uriah used to talk of rib-cages gashed open and blood spurting everywhere,' Bathsheba stammered. She stroked her nipples with her fingertips, as she always did when she was bewildered and perplexed.

'Soldiers' stories are like women's gossip at the well,' he said in a tired voice. 'Rumours and tittle-tattle at the mock well. Lies and exaggerations, nothing more.'

But she had to come to Uriah's defence – he had after all belonged to her. Or she had belonged to him. 'Uriah was truthful! His lips did not know how to form a lie!'

'Uriah was like everyone else,' said Mephibosheth obstinately. 'He was like Joab and David and Absalom and Asahel and Elhanan and Elika and Helez and Zelek and Igal.'

Bathsheba said no more. Mephibosheth's generalization merely revealed the dreadful confusion that reigned in his soul; his soul was like the world before God created it, before He distinguished between living beings and inanimate objects. None of these men was like any other, none was even similar to another, people cannot be classified.

Counted, but not classified.

Shebaniah, then, rode in front. At the second house beyond the city gate, a low and humble house, stood a group of boys. They had stayed in hiding while David and his retinue filed past, and now stood close to the wall of the house looking around in fear and consternation. Their clothes were ragged and dirty; they were all about Shebaniah's age or a little younger. They were leaning on each other for support, some with their arms round one another's shoulders, the youngest shyly holding the hands of the older ones.

Shebaniah sat unnaturally straight and tense in the saddle, the short sword in his right hand standing up before him as if aroused.

The boys looked at him: the sword and the light, rose-coloured cloak, the broad leather girdle with yellow stones, the silver headband the King had given him. And one of them tried to smile at him.

That at least was what Shebaniah saw: one of them smiled.

And he thought: The enemy is smiling.

No, it was not even a thought, it was a fleeting impression that flowed or rushed in his blood straight from his eyes to his limbs.

The enemy was smiling at him.

And he jumped down from the back of the mule, he jumped with such a bound that the tip of the sword nicked a wound in his throat and the mule started as if it had been lashed with a whip. He lunged forward at the boys, who huddled closer together when they saw him coming. He brandished the sword clumsily and inexpertly before him; he could no longer remember or see which one of them was the boy with the smile.

He struck down the first one almost with reluctance, with a groan on his lips and anguish in his heart; he stuck in the sword between the youth's ribs so deep that he could feel the rough cloth of his tunic against his hand on the hilt of the sword, and then drew it out again with a hasty wrench.

He attacked the second by the throat, slashing at him for as long as the boy stood on his feet. His anguish was lessening now; his main feeling was an excited astonishment that the soldier's profession was not more difficult.

And the boys did not attempt to flee, they just clung closer together, stricken with fear.

He stabbed the third one in the back, on the left side beneath the shoulder blade just where the heart is. He felt the glowing fervour of battle rising within him, and the sweat streamed down his face and made his eyes smart.

And he fell upon the fourth with emboldened rage, his mouth foaming. It was almost unbelievably easy to do battle and vanquish enemies!

Then he went on in a state of holy madness, his arm, previously used to holding only a trumpet or the little harp, seemingly lifted by a miraculous force from above, his legs moving lithely and agilely, and his back imbued with a strength he had never before even suspected he possessed.

And he heard and saw nothing but the fearful battle he was fighting, he did not hear Bathsheba continually calling his name in horror and distress, and if he had heard it he would no longer have known that it was his name: 'Shebaniah! Shebaniah!'

When David caught sight of the carriage he recognized it immediately; the covered carriage which his father-in-law, Talmai of Geshur, had given him. It stood barely a stone's throw from him, almost at the city gate.

Bathsheba! Bathsheba!

And he threw away the gnawed partridge breast and began to run. He ran with a heavy, waddling gait, yet made good headway. Absalom and the ass and the mules and the carriage with the royal crown and Amnon were soon left behind. Something terrible must have happened, he thought. Perhaps it is not Bathsheba but the Chancellor come with some dreadful news about Bathsheba. He should not have left her alone, or almost alone, in Jerusalem! He panted and groaned and lurched and stamped like a charging bull, but did not lessen his pace until he had reached the carriage.

Then he came upon Shebaniah, the ground around him covered with the youths he had slain.

With a howl of amazement and rage he grabbed hold of the wretched Shebaniah and tore the sword from his hand. He lifted him up at arm's length before him and shook him the way one shakes a disobedient child, and shouted at him, 'You miserable creature! You miserable creature!' He could not believe that this was his boy, Shebaniah, the mild and gentle Shebaniah with his fragrance of honey, he who had taken Shaphan's place, he who played the lyre more lovingly than anyone else. What had these Ammonite children done that had roused him to such a desperate pitch of anger?

'Shebaniah!' he cried. 'Shebaniah! Shaphan! Shebaniah!'

What alarmed and upset him was not what Shebaniah had done, but that it was Shebaniah who had done it.

A deed which was fundamentally incompatible with all music.

Finally, since Shebaniah proffered no word of explanation,

and the tears poured from his eyes and froth trickled from the corners of his mouth, he lifted him up on to the mule, which still stood quietly where Shebaniah had left it. He lifted him up into the saddle just as one does with a nervous child about to ride for the first time.

And then at last Bathsheba appeared.

She fell rather than stepped down from the carriage, she crawled up to him on her knees, her face lifeless and blank like a bronze mask. She did not weep; fear and joy were equal within her and cancelled each other out. She grasped his legs with her arms and clung and climbed up his body as if it were the trunk of a tree.

It hurt her to be so dependent on him that she could not get up or stand without his support.

Finally, in a low whimper, she said: 'You are alive.'

He felt how stiff and tense she was. She had feared that an Ammonite, just a single one, might have killed him in a state of holy madness. No other wife had ever asked whether he was alive or dead, not even Ahinoam. He put his head down to her face as if to breathe into her nostrils his breath of life.

'Do not punish him,' she whispered. 'I beg you not to punish him.'

'Who?'

'Shebaniah.'

'Why should I punish him?'

'For the abominable act he has committed.'

So Shebaniah too had a place in her heart. All who came near her found a place in her heart, he thought.

'Why should I punish him? They had to die anyway.'

He meant: sooner or later. He had learned that much about mankind.

'Everything is my fault,' she said. 'That you went out to battle. And Shebaniah.'

That Shebaniah went out to battle, he thought.

'No, not everything is your fault,' he said, as if he meant that there were some particular situations for which she did not need to feel guilty. And he stroked the nape of her neck and her throat where the sinews were slowly beginning to relax.

'Mephibosheth is sleeping,' she said. 'He is sitting in the carriage asleep.'

'Mephibosheth?'

'Yes. His rest will not be disturbed. There is nothing for him to do here.'

'Mephibosheth?'

'I wanted to have him with me. In case I needed someone to comfort me.'

And David thought: Mephibosheth?

'You should not have come,' he said. 'Your place is in Jerusalem.'

'Only in Jerusalem?'

'Yes. Only there.'

'My fear drove me to come,' Bathsheba said in her own defence. 'My nightmares.'

'Dreams have to be interpreted,' said David. 'If God gives us nightmares, then terror and anguish are his message. Nothing more.'

'That is not what Nathan says.'

'Nathan is a befuddled wordmonger who becomes intoxicated by the beating of his fingers on his little drum.'

She felt calmness slowly returning to her and the strength in her limbs being restored. She no longer needed to cling to him, and when she pressed the palms of her hands against his chest and took half a step backwards, he responded by releasing her.

'The little one is already moving in my womb,' she said. 'When he hears your voice he lifts his head as if he were listening.'

And David just smiled. That was the way it should be: sons would always be growing and moving in her womb, and they

99

would hear his voice. He would take her carefully and considerately back to Jerusalem; he would tell the servants that the carriage wheels must avoid all stones and holes on Uriah's Way.

When Bathsheba looked around her and saw the half-eaten bodies of animals and the desecrated corpses and the frightened faces at the windows and the boys Shebaniah had killed, she asked in a low, meditative voice as if really seeking an answer, as if she were asking herself and nobody else: 'How can God let this happen?'

But David answered as if the question had been put to him: 'God is perfect and good. But He is also a creator. And a creator cannot be good. When He creates, He steps out of His perfection and becomes like us. Then anything can happen, then He destroys with one hand and creates with the other. That is the way it is.'

Shebaniah too returned slowly to reality. He sat on the mule, no longer straight and upright, but shrunken and hunched forward. As he came to himself again he also regained his frailness: he shook as if he were freezing, and now he would not even have been able to lift the sword up from the ground.

And Amnon and Absalom stood waiting behind the King and Queen. Absalom held by the bridle the mule that was pulling the carriage that held the crown.

The Ammonite boys, the ones who had survived Shebaniah's onslaught, were standing absolutely still. They were not shouting, nor even weeping, they were not invoking their god, they asked nothing; they clung to each other in silence as if they already knew all there was to know.

And Bathsheba walked the few steps back to the carriage on her own. David made a movement as if to lift and carry her, but she did not see it. She deliberately avoided seeing it.

What remained to be done in Rabbah could now be left to Joab and his men, so King David gave now only the most necessary orders: a carriage for Mephibosheth, the sleeper; the King himself would

travel with the Queen; a man to lead Shebaniah's mule and take
the captured royal crown; two men to bury the children who had
fallen to Shebaniah's sword; and a wine vessel for Mephibosheth. Yes, everything that he could think of in haste that was
useful and necessary.

Shebaniah asked Shashak the Benjaminite, who was to escort
him home, for the return of his sword. David nodded his
approval: there was, after all, something unusual and mysterious, perhaps even holy, about the boy. And before he was led
away Shebaniah turned and counted the enemies he had slain.

Eleven.

As they trundled out of the city and away towards the first
wooded hills, the carriage with the crown ahead of them,
Absalom riding in front, David told Bathsheba about King
Hanun:

'His god had forsaken him, his manly strength had faded, he
was as compliant as a sacrificial lamb for the slaughter.'

'How do you know that his god had forsaken him?'

'He said so himself.'

'And he was like a sacrificial lamb?'

'Yes. Like a lamb for the slaughter.'

And Bathsheba thought long and hard. Finally she said: 'Are
you really sure that God had forsaken him?'

But now David said nothing more. He had fallen asleep with
his head on her shoulder. It was painfully heavy.

In Jerusalem there were only women, and Cherethites and
Pelethites guarding the King's house, and a few of the King's
officials.

No gate of honour was erected, but the women strewed palm
leaves and sprigs of myrtle in their path, and the temple
choristers met them at the gate of Gihon. They all bore
themselves like victors: Absalom with the royal crown, Amnon
with a wine cask across the mule's saddle, David with Bathsheba, Mephibosheth with his own carriage – one of King

Hanun's ceremonial carriages – Shebaniah with his sword, and Bathsheba with David.

Bathsheba went immediately to her room. She wanted to anoint her god with fragrant oil. She had a little Egyptian bottle of thanksgiving oil that Mephibosheth had given her the morning after the King had spent the whole night with her for the first time without going to the women's house.

And when David sacrificed a ram in the tabernacle of the Lord, a thanksgiving sacrifice, and when he had commanded Jehoshaphat, the Chancellor, to go to Rabbah to assist Joab in bringing about peace and calm and loving concord among the Ammonites, he called his scribe.

Write:

The King shall joy in Thy strength, O Lord; and in Thy salvation how greatly shall he rejoice.

All that his lips request Thou givest him, Thou fillest his heart with desire and satisfiest that desire.

Thou settest a crown on his head, yes, a crown fit for the heads of ten kings.

Write: There is no victor but the Lord.

Thou shalt abide with him who conquers, Thou shalt forsake the vanquished, his fruit shalt Thou destroy from the earth. When Thou showest him Thy face he shall be destroyed as in a fiery oven.

Thou shalt aim at the face of the enemy with Thy bow; Thy right hand shall find out all Thine enemies.

I shall sing and praise Thy power.

Thou hast given to every man a fixed measure of strength. When he assists Thee in Thy creation, when he lifts his sword for battle and when he carries out his mightiest deeds, then he leaves his house of safety, then he rests wholly in Thy hands.

And when he falters, nothing can support him but Thy mercy.

In fear and terror and need, we children of men flee to each other. It is in Thee we should trust, it is to Thee we should flee!

Lord, I am afraid for Bathsheba. She trusts not in Thee, I know not in what she puts her trust – perhaps she trusts in nothing. When she hastened to me in Rabbah she took not even her house-god with her.

Perhaps her house-god is not a god of battle. He has no male organ, no, not even a female orifice.

No, do not write that.

She is a wife and yet not a wife; she seems to be a real human being. I do not understand her. I say that with confidence: I do not understand her.

She speaks to me without my having commanded her to speak, she comes to me unasked, she eats at my table, my servants obey her word, I ask her advice, she fetches for herself the jewellery she wants from my treasury. The big golden hairslide she is wearing now once belonged to Maacah, Absalom's mother – I recognize it. She mimics Thy prophet Nathan so that we cannot control our mirth: 'Thus speaks the Lord, O lord,' she croaks, just like the prophet, and pretends to beat on the little drum and opens her eyes wide as he does and raises her hands towards the ceiling as he does, and we fall to our knees with laughter and our eyes stream with tears. I do not think that anything is holy for her.

Why did she come to me in Rabbah? Does she doubt my strength?

She expected a battle, she said so herself, a terrible battle. Not a mock battle.

No, that is not to be written.

She is young. Her youth is a burden that I must bear in my old age. She is the same age as my son Absalom. Absalom could be her husband. No, Absalom could not be her husband. No one but I could be her husband.

When she commands you, scribe, to come to her to write for her, you shall go at once. You shall also be the Queen's scribe.

Ah, no, I did not know that this was already the case – I see from your smile and your nodding that you have been her scribe for some time.

No, do not write that.

Yes, the King trusts in the Lord; Thou dost meet him with goodly blessings, Thou givest him glory and booty.

Against Thee the workers of iniquity are powerless.

Against the Almighty all the evil in the world is like a mere breath of wind, like a drop of rain in the desert. The Lord's goodness and wrath consume everything.

Shebaniah shall compose music for these words, that is an order: music to be played on the lyre. It shall be sung in the tabernacle of the Lord.

When Bathsheba had given birth to her second son, King David named him Nathan, which means God's gift.

But Nathan the prophet expressed misgivings. Of course he felt honoured that a son of the King should bear his name, but he thought it was also risky and dangerous, since a prophetic name implied heavenly visions, holy madness, and foaming at the mouth, all of which were actions or afflictions that royalty should abstain from or avoid.

After all, everyone could remember the ignominy that befell King Saul when he once went into a state of religious ecstasy amongst the prophets.

So Nathan named him the Beloved of the Lord, Jedidiah.

And Bathsheba named him Solomon.

When Solomon was only one year old, he began to converse with Mephibosheth and Shebaniah.

At the age of two he could sing seven of his father's songs. His voice was clear and sweet, perhaps just slightly shrill on the high notes. Shebaniah plucked the accompaniment on his lyre.

Five personal servants and a wet-nurse, two teachers, a baker and a cook looked after him and served him. The nurse was a Chaldean woman whom Mephibosheth had won at dice and given to the King; she herself maintained that she had no name. Solomon called her Deborah, which means honey-woman. Even at the age of ten he sometimes suckled at her breasts despite the fact that they had long since dried up.

When he was three years old, Bathsheba ordered the scribe to note down the most important of Solomon's words. The first inscription was:

'I love this profusion of good things.'

Every year Bathsheba bore him new brothers. She did so simply because it was right and appropriate and necessary. For her, Solomon was enough, he was The Son. King David gave them names, wet-nurses and his blessing, and then forgot them. On the eastern side of the palace, near Amnon's house, in front of the washing ponds, he had had five new rooms built, where his and Bathsheba's sons lived. But for Solomon Bathsheba had two rooms established behind her own. She did this by dividing Mephibosheth's room with a wall and by taking over one of the Chancellor's two rooms.

Joab and the army remained in the land of Ammon for four more years. That was how long it took to conquer the whole country and secure peace. Twelve more cities had to be taken, nomadic desert peoples had to be forced into submission, shepherds had to be taxed, villages destroyed, bridges and walls torn down, olive groves burned, vineyards razed, and men sent as slaves to the mines in Edom.

And everything that had been captured, all objects of gold, silver or copper, all the wine, all the oil, all the woven cloth and dried sheep's cheese and tanned hides and polished stones, had to be sorted, measured, counted, weighed and packed and sent to Jerusalem on the backs of asses and slaves. Joab carried out all this, often irritably and impetuously but with a fundamental patience. Precision and planning always stem from a combination of impatience and patience, the King used to say: The mightiest warriors are always the greatest peacemakers.

But the very same day that David conquered Rabbah, the ark of the Lord was taken back to His tabernacle in the city of David.

In Jerusalem the construction of storehouses was continuously in progress – the King had called in master builders from

Zidon and Zarephath. They were simple buildings with clay floors, walls of brick, and doorposts and lintels of quarried stone. Cellars were dug beneath the buildings for wine and oil.

Bathsheba often stood and watched the slaves making bricks. That easily comprehensible, primitive form of creation from clay and straw appealed to her soul. When the bricks had been knocked out of the moulds they were stacked high in towering piles. She thought that she could sense a mysterious understanding or insight in the skilful blending of materials that craftsmanship involved. Slaves with broad leather straps across their shoulders bore the bricks to the Canaanite workers erecting the walls. But she could not clearly formulate what it was that captured her imagination, what it was that she understood about life and the world during her pensive observation.

On the building sites many different gods were worshipped. All the slaves and workmen and overseers had brought their own gods with them. Some had them suspended from a cord around their necks, or standing at their side while they worked; others kept them only in their minds or as a name. Their gods were made of words and sounds, and nothing else. Not even the prisoners of war from Rabbah had left their god behind in their home country; they continued to fear and pray to Moloch despite the fact that he had failed them, and he had taken refuge in the empty void.

When trouble or misfortune befell, when a half-completed wall collapsed, or a finger was trapped or a foot crushed by a falling beam, then all these gods were invoked. Often, so many gods were called upon at the same time that no individual names could be discerned – the gods were mingled in a general roar or wailing, and Bathsheba thought that this deep-throated, howling chorus of human pain, this confused dissonance, perhaps constituted the real name of the one true God.

When the King gathered his officials around him in the afternoons, before the main meal of the day, Bathsheba was always present. None of them knew how this custom had started –

perhaps he had once asked her to come so that he could seek her advice, just on the one single occasion, and then she had stayed. No wife had ever been present before when he met his chancellor and his secretary and the priests, not even Ahinoam. She sat at the window, half turned away as if to indicate that she was not fully taking part in their discussions, as if her presence were just incidental and completely without significance. And whenever David asked her a question, she always apologized for not having been listening, she was just a poor woman who understood nothing of the administration of the realm, and she made him repeat his question.

Then she gave her answer very clearly and unhesitatingly, and the secretary immediately wrote down her words.

Occasionally she avoided answering: she did not want to give the appearance of having the answers to all questions. Sometimes, too, the King's questions were devious and obscure, as if he were trying to discover the flaws in her thinking, or as if he wanted to demonstrate her weaknesses to his officials. The questions and answers and the superfluous questions and non-existent answers were counters in a game they played with each other. For a long time it was the game of love. Love is a duel where every answer and every question, every word and every gesture must be interpreted and given a meaning.

During those first few years she uttered not a word about the army and Joab.

But she understood better than the King, better even than the Chancellor, the art of numbers. She knew the secrets of the number six and the number ten. (It was Uriah who had taught her – numbers were the only thing in life that Uriah had ever understood.) And she knew the correspondence between written signs and numbers so that she could turn numbers into words and words into numbers. There was a number for David and a number for love and a number for Solomon and a number for God: that was the number one. There was nothing in the whole universe that lacked a number. She could say how measurements and weights should be counted up and how time and distance should be stated. She did all this effortlessly in her head. She never drew a sign and never inscribed a number in her whole life.

She often asked Mephibosheth to put her to the test by thinking up puzzles and difficult questions for her, and her mind was so quick that Mephibosheth never even managed to reach the end of his question before she gave him the answer. And he would give a deep sigh and groan in admiration. He himself could hardly distinguish the number two from the number three, and even the number one, the Lord, he was unsure of.

The one who shall reign after me.

Sometimes the King said just these words, and then fell silent. And the others, too, were silent. They could not talk about this, not even tentatively and uncertainly. Not even Nathan dared speak of it in a state of holy frenzy. Bathsheba leaned out of the window as if some strange or disturbing occurrence in the palace courtyard had attracted her attention, something which concerned her far more than this uninteresting question of who was to reign after him. She knew that the choice between the King's sons would not be decided by thoughts and words: all fateful and decisive steps were determined by actions and events, not by words and fleeting thoughts.

The one.

And he might say: 'Amnon is a good person. He wants no more than contentment. As long as he has wine, and can choose himself a new wife from time to time, he is happy. He could be a prince of peace.'

Or: 'Absalom is regal. He moves like a chosen one, he speaks like a chosen one, his whole figure is that of a chosen one. But he is so alone, he has no friends, he has no advisers, I do not even know whether the Lord is with him.'

Decisions and orders had previously poured from him like notes from a harp in the hands of a master musician. Often, he had only been able to observe in amazement the demands and decrees formed by his voice and lips as if in play. This state of indecision and uncertainty was something new and almost frightening for him; it even manifested itself on his skin and caused itching and inflamed red spots on his face and on the inside of his thighs. He said to Bathsheba: 'The Lord will never forsake me. But He seems to be blurring the world in my sight. He is creating difficulties with my vision and thought, nothing is so sure and certain as before, He is robbing people and things of their individual identities.'

'That is how it has always been,' Bathsheba replied. 'All people have resembled one another to some extent, things have always been linked to one another. But you have not seen it.'

'You mean, our perception sharpens as our sight fails?'

'Yes, that is what I mean.'

'How old are you now, Bathsheba?'

'I am twenty-seven.'

'And already you say people cannot be differentiated, things and living creatures merge into each other without discernible boundaries?'

'Yes, that is what I say.'

'Do you believe it, or are you just saying it?'

'I believe that everything contains something else,' said Bathsheba. 'Behind everything we see, something else is concealed, something which we cannot see.'

'You would never be able to take decisions,' said David. 'You would never be able to issue commands.'

He said this quickly; this he was certain of.

And she answered as abstrusely as she could: 'I never try to do anything other than what is necessary.'

Then he ended the conversation impatiently and with a firm voice: 'Everything is what it is, neither more nor less. Nothing deviates from its kind, the kind that was determined at Creation. Everything has a manifest and unambiguous nature. It must be so. Everything is what it appears to be. God is God.'

Often the scribe had to write down just these words:

'The one who shall reign after me.'

The King could not force himself to think further than that.

And his irresolution spread throughout the whole palace.

Even to Mephibosheth.

'What if the choice falls on me!' he said anxiously to Bathsheba. 'Think of that, my Queen. After all, I have royal blood in my veins. I am descended from the holy seed of Saul.'

'Yes,' said Bathsheba in a serious tone. 'You would be a good and merciful king.'

'I would bear with patience the burdens the Lord laid upon me.'

'Yes, we would all feel secure under your sceptre.'

'I am worried most about all the anger and hatred a king must generate in himself. When I try to feel anger or hatred I just feel melancholy.'

'The Lord gives the king the strength to hate and be angry.'

Bathsheba was forced to turn away so that he would not see her contorted face as she fought back her laughter.

'Perhaps my body would be straightened and be more handsome,' he mused. 'Perhaps my feet would be healed. Perhaps that was what happened when the servant woman who was carrying me above her head dropped me to the ground: my kingly qualities were shaken loose in the fall.'

'No, you must be the person you are,' Bathsheba assured him. 'You must be the same Mephibosheth you are now. And yet king.'

'I do not know if that is possible,' he said sadly.

And he added: 'A king must possess some kind of power. His place must be between men and God.'

'I too could remain the person I am,' Bathsheba went on.

'The person you are?'

'The King's wife.'

'But if I became king, the King would no longer be alive!'

'I could be queen to the new king.'

115

'My wife?'

'Yes. Your wife.'

But now Mephibosheth realized that she was making fun of him. His bloodshot eyes filled with tears and he shook his fists at her and cried: 'Bathsheba! Bathsheba! Have you no pity for me?'

And Bathsheba felt a sense of confusion and no longer knew what to say.

And he continued with a sob: 'You, my dearest turtle-dove! How can you speak of me as if I were merely a fool or a Babylonian ape?'

And she looked at him and recognized how apt this description was, and saw that he was weeping with rage, the laughter within her was turned into sadness and compassion, and she tried to console him.

'I did not mean it like that. I did not mean to mock or taunt you.'

'You insulted me so beguilingly that I was totally unprepared.'

'You must forgive me,' said Bathsheba sorrowfully. 'And of course none of us knows anything for certain. Perhaps there is a king deep down inside you.'

But then Mephibosheth said, in a low but firm voice, catching her nervous glance with his morose gaze: 'I am human, I am very fond of you, Bathsheba. I have a man's face, with cheeks and lips and eyes – see how indescribably handsome I really am. I love you, Bathsheba.'

And when she saw that he really meant what he said, Bathsheba, too, began to weep. So, after all, he had conquered her.

Shebaniah, who was convinced that it was Bathsheba who would ultimately decide on the one who would succeed the King, spoke to her subtly and persuasively.

'I pray to the Lord every day that he let Amnon be chosen. I have even sacrificed a dove for his sake. He will fill the palace with song and dance and he will redeem the oppressed because he will not bother to oppress anyone, and every evening he will provide music with seventy stringed instruments!'

'Why seventy?' Bathsheba asked.

'That is the only number I know,' Shebaniah admitted.

And Bathsheba remembered Shebaniah's battle in Rabbah. If Amnon became king, Shebaniah could be given command of the army.

'I tell you that the King will live and reign for another thirty years,' cried Bathsheba. 'Certainly no less than thirty years!'

'I do not understand that,' said Shebaniah. 'How long a time is thirty years?'

'He is as strong as a young man,' she said. 'Yes, stronger, for he also has the stamina and perseverance that come with age. He is like a stallion in Pharaoh's team of horses and like a beam of weathered cedarwood. No one will succeed him for a long time yet.'

Shebaniah fell silent. And then he said cautiously, 'Yes. No one but you can know how strong he really is.'

'No,' said Bathsheba decisively. 'No one knows his strength as I do. Every night, again and again, I can bear witness to it from my own experience.

But that was not the complete truth.

He often lay beside her now without taking her. He might even lie at her side without knowing her during the days of her monthly purge. He would place his sword between them in the bed, and they would talk each other to sleep; sometimes he would recite songs to her that he was trying to compose in his mind, and she would help him to count the number of syllables or to choose some particularly elevated word, or help him to hum the wandering tunes that were to accompany the words.

Sometimes he would prop himself up on his elbow in the bed afterwards and turn his face towards her, and she could read the proud question in his eyes, 'Do you see what it means to have created this magnificent song?'

And when Ahinoam died he did not touch any woman for two months. He ordered a time of mourning and abstinence for himself and all his men. She was the first wife to have borne him a son, and he wished her to travel in peace down into the realm of death. Her journey should not be disturbed by the panting embraces of the living.

But Bathsheba thought: Ahinoam was not like that, she would not have looked on the lovemaking of the living with disapproval or bitterness. She had only gone to thank the Lord that she herself no longer needed to exert herself in this respect.

She died in the fourth year after the fall of Rabbah. She died of old age, this mother of his first-born who was two years younger than David.

He had not desired her for many years; she had been an old woman who came and went as she wished in the palace, a toothless old woman with pearl-grey hair. Many of the younger ones did not even know that she was a wife. But now that she was dead, she seemed to be reunited with him again. He composed a song of mourning for her: I have behaved and quieted myself, as a child that is weaned of its mother.

And he told Bathsheba of the occasion in his youth when the Amalekites, those wild and nomadic desert people, had stolen Ahinoam from him. It was when he was living in Ziklag. Yes, she was as beautiful as the moon and as radiant as the sun. He had pursued the Amalekites to the south, at first with 600 men; but one after another they tired, and when he finally caught up with the band of robbers 400 of his men had given up. He slaughtered the Amalekites and their camels – yes, even the camels. For a whole night and a whole day he did nothing but cut the throats of men and camels, and when night fell he begat his third son with Ahinoam. Bathsheba felt like a child listening to an old man's stories.

Amnon mourned for his mother so deeply that he clothed himself in black sackcloth and smeared ash over his face and did not wash for several months and drank nothing but camel's milk.

But he let it ferment in the way Ahinoam had learned from the Amalekites and which she had then taught him, and his mourning thus became bearable, even, almost, enjoyable.

And David wondered at the strength of character Amnon displayed in his grief, at his gentle dignity and manly smiling seriousness.

The one.

At that time David's hair began to go grey and thin. Perhaps it was during the days Ahinoam lay dying in Amnon's house, when they all realized that her ageing was an illness from which she would not recover, or perhaps it was during the months of mourning. The grey colour was difficult to discern because his hair was so fair, but Bathsheba saw it, and sometimes in the evenings she would rub her palms with almond oil and yellow antimony and smooth it on his hair without his noticing it. She dyed his hair to protect him from old age.

Nor was Ahinoam the only wife who died. No, the decline and fading seemed to be spreading like an epidemic through the women's house. Bathsheba was forced to beseech and implore David to go down there at least occasionally; the wives no longer seemed to miss him at all. The few who were still having their monthly purges lived hidden and withdrawn in the innermost rooms; the children had disappeared; the women who were afflicted with old age got together in small huddles like flocks of birds in the winter cold, and talked of nothing but tooth-rot, gout, varicose veins, discharges, bad dreams, corns, shortness of breath, and God.

But the King did not notice that his wives were becoming fewer and fewer – in former times their number had steadily increased, and his wives had gladdened his heart as they had added to the rest of his constantly growing riches, but now he closed his eyes to their delights.

The women's house was almost never clean. Death is unclean.

During the first seven years after the fall of Rabbah, there died, apart from Ahinoam, Michal, Saul's daughter, who was childless, Maacah, Absalom's mother, and ten others. And the King mourned them with an ever lighter heart.

And the women of Jerusalem talked incessantly about the passage of time. When they met at the well they muttered continuously about the days, months and years that were passing. Most of them could not count them and did not know their names; they knew the names only of the months that had special significance, the months of conception and birth. This uncertainty and confusion transformed time into something mysterious and frightening – time gnawed at their skin and withered their flesh and they could not protect themselves against its ravages. Time robbed men of their strength and children of their softness, time was a hole at the base of existence, and life and joy and beauty seeped out through that hole. Everything was constantly in the process of waning and drying up and draining away. And at the end nothing more remained of human beings than there was water in the King's mock well.

And they were amazed when they found that their thoughts about time had brought them to that tired and terrible admission: Yes, the well was empty, it had always been empty, nothing could be drawn from it but emptiness.

Scribe: I cannot say to her, 'Without you, Bathsheba, I could not go on. You restore my soul, you lead me in the paths of righteousness, you anoint my head with oil.'

I can never say that to her. I am entirely in her hands. If I said that, I would be giving myself up to her as a lamb is handed over to the priest for sacrifice. Then I would no longer repose in her love but in her pity.

I, King David, need to seek advice from someone about Bathsheba. But officials do not understand afflictions of this sort, they do not know of the conjunction of heart and body. Joab? Mephibosheth? Hushai? No, the only one who might be able to give me advice is Bathsheba. But I cannot ask Bathsheba about Bathsheba.

So I must say to Bathsheba: 'You must never forget that I am King. You must never allow yourself to humiliate me in your own eyes. You must defend my eminence in your own mind. You must never become my only refuge. You must remember that the Lord has chosen me and none other. You shall be subject to me, for you are my only refuge.'

But I shall never be able to force my tongue to say that to Bathsheba.

When I was young I had a friend who was as close to me as Bathsheba is now – that was Jonathan, son of King Saul, father of Mephibosheth.

We mingled blood with each other as Bathsheba and I have also mingled our bodily fluids, we lived as brothers in his father's house, we fought together against the Philistines, we sang together.

He tried to persuade his father, Saul, to accept the idea that I was the one who would reign after him – no, not the idea, the certainty. He wanted to make peace between us, he thought that I would be able to bide my time, that I could be patient and mark time in the happy conviction that my day would come.

What a terrible burden my friendship with Jonathan was! No, not friendship. Love!

Love, which never fails, is a consuming sickness. It is impatient and insistent, it is full of envy and puffed up, it behaves itself in an unseemly manner and seeks its own self-interest. It rejoices in iniquity and deceit, it hopes for everything but believes nothing and endures nothing.

When Jonathan fell on Mount Gilboa I was stricken with a grief that almost turned me into water, and by a joy of liberation that compelled me both to weep and to sing.

Your love to me was infinitely wonderful, Jonathan, very pleasant have you been to me. Brother Jonathan, your love to me was wonderful, passing the love of women.

I wish that Bathsheba were like Ahinoam. Ahinoam never gnawed her way into my being, she remained outside me. She was true to me, I was true to her. We lived our life in lasting loyalty.

Ahinoam's fragrance changed, about the time when Maacah bore Absalom; she stopped smelling like a woman.

And I said to her: 'You no longer smell of passion.'

'I no longer feel any desires,' she replied. 'My body has given up its desires.'

'Have you yourself renounced your passion?'

'I have tired of feeling passion. I have exchanged my passion for reflection and peace of mind.'

I felt warned by her words, even excited by them.

'So you have felt passion?' I said.

'I thirsted for you as the desert nomads thirsts for water.'

'With the whole of your being?'

'My body thought of you constantly, my body woke me at night and cried: "David!"'

122

'What did you do then?'

'I created a David for myself in my loneliness, I was my own David. Then I could sleep again.'

And she added, 'But I often wondered about that: how wonderful it must feel actually to be David, to feel one's skin and one's bones filled with oneself, to be the one who is. And I could never understand why you needed to go to others, for you had yourself.'

'I have always had too much of myself,' I replied. 'That is why I have continually felt the need to empty myself.'

And I asked her, 'How can you bear to be constantly filled with reflection and peace of mind?'

'I think. I am myself. It is not much, but it is something. It is not the same as being filled with David, but nor is it complete emptiness.'

'Complete emptiness exists only in the realm of death,' I said. 'The whole of creation is full of states and changes and arrivals and presences. The only thing the Lord has not created is emptiness.'

'Yes,' she said. 'The Lord be praised.'

'Yes,' I said. 'Praised be the Lord.'

Then I asked: 'You no longer want me to come to you?'

'I have never required you to come,' she said.

'I have given you my promise before the Lord,' I replied.

'What the Lord demands of you, I do not know,' she said. 'I, Ahinoam of Jezreel, demand nothing.'

'Is this demanding nothing what you mean by reflection and peace of mind?'

'Yes,' she said. 'It is.'

Bathsheba has a fiery aura of passion. Everyone who comes near her senses it. It shows in men's faces, their skin tautens, their eyes open wider, their nostrils quiver. Men who sense her aura straighten their backs, run their fingers through their hair, stamp their feet uneasily, stroke their beards, fill their lungs with air. The aura of passion excites them as much as the call of the trumpet.

And I am filled with fear when I see it.

No, not fear that some man will steal her from me. But the fear of unheeding passion.

It seems to me a passion without object or direction, a passion that exists only in itself. A passion she throws out like a spear and bears like a shield before her.

I wish that she could lust for holiness and the Lord. But she is not able to – not simply that: that passion can be felt only by a man.

I fear that she has a passion to rule. She does not know what it is to rule. I am worried that she might be consumed by it. Anyone who comes close to power without really taking command of it will burst into flames and be reduced to cinders by its heat. Power must either be won and wholly possessed, or left well alone.

If she perishes, so will I.

She is putting on weight. Her breasts are getting heavier, her belly is rounded now even when it is not harbouring a new son. When she straightens her arms I can see hollows in her elbows. I can also see a fold in the skin on her neck, a fold which was not there before.

I am always offering her all the delicacies that my house and stores can offer.

It is my wish that she shall be wrapped in fat. For it is so: passion cannot force its way through a layer of fat, passion is shackled and imprisoned by fat.

I must surround her with walls and fences and ramparts. With armed men, cunning, love, blocks of stone and fat.

For I must keep Bathsheba unto eternity.

Maacah, Absalom's mother, had also given David a daughter called Tamar. She had now grown up and become one of the most beautiful women in Jerusalem. When Rabbah fell she was fourteen years old. She was slim and slender-limbed, but her bosom was high and full and her hips were broad; her hair, which she never tied up or plaited, was long and curly and as ruddy-brown as cornelian. She never used make-up or jewellery: all such things would have been insults to her beauty.

David came upon her one morning in the courtyard of the palace. The sun and wind were playing in her hair so that it looked like glittering serpents – serpents are holy for they represent eternity – and he asked her who she was.

'I am Tamar, youngest daughter of Maacah.

'Dearest Father.'

And he commanded that she should move into his house, she should adorn it with her presence. He felt pride and joy, but also relief when she said who she was. A beautiful woman to whom he need not make love, indeed whom the Lord's law forbade him to love, and whom he could thus enjoy with his eyes restrainedly and shamelessly. She would never put him to the test.

She was gentle and quiet; with men she spoke only when she was forced to, with women she was taciturn in a way that could sometimes be interpreted as shyness, sometimes as secretiveness.

But she could dance. Not like a dancer, but like Bathsheba before she began to bear sons.

Bathsheba and Tamar.

They could themselves see how much they resembled each other. Not in detail, not if one compared them hair for hair, eye for eye and neck for neck. But as a whole, that imperceptible whole.

Tamar's presence disturbed Bathsheba.

Bathsheba's presence disturbed Tamar.

And when Bathsheba saw Tamar, the untouched, unspoiled Tamar, she could not prevent her hands exploring her own body, running over her breasts, which had already begun to droop, over her belly, which had swelled and sagged and lost its shapely curve, over her hips, which had become higher and broader and resembled the flanks of a mule, and she thought: It is the sons who have forced their way out and deformed and destroyed my body.

Now, by the seventh year after the fall of Rabbah, she had borne King David five sons, not counting the Blessed One. She was twenty-seven years old. She went to Nathan the prophet and said: 'I no longer want to be fruitful.'

He looked at her and did not understand her words.

'My life is being squandered,' she said. 'I have borne Solomon and four other sons. And I gave birth to the Blessed One. My days and years are ebbing away!'

And he smiled at her, not comprehending what she was trying to tell him.

'You still have time to bear another ten,' he said. 'Or even more.'

He knew no suitable number above ten; the next he was familiar with was seventy.

'I want to be released from my fruitfulness.'

'Every time you give birth to a son you are delivered,' he said. 'You are released from one small part of your fruitfulness.'

He still smiled, but there was now a hint of suspicion in his eyes.

'I am being consumed by continually bearing sons. They are devouring me from within.'

'Man's seed must find somewhere to grow. You are the vineyard in which the holy sap can rise.'

'I am not a piece of land. Not a furrow in the earth.'

'All fruitfulness is a gift from God.'

And he tapped his fingers absent-mindedly on his drum.

But now she said absolutely clearly: 'I want you and the Lord to release me from the fruitfulness that is visited upon me. When Sarah was ninety the Lord made her fruitful so that she bore Isaac. So he must also be able to bring fruitfulness to an end.'

And now, finally, the prophet began to foam with rage. Bathsheba had realized that she would be forced to drive him to that.

'You blaspheme against the holy name of the Lord!' he screamed. 'He who blasphemes against the name of the Lord shall be punished by death!'

'Fruitfulness can also lead to death,' Bathsheba replied very calmly. 'If Ahinoam had not borne children so assiduously, old age would not have felled her so soon. She would still be alive now. And why should I bear superfluous sons, sons who are not needed on earth?'

'Every person that is born has a purpose!' cried Nathan. 'All your sons are created by God!'

'I know nothing about that,' said Bathsheba. 'I only knew that King David had begotten them.'

'Your sons will become great soldiers and priests and princes! Even the unborn ones! You will be remembered for your sons, not for anything else!'

'We even named one of them, the fourth, Nathan,' Bathsheba said quietly.

And now the prophet's anger subsided; the reminder of his name's renown calmed him.

'I implore you,' he said, 'eradicate these thoughts from your little mind. I do not even know how one would go about it.'

'You are the one who is the prophet of the Lord,' she said. 'You must be able to find the right course of action.'

And in the end he actually did it. That was how things almost always were with Nathan: he had to be entreated and persuaded. He anointed her with the oil that he normally used to drive our evil spirits from wine-drinkers and gluttons. It was an oil he happened to have at hand. He found that it was not at all difficult or unpleasant, and the voice of the Lord within him was silent.

Thereafter Bathsheba bore no more sons.

And what she thought about all the sons there already were and about the one who would reign after David she confided only to her scribe, which was the same as confiding to no one.

The King never allowed his hands to touch Tamar. He distrusted his hands. He had many times seen them perform actions he had forbidden them. When she was with him he held them clasped over his chest. Tamar thought he always held them that way; it looked as if he were worshipping her.

He always wanted her to sit so that he could see her face. The servants often had to move lamps and candles so that the light would fall on her eyes and lips; it was her lips in particular that he absolutely had to see.

Sometimes he ordered her to walk around in the room, just from one wall to the other, so that he could observe her calf muscles, the rise and fall of her heels, the swaying of her slightly projecting hips, the quivering of her breasts, the gentle swing of her arms and the anxious stroking of her hands over her thighs and stomach.

And he looked upon her and sighed as if he were bound in chains.

He constantly enquired of her servants about her cleanness, and whether she had carried out her sacrifices, whether she had performed her ritual toilets. He always knew when her monthly purge was due, and used to say, 'Today she shall be with me from morning to evening, for tomorrow I must be without her, tomorrow and seven days thereafter.'

But he never spoke to her. He feared and mistrusted words as much as hands, and if ever she seemed to be about to open her mouth to say something, he immediately called to the servants to ask her to be silent. He was afraid that something unclean would pass her lips, or that she would incite him to begin to converse with her. He thought with horror of how one thing could lead to another: words, hands, bodies.

And that was Bathsheba's only consolation: that David never spoke to Tamar. If they had also started to talk to each other, Bathsheba would have come to regard herself as conclusively rejected.

No, the one with whom he conversed, that was Bathsheba.

Scribe: I, Queen Bathsheba, have chosen Absalom. He gave me Korban, the turtle-dove.

No, do not write that – no, definitely not!

You think that every word I speak is true and must be written down. You do not know me!

I believe that he is the Chosen One. But I do not know why.

He holds himself so beautifully, he twinkles his eyes at me, he stretches out his neck and calls softly and intimately straight to my heart, he struts and sings so that I shall not forget him even for an instant.

No, not Absalom – the dove!

He is so reserved and noble and self-assured, his movements are never hesitant or irresolute, his figure is firm and taut like a pillar of the royal palace, his head alert and continuously watchful like a guard at the top of a tower.

No, not the dove – Absalom!

He is the only one who dares turn his back on King David. And the only one who is allowed to do so.

When he converses with the King he always stands at the window; he makes sure that their eyes never meet; he looks out over Jerusalem as if the city were already his. And his answers to the King's questions are short and precise, his voice is low and deep but clear. I once heard him say to the King: 'When my time comes.'

Just like that: 'When my time comes.'

It seemed to be something self-evident: there will come a time which is his and no one else's.

But I think that his being chosen must be given a little impetus.

One thing I have forgotten to say, and which has thus not yet been written down: he is the most handsome man I have ever seen.

Tamar is his sister.

Their mother, Maacah, daughter of King Talmai of Geshur, is said to have been the most beautiful of all the King's wives.

I saw her only once, after she had lost her hair and her teeth and had necrosis of the face. Then she died. She was hideous.

'Before he met you, Bathsheba, he had no wife more beautiful than Maacah.' That is what people tell me. That is what everybody says to me.

Absalom killed ten Amalekites unaided at Sela in Edom. Just with his sword. And they, too, had swords. He brought their heads and their camels back here to Jerusalem. He himself says: 'Now no more of the descendants of Amalek are left alive.' I do not know.

I wish I knew why my choice had to fall on Absalom.

He is the same age as I. I am a woman who has borne five sons. He is still a young man whose time will come.

His hips are narrow and his chest is broad and deep. He has a gold ring in his right ear, but it is visible only when he pushes back his luxuriant hair. He often carries his cloak in his hand or thrown over one shoulder; dressed only in his leather girdle he is almost painfully attractive. His skin is darker than David's.

The one.

No, not Amnon. He is just an ordinary person. If he were to be the one, then the palace would be filled with advisers, all men would be officials – he has such a generous heart. Nobody has as many friends as Amnon. He is immoderate in the matter of wives and friends. But he has no enemies. Enemies provide power.

Among his friends Amnon sometimes refers to 'My friend'.

Then he means Jonadab. Jonadab is his friend, the others just friends.

Jonadab is a wanderer, no one knows where he lives – he does not know himself. He sleeps mostly in Amnon's house. He is the son of the King's brother, his father was Shimeah, brother of King David.

He is as smooth and shiny as a copper mirror.

Why do I say that?

Because he always gleams with sweat. And he lacks any distinctive characteristics: his mind seems as if polished, he has no character of his own, he is like clay before the hand has shaped it. He is as everyone wants him to be, and so it cannot be said that he is anything at all. It is strange that he even has a name. One can never say, *That* is the kind of man Jonadab is.

That is exactly the kind of man Jonadab is.

He is Amnon's friend. His own friend is Shebaniah. Amnon confides the innermost thoughts of his vacillating mind to Jonadab. Jonadab confides them to Shebaniah.

My Shebaniah.

Poor Shebaniah. He is no longer a boy. And he dares not be a man. He was checked in his growth on that occasion in Rabbah when manliness broke out in him like a deadly fever. His voice has become deep; his voice and David's now rise and fall together in song. His cheeks are covered in beard, and he goes to prostitutes, according to Mephibosheth.

But still he says: 'I am the boy who plays the lyre for the King, I am the boy who comforts King David.'

He drinks wine with Jonadab. And sometimes he too stays at Amnon's house. And everything that Amnon tells Jonadab, Jonadab tells Shebaniah, and Shebaniah tells me. He has to tell someone. He thirsts for involvement the way other men thirst for wine and water. He believes this drunken chatter is significant and serious.

One thing I forgot about Jonadab: he sweats with fear. Exactly as the earth is covered every morning by dew and fear of the day to come, so Jonadab is constantly covered in sweat. He fears everybody. That is why he tries to make everybody believe that he loves them.

That is why he has indeed got to love everybody.

He has a god on a chain around his neck, a god without a face, a god that could be any god at all. Whoever he speaks to, he can say, 'Yes, it is your god. It is God.'

Perhaps that is God – I do not know.

Amnon has told Jonadab and Jonadab has told Shebaniah and Shebaniah has told me how Absalom behaves with women.

Absalom goes to women only out of necessity, because he must be released from his lust. The only thing he wants is salvation, nothing more, and when he has found it, he gets up from the bed at once, without even a friendly or grateful word. He has to escape; he turns his eyes immediately in other directions.

That is the kind of man he is.

Can you hear him calling?

Can you see him strutting about? Can you see his taut neck quivering with excitement?

No! Not Absalom!

The dove!

Amnon was standing on the roof of his house when he first really saw Tamar, his sister. She had come out into the courtyard behind the palace, and was drying herself with a big linen cloth; her hair was flowing loose. He saw at once how frighteningly beautiful she was. He had seen her before only as his father's daughter, a sister whom his father had taken in to adorn his house.

And he immediately called Jonadab.

'Do you see her?' he said.

'Yes,' replied Jonadab. 'It is your sister, Tamar.'

'I do not see a sister,' said Amnon. 'I see a woman.'

And Jonadab agree: she was without doubt a woman.

'It is strange,' said Amnon, 'I do not even know whether she has a husband.'

'King David has forbidden her to have a husband. He wants her to remain untouched as long as he lives.'

The colour had drained from Amnon's face, all his blood seem to have sped elsewhere, and he was shaking as if from a fever.

'Do you see?'

'Yes. I see.'

'Her hair is like a herd of goats streaming down from the Mountain of Gilead.'

'Yes.'

'Her teeth are like a flock of newly clipped ewes.'

'Yes.'

'Her cheeks are like ripe pomegranates.'

'Yes.'

'I must possess her.'

Now Jonadab was shaking too, but with fear, with fear pure and simple. He took hold of the god that hung around his neck and rolled it between the thumb and forefinger of his right hand. The sweat ran down his forehead and obscured his vision.

'Must your love always be lust?' he said.

'There is no other love.'

'You should temper your love with fear and dread,' Jonadab argued. 'Then lust would never arise.'

'Terror and lust and love,' said Amnon. 'I cannot distinguish between them. There are no such orderly divisions in my heart. All I know is that I sometimes begin to tremble with excitement.'

'The Lord forbids it,' Jonadab persisted. 'He will destroy you.'

'The Lord cannot be like that,' Amnon groaned. 'The Lord is love.' His gaze had welded itself to Tamar, who was still standing there drying her body.

'The King will have you stoned.'

'My father is merciful. No one knows as much about love as he.'

'Precisely,' sighed Jonadab. 'Precisely.'

What he meant by that was impossible to judge.

When at last Tamar was dry she wrapped the linen cloth around herself and disappeared into the palace.

Then Amnon discovered that his legs would no longer support him. His friend had to put his right arm around him and half guide, half carry him down to his room. Desire had weakened him so that he could hardly keep his head up; his hands were shaking and he was panting and having difficulty in breathing.

His friend laid him in his bed and gave him a cup of fresh wine spiced with the resin of the myrrh tree. When Amnon had drunk from the cup, he began to weep.

He wept so violently and desperately that he could neither hear nor speak.

Then Jonadab went to Shebaniah and related what had happened.

135

And Shebaniah went straight to Bathsheba.

Bathsheba realized at once that what had afflicted Amnon could be both fateful and fortunate.

Someone must take on the task of assisting both fate and fortune.

She was not over-hasty. Shebaniah and Jonadab and Amnon were in urgent need of advice and support, and perhaps Tamar also needed help. The thoughts she conceived now would flow out into the world like water in the furrows of the field, and bring forth fruit.

And she could not stop her heart from thinking: Absalom.

'He is lying as immobile as if he were unconscious,' said Shebaniah. 'His eyes are red and sunken, he has emptied them of tears. And he is as white as camel's milk, just like a leper. All his blood has gone to just one part of his body.'

'Go down to the tabernacle of the Lord and sacrifice a perfect ram for Amnon's sake,' said Bathsheba. 'It will be a trespass offering. And a goat and three loaves of unleavened bread. That will be a thank offering.'

'Yes,' said Bathsheba. 'The breast shall be held up before the Lord. A thank offering. And the kidneys and fat shall be burned.'

And Shebaniah did as he was ordered. Bathsheba had never yet misinformed or deceived him.

That was the nature of his life: to carry out the deeds of others, to adopt the views of others, to put himself in someone else's place, to be involved with others.

When Bathsheba faced particular difficulties or pressing temptations she often went to Mephibosheth. He was asleep now, lying on his back with wide-open eyes and gaping mouth. She was pleased: when he was awake he disturbed her train of thought – he always tried to help her with his own ideas and gloomy fancies – but when he was asleep he inspired in her precisely that state of productive tranquillity she needed. His naked, vulnerable face was like a landscape in which the gaze could wander freely and find nourishment. It was worn and ravaged, yet rich and full of potential. There, in front of the unconscious, snoring Mephibosheth, she thought out the necessary plans.

It was the first time she had contrived the occurrence of momentous events in this fervent yet self-possessed manner, even devising hitherto unfamiliar events. It was far more momentous and significant than saying to the King, 'Yes, you must take Rabbah!' or saying to Solomon, 'No, you must not drink any more of that sweet wine.' It was an exercise in thinking as a holy act.

When she turned to go she discovered that Solomon had crept in to her. She took him by his soft yet demanding little hand and went back to her room.

And she explained to Shebaniah, who had now returned after seeing to the necessary sacrifices: Amnon's union with Tamar was inevitable. His predicament was grave, the fever of desire might totally consume him, his soul might drown in the tears of lust, his flesh might rot and wither from this constant seething state of arousal, rot and wither.

Shebaniah nodded: Yes, that was true.

Tamar was his sister, of course. But not his full sister: it was only the King's seed that united them. And the peculiarity of royal seed was that it never curdled, it was nothing like ass's milk. No, it would tolerate mixing in all possible ways and yet remain pure. It could even be mixed with itself without turning sour or rancid. Indeed, some kings completely forbade their seed to be mixed with anything but itself: their sons were not allowed to take wives who were not also their sisters.

'That is the way it is in Egypt.'

Yes. That is the way it is in Egypt.

'By this method,' Bathsheba continued, 'a much purer royal

line ensues, an undiluted and untainted lineage of chosen people which perhaps eventually results in the begetting of gods.

'If Amnon takes his sister unto himself, it is just another step on the path to being chosen.'

Bathsheba was sitting on the Egyptian chair at the head of the bed. Korban, the turtle-dove, was huddled in mute silence in its cage. She had Solomon on her knee, Solomon who had long ago reached the age when sons reject their mother's knees.

'But the Lord?' Shebaniah said fearfully.

But she had also thought about the Lord.

'The Lord can always be appeased,' she replied. 'The world is full of the Lord's mercy. Amnon will have to sacrifice a ram. Or twelve rams.'

'Whosoever uncovers the nakedness of his father's daughter shall be cut off from among his people,' said Shebaniah, almost in tears. 'Then no sacrifice will help.'

'What applies to the people does not apply to the King's sons. The whole of the King's house is chosen and holy. The Lord would not have breathed this lust into Amnon's flesh if it were forbidden.'

Shebaniah looked at her. She appeared confident and untroubled. Imperturbable. And suddenly he noticed what he had not noticed before despite his daily proximity to her: her limbs had lost their slender, youthful look, she was no longer a young girl with a figure like a lily stem, her whole body was broader and heavier, her shoulders had grown as if to enable her lift and bear the burdens of men. He had not thought that she would ever change. He had believed she would remain as she was that first night when he had sat guard over her sleep in Uriah's house.

It gave him a feeling of calm confidence to discover suddenly that even her body had become that of a queen. He was sad to see it.

'And the King?' he asked.

'In his heart he knows he must lose Tamar. A beauty such as

hers must be used. What is the purpose of beauty if it is not put to use?'

'I think she is holy for him,' said Shebaniah, his voice thick with anxiety. 'And whatever is holy for the King, he can never do without. He will kill Amnon and take her back.'

'You do not know the King. Not as I know him,' said Bathsheba. 'He will admire Amnon's courage. Superhuman courage is needed to carry out what God has forbidden. The King himself no longer has that degree of courage.'

'I can feel with the whole of my being that this will lead to disaster and death,' Shebaniah whimpered. 'I am sick with fear just as Amnon is sick with desire.'

His whole body was indeed trembling, and he was forced to support himself against the doorpost.

'You will always remain a boy who plays the lyre,' said the Queen, her words accompanied by a gentle, affectionate and perhaps rather condescending laughter.

'Yes,' Shebaniah replied. 'That is my hope.'

Then Bathsheba explained to Shebaniah what he should say to Jonadab and what Jonadab should say to Amnon. It was not just good and well-meaning advice, it was the only possible advice. It was the inevitable course they had to construct and follow.

Amnon was to stay in his bed. Even if the fire within him diminished he should remain lying there and send a message to the King that a deadly fever had afflicted him, that he wanted to see his father one last time and receive his blessing, that he must have a royal word of blessing to accompany him on his journey down to the realm of death, that the fever was consuming his spirit and his blood. He should say, 'You must not forget my birthright.'

Bathsheba rocked the adolescent Solomon on her knee, deep in thought. His fingers were playing with the huge gold chain hanging round her neck. She pressed her cheek against his curly hair as if it were to him she was really speaking.

'And when the King comes, Jonadab must cover Amnon so that only his blood-drained face is visible. He must not let the King discover what part of his body has sucked all the blood to itself. And Amnon must tell his father that he is looking forward to death as a deliverer, that life has never given him any real joy, that he will feel at home as one of the shadows of the realm of death, that he has already begun to practise the state of bloodlessness and transparency. And when the King has of necessity laid his fatherly hand on his forehead, he must say with a sigh: "It would be one last comfort before I surrender my spirit if my sister Tamar could come to my bedside. You know Tamar, Absalom's sister, she of the small voice and lowered eyes, your daughter. If she could only come to my death-bed and make me a loaf of wheat and barley. That bread would be my food for the journey."

'The King will not begrudge Amnon that one little pleasure.

'And then when Tamar comes down to him, when she has baked the bread and hands it to him, then he must draw her to him and take her. A woman offering a man a freshly baked loaf is completely defenceless, she is hot from the work and the glow of the oven, and her heart is overflowing with feelings of generosity and love. Afterwards she can lie in his arms and they can share the loaf between them.'

'Is that all?' Shebaniah asked.

'Yes,' said Bathsheba. 'That is all.'

'And what will happen next?'

'Nothing more will happen. She will belong to him then. The King will be pleased when Amnon recovers. He will think the Lord has spared him.'

'Spared?'

'Everything that is to be chosen must first be spared. That which is rejected can never be chosen. This too Jonadab must say to Amnon: "First one is spared, then one is chosen."'

And Shebaniah went to Jonadab and Jonadab went to Amnon. He lay in his bed, he did not touch the wine that his friend offered him, he said that he did not even want any bread. But he listened attentively to the cunningly contrived plan which Jonadab put to him.

'Without your friendship I would not have been able to endure this,' he said.

'You are surrounded by more friendship than any other person I know,' Jonadab replied.

King David recognized immediately the suffering that afflicted Amnon. Yes, he was familiar with this complaint in the same way that a leper is familiar with bleached skin and purulent sores.

'Who is she?' he asked.

'No one,' Amnon replied.

'You must tell me who she is. You shall have her, I shall give her to you with my own hand, whoever she is.'

'She is the Lord's shadow. The shadow who reigns in the realm of death.'

'The Lord's shadow?'

'Yes.'

'Yahweh's shadow image?'

'Yes.'

'Do you really believe that is so?'

'Yes, father, that is the case.'

'She is the Lord?' said David searchingly and not without distaste.

'We are all transformed into shadows in the realm of death,' Amnon explained in a tired and indifferent voice. 'Even the Lord.'

'I have brought a raisin cake and honey for you.'

'Thank you, Father,' said Amnon. 'But I am already full with suffering.'

'A few drops of honey?' David tried.

'No, not even that.'

Amnon's cheeks were no longer rounded as they always used

to be, and the rolls of fat beneath his eyes had given way to furrows in which the tears had gathered in beads.

'I have fasted,' said the King. 'But I have always felt hunger. It is the hunger which gives fasting its religious significance. If one is not hungry, God does not notice that one is fasting.'

'Jonadab brought a cup of wine,' said Amnon. 'But I could not make myself drink.'

'Fasting without hunger and thirst is meaningless,' the King assured him. 'You might just as well eat and drink.'

'I am not even hungry for life,' said Amnon. 'My soul is only thirsty for the coolness of death.'

And the King saw that he was powerless, and decided to surrender himself to his impotence: he was strong enough for that. He was afraid of what Amnon would say if he forced him to reveal who she was – who it was that had smitten him with this desperate desire. He did not have the courage to hear her name. He bent forward over the bed and reluctantly and sick at heart laid his hand on Amnon's forehead, saying: 'Is there then nothing you want?'

'Besides your blessing?'

'You have that already.'

'Besides that? No, nothing.'

'Nothing?'

'Unless, just to please you, I were to think up a totally superfluous wish,' said Amnon, in a half-smothered voice.

'Do so,' said the King.

'In that case I would like a loaf of bread. A simple round loaf for my journey. Made of corn and barley.'

He spoke very slowly, as if he had to find the words one at a time.

'Yes?' said David.

'If Tamar, your daughter, my sister, who is more truly sister to Absalom, could come down here and bake the loaf, it would give me a few moments of comfort.'

As he said her name a shiver went through the King and he lifted his hand immediately from Amnon's sweating forehead.

It should have been I who forced him to say the name, he

thought. But I allowed him to say it voluntarily, almost innocently. I am powerless.

'She would be able to make the bread before my eyes. Perhaps I would be able to enjoy life one last time if I could see her hands kneading the dough and smell the fragrance of the leavening.'

'Before the final journey the bread shall be unleavened,' said the King, who heard clearly the desire lying hidden in his son's mournful voice.

'It is a very short journey,' Amnon countered. 'For me it is just one step down to the realm of death.'

'I shall send her to you,' said the King. 'I shall send her straight away. And the flour. I shall send the flour and the leavening, too. I shall give you everything.'

Then he got up quickly and left. He took the raisin cake and the honey with him. The only thing he left behind was his blessing.

But before he let Tamar go he went down to the Lord and asked His advice. But the Lord only answered as He always did:

'A king's promises are given before God.'

It was Shebaniah who told Bathsheba what happened next. He spoke softly and carefully: he felt embarrassed despite the fact that she had foreseen the whole thing. He tried to conceal some of his words by clearing his throat or stammering, and he also avoided all the descriptive gestures and hand movements that normally accompanied his speech.

'Tamar kneaded the dough beside Amnon's bed. The whole room was filled with the smell of grain and leavening. Her fingers were lithe and supple but strong. It seems to have been her innocent yet strangely experienced fingers that particularly held the sick man's attention. They flexed and straightened in confident rhythmical movements – when she pressed them into the dough a gentle hissing sound could be heard, and when she drew them out again there was a sucking, smacking noise from the moist texture of dough. She was panting in time with her movements, and her cheeks glowed as red as a pomegranate.

'Do you understand?'

'Yes, I understand. Go on!'

'When she had shaped the loaf – it was a round loaf with a soft deep slit in the middle – she put it in the tin and went out to the oven at the back of Amnon's house. Amnon was now in such agony that he fell into a faint when she left him. Jonadab splashed his face with aloe and I rubbed his chest with oil, but he did not recover his senses until she returned with the baked bread.

'And she asked: "Shall I break it?" Her voice was low and hoarse, and she was still panting.

'"Yes. Break it," said Amnon.

'And she lifted it from the tin and broke it and asked, "Shall I put it here on your plate?"

'"No," said Amnon, "pass it to me in your hand."

'Then he ordered us to leave them alone, him and his sister Tamar, and we crept quietly from the room, Jonadab and I – yes, we really crept, because we too felt that we were close to being afflicted by the shameful fever ourselves. So it is almost inexplicable that I am able to tell you the rest – yes, even the end – of this story.'

'Yes, I see. I know you, Shebaniah. Go on!'

'She went up to his bed, she held the broken bread in her right hand, clutching her tunic together over her breasts with her left, and she proffered the bread as one proffers food to a captured wild beast. The bread smelled like a field of grain in the midday sun.

'"Come closer," he said. "Come and sit here on my bed."

'And she did so, but she perched cautiously on the edge as if she were about to get up again the whole time, and she asked, "Is it really true that you are going to die?"

'"Not any more, not now you are with me."

'"But it was true?"

'"Yes. I was going to die."

'"Why are you no longer going to die?"

'"You have come to me with the bread of life."

'"You are not eating any of the bread."

'"Lie down here with me! Then we shall eat the bread."

'And he pulled her down to him so that she was lying on her back by his side. His face had regained its colour and his arms their strength. She held the pieces of bread before her like a shield, and she asked, "You, who have been brought up by priests and know the law of the Lord, has the Lord not forbidden this?"

'She threw out the Lord's name at him as if it were a copper-plated javelin.

145

' "No, in the Lord's law there is not a single word about this." '

' "Is that really true?" '

' "As true as the Lord lives, my sister. Not one word!" '

' "I am still a virgin?" '

' "Yes. You have been spared for me. And I have chosen you. First one is spared, then one is chosen." '

' "It is my virginity which has given my life its value. If I am robbed of my virginity, then I also lose my special quality." '

' "For me you will always remain an untouched sister!" '

' "My father will cast me out." '

' "All fathers cast out their daughters when they lose their virginity." '

' "I want to remain pure." '

' "It will be over quickly. You will not have time to become impure." '

' "Even the Lord will take His hand from me." '

' "I shall protect you and keep you all your life. You shall be my queen. May I be eternally damned if I do not remain your protection and your strength until I am old and toothless." '

'And he tore off her clothes with his eager fingers and exposed her private parts and pulled her to him and bedded her. He did it frenziedly and with jerky convulsive movements. She wept and wailed but he did not hear it – everything happened so fast that he hardly had time to think about the noises she was making. Can you tell me, O Queen, what basic difference there is between loving and violating?'

'There is no distinction between love and violation.'

'And afterwards he jumped up from the bed, his pallor all gone – he was like a young stag, he was naked and glistening, and he immediately began chewing a piece of bread that Tamar had dropped on the floor. The Lord had indeed wrought a miracle with him. And he said: "You are a bitch, Tamar! You are a bitch like all the rest!" '

' "Now everything is finished," she whimpered. '

' "Yes. Now you have got what you wanted," he said, "what

you in your virginity have constantly dreamed about. Now I have nothing more to give you."

' "You promised to protect and keep me."

' "I was sick. I was dying. I was delirious."

' "You must take me to wife. The King will give me to you."

' "You fill me with loathing," he said. "Your bread is excellent, but you yourself are doughy and stink of leavening. Go away, I never want to see you again!"

' "If you cast me out you will be committing an even graver crime than when you violated me."

' "The Lord gave you into my power. What could I do?"

' "You could have loved me with brotherly love."

' "That is what I did. I loved you with the love with which the Lord has filled me."

' "Do you know that for sure?"

' "Yes. I am certain of it."

'She was silent for a long time, weeping quietly. Then she said, sitting huddled up with her head on her knees, seeming to direct the question inwards, towards her own body: "What then is the nature of the Lord?"

' "Why do you ask that?"

' "I am not asking you. I am just asking."

' "I have never seen him," Amnon replied. "I know Him only through His deeds. But He seems to be terrible. Terrible and omnipotent."

'And he added: "He is so capricious that I have ceased to fear Him."

' "You do not know Him at all. You only use His name to blaspheme and jeer."

' "And you are like Absalom," said Amnon. "I did not see it before. But now I see it. You imagine that the Lord has chosen you! That in His indiscriminating goodness He intends to exalt you!"

' "Absalom is a chosen one!" she cried. "He is a chosen one, but you are not!"

147

'"Be gone!" Amnon screamed. "Be gone and never come before my eyes again! I do not know whether I am a chosen one or not, I do not want to know, I only want to be magnificent and free!"

'And then Tamar got up from the bed and hastily pulled her full-length tunic over her body. She was still just as beautiful. Jonadab and I could not see that anything had happened to her. And she took the blood-stained sheet under her left arm and ran off, saying nothing more, not even weeping any longer, and she fled straight to David's house. She is hiding in Mephibosheth's room.'

'Was that all?'

'Yes, that was all.'

'Then go to Tamar and tell her that she must move into Absalom's house. She must tear her maiden's garments to pieces and strew ashes in her all-too-lustrous hair. She must say that she wants only a simple storeroom, she is no longer worthy to live in a room fit for a person. And she must tell Absalom everything.'

'Yes.'

'Then you and Jonadab must seek out the King. You must say that your message concerns the kingdom and the one who will reign after him, and you must tell him the indisputable truth about his daughter, Tamar, and Amnon, his son.'

'Jonadab is lying sick and weeping in Amnon's house,' said Shebaniah. 'He does not have the strength to raise himself, and he has even less strength to divulge truths.'

And so Shebaniah carried out what Bathsheba had commanded him.

And the King shook his head. He sat with his little flute in his hand, and as he listened his face went horribly white and he snorted like a ram being clipped. He broke the flute clean in two between his fingers. Finally he said what he had to say, the only thing it lay in his power to say:

148

'I am powerless.'

Then he looked round hastily to reassure himself that no one other than Shebaniah could hear him, and whispered: 'Do not report that to Bathsheba! She would not endure hearing it, she has not strength enough to bear powerfulness, her poor female heart would break within her!'

But then he said, and it was as if he dimly remembered that she too had some unfathomable guilt to atone for, 'No, go to Bathsheba and tell her the truth! Why should she be spared and protected? She has no right to stand outside this – no living being is righteous or innocent. Force her to hear everything!'

Scribe: Perhaps this can be a song.

I praise the Lord who taught my hands to war and my fingers to fight, He who is my shield and in whom I trust, He who subdues my people under me.

What is man, that Thou takest knowledge of him! Man is like to vanity, his days are as a shadow that passeth away.

Tamar. My daughter Tamar. Anyone could have stolen her from me. She was the lamb that no one watched over. I was her shepherd but I did not watch over her; she was too dear to me. Now I have lost her for ever. I have sacrificed her.

Scribe: Help me to remember, I must sacrifice a ram for Amnon's sake, a guilt offering, a sacrifice for one who sins by withholding something which is holy to the Lord.

I no longer pay heed to sacrifices as I should. Help me to remember that, scribe. Perhaps I think, as I now begin to perceive the limits of my years, I have sacrificed enough. This thought makes me inattentive and I neglect my sacrifices. Bathsheba says: 'You own everything, and therefore you have nothing to offer in sacrifice.' I wish I could sacrifice everything in exchange for being as young again as Amnon. Or Absalom.

I shall not punish Amnon. I am not able to. Lord, I beseech Thee, do not punish him!

Only Thou hast the right to punish him. O Lord, smite him with Thy wrath if there is no other way!

Bow Thy heavens, O Lord, and come down, touch the mountains and they shall smoke! Deliver me out of great waters!

Nor may Absalom punish him for violating Tamar. Absalom believes in punishment. There is not the slightest little lie in his life, nor any cheating; he never falters. I must remember this: I shall have to forbid Absalom to lift his sword against Amnon!

Bathsheba is not coming to the evening meal. She has sent a message to say that she is staying in her room, out of grief for Tamar, grief for Amnon, grief for Absalom. She is staying with Solomon.

Solomon has begged me to give him a palanquin of acacia wood and ivory. I shall give him a palanquin of acacia wood and ivory.

No, I am not laughing. That horrible sound which you unfortunately misunderstand comes from deep inside me: it is my throat constricting with cramp from despair and impotence, it is my tongue rattling in the knowledge of all the contradictions which cannot be reconciled and yet which are constantly merging, which the Lord is incessantly entwining and fusing. I beg you: Forget it!

I must turn my hatred of Amnon into mercy. I must forgive him. He only carried out my deed. It was I myself in him who violated Tamar. Oh, how I hate my beloved, first-born son! How hatred and love darken my soul!

I never want to see the defiled Tamar again. I must tell my heart: She is dead. My heart is frozen in my breast, I mourn her as if she were my dearest child. She is my dearest child.

When night comes I shall sleep on the ground like an animal or a poor shepherd boy. I am a shepherd boy who has lost his dearest lamb.

May our sons in their youth be like plants full grown, our daughters like corner pillars cut for the structure of our palace; may our garners be full, providing all manner of store; may our sheep bring forth thousands and ten thousands in our fields; may our cattle be heavy with young; may there be no breaking in, nor going out and may none of us be taken as prisoner; may there be no cry of distress in our streets. Happy the people to whom such blessings fall. Happy the people whose God is the Lord!

Yes, scribe, it turned into a song.

It was Absalom who taught Bathsheba to shoot with a bow. He had suspended a lion's skin between two pillars in the courtyard behind his house. Nathan and Mephibosheth sometimes stole in to watch them, Mephibosheth sitting in a palanquin that really belonged to Bathsheba, and they wondered why she was practising this senseless art.

Absalom stood behind her, shouting out brief instructions: 'Left foot further forward! Elbow higher! Head back! Only two fingers on the string! No, raise the bow to eye level!' He never asked why she sought this tuition. He made her stand for long periods immobile with drawn bow to develop her resistance to trembling of the arms. He had also made her a gift of the bow, a wooden bow covered with braided cord, the string made of the plaited sinews of a ram. She used hollow arrows with bronze tips.

But the morning after Tamar had moved into his house and she and Shebaniah had told him in detail all about Amnon, he gave Bathsheba no help with her practice. No, he himself stood in the marksman's place, and she could only look on in astonishment as he shot arrow after arrow through the eye of the lion. Not a single shot missed its mark, and Bathsheba was well aware of whose eye he was really shooting at, who empty hide he saw before him in his mind.

A lion, thought Bathsheba. It ought to have been an ass.

No, Amnon was not a lion. Absalom.

And then when he had emptied his quiver ten times and had wearied of shooting, when he had hung the bow over his shoulder, she asked: 'When will you do it?'

But he replied: 'I never hurry. I shall do it at the appropriate time.'

Tamar's name could never be mentioned in front of David. Amnon, on the other hand, could be spoken of: he continued to be alive and real in the King's mind; but he was not allowed to enter the palace, he was no longer invited to meals, and he never followed with the King's retinue to the tabernacle of the Lord. She was annulled; he was allowed to keep his name.

In the storeroom in Absalom's house where she lived Tamar gave birth to the son that Amnon had begotten. But Absalom had him sent away at once; he was never given a name, he would never have been anything but unclean – he did not even have him circumcised. A servant had to carry him out at night to the Valley of the Sons of Hinnom and give him to Moloch, the child-eater, the nocturnal form of the Lord. In the dark all that remained of God was his wrath and his rapaciousness. No, Tamar's son never belonged among the living.

And Solomon continued to grow. He was quiet and tranquil and smiled almost continuously. When he was eleven years old, he was given a flock of sheep and two shepherds by the King, and he went up to Hebron with Mephibosheth to see his sheep, and counted them for himself: 100. He was the only one of the King's sons who could count and name the quantity of his sheep in one single number.

All the King's sons had flocks of sheep which King David had given them. He knew everything returns to its source. Perhaps one day his seed might have to return from Jerusalem to the pastures around Bethlehem – after all, a kingdom is like a woman's love. Then the sheep would be waiting; his seed would not perish from hunger.

It was also of great importance that the King's sons should have their own animals from which they could take their sacrifices for the altar of the Lord.

When the sheep had to be shorn, all the King's sons rode out on their mules to see that everything went well, that no wool was defiled or misappropriated, and that the ears of all the yearling lambs were properly marked. They rode together from flock to flock, they had their servants with them and they took with them wine and fruit and musical instruments on open carts, and sometimes dancing girls too. And when they came to the last flock they celebrated the shearing festival: they clipped their own hair and weighed it. Absalom's hair was always heavier than ten of the others together. They roasted lamb over open fires and drank wine, all the wine they had managed to carry, and the festivities did not finish until the servants loaded the King's sons on to the now empty carts and took them home to Jerusalem. They remembered nothing then of what they had seen or heard, and from this comes the saying 'to know someone as David's sons know their sheep'.

The King had formerly been wont to celebrate the sheep-shearing with his sons, but nowadays he refrained. He still loved the sheep, of course, but felt he could no longer hold the wine.

Bathsheba had often begged him to let her ride out with his sons. She could help them count and remember all the numbers and sums, she could ride the King's ass and be like a mother to them – yes, she felt as if she were a King's son herself. But David would not allow it. Since she had stopped bearing him sons he seemed to have become increasingly anxious about her health and welfare. And Nathan had told him that her infertility was a sign from the Lord: He had spared her and chosen her for some purpose which would gradually be revealed, which, indeed, for the clear-sighted, was very soon to be revealed.

Scribe: I want to think about Goliath, the giant.

I, Queen Bathsheba, do not know for certain what to think about Goliath.

This is what David has told me:

He was guarding his father's sheep outside Bethlehem. His three eldest brothers were encamped with King Saul in the Valley of Elah – it was during one of the wars against the Philistines. His father, Jesse, sent him out to his brothers with bread and roasted corn, and with ten cheeses for the Commander of the army.

While he was with his brothers and the army, Goliath stepped out from the army of the Philistines, who were encamped opposite the army of Israel, and mocked and jeered at the people of Israel, crying: 'Here I stand alone. Is there not a single man among you who dares to fight me? Are you all like frightened asses' foals and nervous lambs? If one of you is able to fight with me and kill me, then we will be your servants. Not just I who am slain, but also all the living will fall to the ground before you, you suckling babes, incestuous dogs and eunuchs!'

And the children of Israel drew back in fear when they saw him and heard his terrible voice.

And they told David: 'This is what Goliath does every day!'

David was still just a boy. 'I was like Shebaniah,' he often says – his beard had not yet grown and he had not yet lain with a woman.

Goliath was indeed dreadful to behold.

He was seven ells tall, the copper helmet on his head could be used as a cooking-pot and would hold two kids, and his armour was the weight of two horses. The shaft of his spear was like a pillar of the palace, and three men were needed to lift his shield.

But when David saw that the whole army fled before Goliath, he said: 'What will his conqueror receive?'

And they answered him: 'He shall have King Saul's daughter, Michal, and his house shall be free of the King's tax.'

Saul's daughter Michal.

But his eldest brother said to him: 'I know you, David. You are evil and inquisitive, you have come here just to see us slain. Go home at once to your little sheep in the desert.'

This angered David, and he replied: 'I shall fight Goliath and I shall vanquish him. I have slain lions as well as wolves and bears that have attacked my sheep. Yes, I have caught lions by their beards and slain them. Am I to fear an uncircumcised Philistine?'

And they put King Saul's armour on him, but the armour weighed him down and dragged on the ground so that he could hardly walk.

'No,' he said. 'I am a shepherd and as a shepherd I will meet this heathen ram!'

And he took his sling and his staff, which was also a sling, and went to meet Goliath.

And Goliath cried: 'Am I a dog, that you come to me with staves?'

And when he shouted this the whole of the army of Israel took fright and ran back seven paces.

But David took a stone from his bag and cast it at Goliath, cast it with his sling at a distance of forty paces, and the stone smote the giant's forehead and stuck there like a horn, and he fell unconscious to the earth.

Then David ran forward and slew him and took hold of his beard and cut off his head, and the Philistines fled.

And David's three brothers took Goliath's head by the hair and dragged it to King Saul and laid it at his feet.

And David kept his sword and his helmet. The washerwomen have the helmet now; they use it for washing the bed linen.

And the men of Israel and Judah arose and shouted when they saw that Goliath the giant was dead, and they pursued the Philistines to the gates of Ekron. Ekron is the capital city of the Philistines on the borders of Judah, in the mountains.

Seven ells tall?

Can such a man really have existed?

And the spear that was like one of the pillars of the palace? Would not a giant, if giants existed, be better served by a perfectly ordinary spear which he could throw with ten times the strength of an ordinary man?

And must he not have been able to recognize the sling that David carried? Not even a Philistine giant can be so ignorant as not to recognize a shepherd's sling and know that it can fell the mightiest of wild beasts!

Why did he not even raise his shield?

Is a man really less wily and prudent because he is not circumcised?

The first time King David told me about Goliath, I felt a mixture of terror and pride. The second time I listened more attentively, since I knew the end of the story, and I thought: The words are exactly the same, only the measurements have grown a little, a quarter here, an inch there.

Then I realized how it is: David's kingliness caused everything in his vicinity to grow, even stories; his power does not allow anything to remain as it was.

Perhaps Goliath was very tall. But he was a totally ordinary man. His sword was made long after his death to support the rumour of his giant stature. He was heavy and clumsy, and David felled him with a stone from his sling at close range, and that was well done. But it was not a miracle of the Lord, it was hardly even the heroic feat of a Benjaminite shepherd; it was only what could have been expected of David.

So I often think of Goliath now, the terrible giant from Gath.

Absalom would have attacked him with his sword. Perhaps he would have been slain, perhaps not.

Bathsheba practised at her bow with Absalom one last time. She could now penetrate the double hide at a distance of thirty paces. Her arms and fingers no longer trembled when she shot and she had ceased blinking at the instant she let go of the string.

It was the day before the sheep-shearing, and they were talking of Amnon. She said: 'Two years have passed now.'

But he said nothing.

'I cannot understand your patience,' she continued. 'Patience can turn into forgetfulness.'

But he was silent.

'And forgetfulness turns into forgiveness. You will soon be inviting him to eat at your table.'

But he seemed not to hear.

'Tamar will soon be expunged from existence. She walks around in your house like a shadow, Absalom. Do you not remember how beautiful and lovable she was? Your sister Tamar?'

And she waited a moment for his answer; she stood with her bow raised and drawn.

'You cannot simply await your opportunity, Absalom! We must ourselves create the opportunities we need!'

'Lift your shoulders!' he said. 'And raise the bow a hand's breadth higher!'

She let the arrow fly, and it whistled straight through the lion's eye.

Then she lowered the bow, her arms and fingers began to tremble and she closed her eyes.

Absalom.

He said nothing, but she was aware of the warmth of his body. He stood behind her, the Chosen One, so close that she could feel his breath and the heat of his gaze on the back of her neck. When a gust of wind blew in through the gate she could hear his thick hair wafting and waving. She could smell the odour of his skin and his sweat-dampened leather girdle.

Absalom!

If she took one single step backwards she would be in his arms.

He would finally touch her; her shoulders would be leaning against his chest.

Just one short step.

But when at last she took that one step, when she could no longer stop herself from pretending to half stumble, half fall backwards, what happened was not what she had imagined and feared and desired.

No, he raised his hands, and, pressing his palms against her shoulder blades, pushed her away from him as if she were a dead thing, as if she did not need to support herself against anyone – yes, as if her body gave him a feeling of loathing and disgust.

He rejected her.

And she threw the bow to the ground and turned round to face him. She tried to see him but could not, she could only faintly discern his face. A billowing veil of darkness had descended over her eyes, her mouth filled with saliva and her throat was constricted with cramp. And she felt for his face in a state of helpless bewilderment, that face which suddenly seemed to have lost all its distinctive features and been transformed into a blank surface, a polished mirror. She reached out for it with her taut, hooked fingers, her nails dug deep furrows in his skin and flesh. And he let her do it, he offered up his face to her as if he were prepared to sacrifice it for her sake. Only when he could endure no more and when he felt she had inflicted enough punishment on him did he seize her by the wrists and stop her. With blood streaming down his face and into his eyes he gripped her tight, until her body went limp and the suppressed tears began to well forth from her eyes.

The rejected queen.

Thus they stood for a moment, confused and afraid. They had been cast into this predicament by some unknown force; perhaps it was a state of holy madness. They would both have to grope their way back to the beginning and to their senses. But finally he let go of her and took two steps back from her, and then walked off slowly towards the lion's skin. It had to be taken down and rolled up. His movements were measured and controlled, as they always were. Had it not been for the blood on his face no one could have seen that anything unusual or ill-fated had happened to him.

But Bathsheba ran up to the palace. She ordered water to be brought. She had to wash herself clean. She rinsed her eyes and lips over and over again and rubbed and brushed her hands and nails as if the deed that had emanated from them had been an unclean discharge. She took a switch of hyssop and a linen cloth, and she did not stop until her skin had forgotten Absalom and begun to smart as if it had been purged by fire.

Then she called Shebaniah to her: Korban the turtle-dove would be sacrificed. Shebaniah was to carry the cage down to the priests; he was to say that it was the Queen's dove.

But Shebaniah hesitated.

'He has been very dear to you,' he said, cautiously.

'He is foolish and ridiculous,' said Bathsheba. 'And he is old. If I do not sacrifice him, he will soon die of old age.'

'I have never seen a more beautiful bird,' said Shebaniah. 'And you will miss his singing.'

'He does not sing. He coos, that is all. When King David was young, he had a bird that could imitate the sound of a sword being sharpened and the twang of the bow-string.'

She said this as if to explain to him that there were birds for every possible requirement or occasion, but that Korban was not the bird she needed any longer.

'Is he to be a burnt offering?' Shebaniah asked.

'Yes. A burnt offering.'

And then she added: 'And a promise offering. I shall say the appropriate prayer myself when I am alone.'

And as soon as Shebaniah had gone, carrying the dove pressed to his breast as if he wanted to protect it and in some mysterious way save it for her, Bathsheba said her prayer to the Lord. She raised her arms and turned her palms towards the ceiling as she had so often seen David do. She prayed that Absalom should fare as he deserved, that he should not be chosen in any way, or that he might perhaps be chosen as Korban the turtle-dove had been. She closed her eyes and said: 'He is faithless and false, trust not in him, he is an adder that has turned into a rigid staff!'

And Absalom went to King David. One of the sons always had to ask him: 'Will you ride out with us to the sheep-shearing?'

And the King answered as he had answered for the last ten years: 'No, I will remain in my city.'

And Absalom said what he had to say: 'We beseech you to accompany us, O King. For the fertility of the sheep and the lustre of the wool.'

And the King answered as he had to: 'My sons are my fertility.'

That was all.

Absalom looked at David: he half lay on his short couch behind one of the embroidered screens that the servants had constantly to put up around him. The screens were covered with birds and fruit trees and coiling serpents; nobody knew what they were supposed to protect him against. His stomach hung loose and heavy against the goat-hair blanket; he squinted at Absalom as if at an irritating light; his right arm and shoulder were trembling slightly with the effort of supporting his torso. Absalom noticed with satisfaction how his father was ageing. Every time he met him now he found a new wrinkle in his face, a new slackness around the eyes or mouth, a new liver spot on his increasingly withered skin. His eyes were sinking deeper and deeper into his head, and his face more and more often gave an impression of absent-mindedness or even indifference. Perhaps he was practising self-absorption and callousness the better to be able to endure decline and death.

'What has happened to your face?' the King asked.

And Absalom drew his hand across his wounds where the blood had now congealed.

'I rode through a rose thicket,' he replied. 'And my hair got caught in an oak tree. And the mule was frightened by the rose thorns and ran off.'

'That rose has nails like a wild and embittered woman,' said the King. 'Such rose thickets are best avoided.'

'It is only in one's youth that one rides like that,' said Absalom.

'Roses can be dug up with their roots and tamed in one's garden,' said the King.

'I shall cut them down,' said Absalom. 'I shall hack them down with my sword.'

And then he asked, as if wanting to change the direction of their conversation as quickly as possible: 'Will you be sending my brother Amnon with us?'

'Amnon?'

'Yes, Amnon.'

The King lay quite still. Absalom could not see his eyes: he could only feel his penetrating gaze.

'I beg you, O King,' he repeated, 'if you cannot come yourself, then send Amnon in your place!'

'Amnon in my place?'

166

'Yes.'

But that request was incomprehensible to the King. He could not imagine such interchangeability, Amnon in his place, he the King and Amnon the defiler of his sister. Why not a mule or a mad bull in his place? Why not a rotting corpse in his place? And he screamed at Absalom, he heaved himself up and screamed so that his stomach rose up from the goat-hair blanket like the wall of a tent in a storm:

'Amnon! That sullied boar! That pestilential abscess who infects everything around him!'

And he went on: 'Nobody can ride in my place! If I am not in my place, then that place is empty!'

And when Absalom turned to go in a dignified and self-controlled manner, he noticed another good sign: his father's breathing after this outburst was rattling and wheezy, as it often was with old men when they have begun to lose the strength to breathe and to cough up the impurities in their lungs. 'Nobody can ride in my place.' And he went back to his house to have his wounds attended to and to make himself ready for the sheep-shearing.

But David went to Bathsheba. It was not yet time for the evening meal.

'Where is the turtle-dove?' the King asked.

'I have presented him to the Lord,' Bathsheba replied.

'Have you sacrificed him?'

'Yes.'

And the King did not want to ask what kind of sacrifice Korban had been. Perhaps she had only wanted to enhance her state of cleanness or pray for fertility. It is always the cleanest people who strive to become cleaner, he thought. He took a lock of her hair in his hand and put it in his mouth – this was something he had begun to do in the last few years, to suck on her hair. They lay on her bed; she had been lying there when he came in.

167

'He was free of blemishes?'

'Yes,' she said. 'If old age is not a blemish?'

But he made no response concerning old age.

'That which is dearest to us shall be sacrificed,' was all he said. 'Thus we transfer our love to the Lord.'

And Bathsheba asked, as if she honestly wanted to know, as if God were unknown to her: 'Does the Lord really want our love?'

'He thirsts for it as the desert thirsts for rain.'

The desert.

And he continued: 'He created love in us so that we would give it to Him.'

'Did love not exist in the chaos before Creation?'

She said this softly and wonderingly, but he did not hear the undertone of longing in her voice.

'No,' he said. 'In isolation God could only love Himself, in meditative introspection.'

'He filled us with too much love,' said Bathsheba. 'Love surges forward like a storm in the desert.'

'Yes,' said David calmly, as if he had not noticed the strength of her emotion. 'It is like the east wind that stirs up everything that lies loose and unsecured in its path. But in the end it rises upwards. All love ultimately returns to God.'

And she thought: How simple and obvious everything seems to him. The way he teaches me is also the way he teaches his sons and his officials and the priests. Who will be able to explain the nature of the Lord when he is dead? Will the Lord dissolve and die at the same moment as King David?

'Absalom wants Amnon to ride out in my place,' he said. He said it quickly and almost casually, to check whether she would notice the godless and terrible nature of this proposed exchangeability. He wanted to put her to the test.

But she replied: 'No one can perform anything in someone else's place. People cannot be exchanged like stones for pearls or meat for hides.

'But Amnon ought to ride out with his brothers,' she continued, a soft and caressing tone in her voice now. 'He has been deserted by everybody, he is a prisoner in his own house.'

'He has Jonadab,' said the King.

'Jonadab. In other words, nobody.'

'Yes, that is true. Jonadab is nobody.'

'Amnon is becoming a stranger to his brothers,' she said. 'A defiler of his sister and nothing more.'

'He certainly is nothing more. An ass and a defiler of virgins.'

'But he is of your seed.'

'Of my seed?'

'Yes. Your seed.'

'Why do you say that?'

'Nothing is as certain or as true as you think. Shameful love is also a kind of love.'

'You are trying to persuade and inveigle me into something,' he said.

'I am afraid of order and immutability,' she said. 'Everything that has come to a halt, grown dormant or become paralysed frightens me.'

'Yes, Bathsheba. I have come to understand that much of your nature.'

'People who are stopped in their movements. Men who are locked in their houses. Events that are not allowed to happen. Days that are postponed to the next day.'

'And destruction and death that are prevented?'

Bathsheba smiled at that: 'When did your nature change, King David? When did you begin to fear the death and destruction of others?'

'Perhaps my nature is in the process of changing.'

Bathsheba fell silent. She did not want to say anything about how his nature might possibly be changing. Nor was it about him she wished to speak. It frightened her to see him ageing: the old man in him was a stranger who made her uneasy and apprehensive. And who attracted and tempted her as all strangers did.

Finally she said: 'You must command him to ride out with his brothers.'

He invoked no more protests or excuses now, he did not even ask her to expand her thoughts on the necessity of movement and change. He merely sighed in affirmation as if she had succeeded in clarifying for him what his duty was in the eyes of the Lord.

But when she suggested that one of Solomon's servants should be sent down to Amnon's house with the order, he refused. Solomon's servants were eunuchs: Solomon was such a handsome and lovable boy that Bathsheba and the King had not the courage to let real men watch over his sleep.

No, a task that was so delicate, and that might perhaps even turn out to have a significance akin to the holy state of being chosen, could not be entrusted to a eunuch. But Shebaniah could go – yes, Shebaniah.

When they were alone again, when Shebaniah had run off in delight and excitement with his message for Amnon, Bathsheba was seized by a sudden and inexplicable passion. She loosened her robe and let it slide down off her body. It was a deep passion that seemed to come from within her breast. She freed her arms from the wide, gold-embroidered sleeves. She wore no girdle.

It was not yet time for the evening meal.

David did not immediately notice that she now lay naked at his side. His thoughts still dwelt on Amnon and Absalom and the sheep-shearing. But when he stretched out his hand fumblingly towards her to take a new lock of hair to suck on, it met her warm, damp skin, and he hurriedly drew back his hand as if her ardour had burned him.

He tried to recollect how long a time had passed since he had last lain with her, but he could not.

And he thought: It is expected of me.

This I cannot avoid.

And he sat up and shook off his cloak and untied his girdle so that he could shakily wriggle out of his knee-length shirt.

And Bathsheba thought: I have kindled his desire.

Then he came to her; he climbed on to her as an old man mounts a horse. But all he could do was crush her beneath his huge weight as he sobbed. Despite her utmost efforts to make appropriate and pleasurable movements beneath him, his manhood was not aroused.

And she whispered in his ear: 'Think of some other woman! Think of your Nubian slave-girl, think of Naomi, the dancer, think of Tamar!'

But it was no help, his sobs just became more violent. And finally he rolled off her, limp and heavy and exhausted.

She took his penis in her hands: it was soft and warm and peaceful, and as she rubbed it gently between the palms of her hands it seemed to come alive and move. At first she imagined that she could feel the beating of his heart within it, but then she realized that these movements were only those that a dead bird makes when a child blows on its wings.

And she was suddenly conscious of how deeply and sadly she loved him.

And she knew that he was thinking: Perhaps the Lord has forsaken me.

He continued to sob, and he was panting as if his failure had drained his strength; not the vain physical exertion and tremendous effort of will, but the failure itself.

At last she said: 'I do not think that He has forsaken you at all.'

'Who?'

'The Lord.'

'Who says the Lord has forsaken me?'

His voice was sharp, and he sat up and looked at her. And for the first time in a very long while, she saw his eyes.

'No,' she retorted, 'you must never let that suspicion enter your head.'

But now he cried: 'You suspect that He has forsaken me! You have long believed that the Lord my God has forsaken me!'

171

She tried to keep calm; she could see that his spirit had been roused.

'That thought has never even occurred to me!'

'Has Nathan said anything?'

'No, Nathan has said nothing.'

'But it is being said in my house. It is being whispered among the slaves and the priests and the people: "The Lord has rejected him!"'

'Never have I heard a single word that could be construed in that way!'

She said this calmly and very humbly. But not humbly enough.

'You are trying to sow doubt in my mind! But the Lord can never turn his back on me!'

He leaned forwards over her and screamed his words in her ear.

'Even if I reject Him, He will not take His hand from me! Wherever I am, there is the Lord also!'

'Yes,' she whispered, submissively and fearfully. 'I know that you belong to the Lord and the Lord to you.'

But the turmoil in his soul was not to be quelled.

'He lives in my heart and in the air that I breathe. When I move it is He who moves within me, the acts of my limbs stem from his strength!'

And then he came to her, he took her in his wrath. Now his manhood was irreproachable, and she felt again like a young girl. She trembled with fear and she rejoiced for his sake.

When morning came, the sons went off to the sheep-shearing. Absalom rode at the head and Amnon was last. No one but Jonadab would ride at his side, but he now had his place again among the people and in the retinue of the King's sons.

While Absalom was away at the sheep-shearing, Tamar died. As long as her brother was in the house she was nourished by his very proximity, she drew the strength she needed from the sound of his footsteps and from his voice and from his breath.

When she was left alone, she no longer had the nourishment she required, and she simply faded away. She was buried by Absalom's servants, the ones who had stayed behind. David and Bathsheba did not hear of her death; they did not know what had happened until much later.

Absalom had said: 'She must disappear.' That was all.

Absalom had also given orders that if she died she was to be buried without mourners, without songs and funeral feasts, in an unmarked grave.

So nobody knows where her burial place is. There is a burial stone for Tamar, but her grave is not there.

But there must always be a Tamar, someone who is loved much too passionately by the wrong men. So her name was given again and again to new-born baby girls. At about this same time, the last daughter born to David was named Tamar, and one of Absalom's wives gave birth to a Tamar who her father loved to distraction. The name means palm tree, and the palm is the tree of life. Absalom's daughters also had daughters who bore her name. Yes, to this very day there are still daughters and sisters who are called Tamar.

But never was there a son born to Absalom who remained alive. They all died at the moment of birth.

While the other sons were overseeing the sheep-shearing, King David gave Solomon a first wife. He was much too lonely and much too carefree and much too childishly wise. Her name was Orpah and she bore him a daughter whom she called Tamar.

When the time came for the sons to return from the sheep-shearing, a messenger arrived. It was one of Amnon's twelve men. His mule had burst its lungs and was bleeding from its nostrils in front of the palace steps.

And the messenger told his story to the King and Bathsheba. The King let him sit on a chair since his legs would not support him. 'It was at Gibeon, and all the sheep were shorn, even Absalom's sheep, which were more than all the others together . . . yes, all the sheep were shorn and all the men were drunk, it was the second day of feasting, and Absalom – not even allowing the wine to mellow his heart – said to his men: 'Now they are so drunk that life and death are all one to them. Draw your swords and cut them down!'

'And Absalom's servants slew all the King's sons and half of all the men. All the newly shorn fleeces were soaked in blood. We who could stand up clambered on to our asses and fled. I was the only one who was brave enough to flee here to Jerusalem to tell you what had happened.'

And everyone could see from the King's expression that this was what he had expected. He did not fall into a faint and he did not weep. The news could equally well have come from his own suspicions and presentiments as from the pastures of Gibeon. The messenger could have been the embodiment of David's paternal fears, a dream image clothed in flesh. The King's face turned pale and his shoulders bent a little, as if yet another burden had been laid upon him, but he neither shouted nor spoke a single word. Possibly Bathsheba, standing at his side, might have heard a slight moan, though it could equally well have been a wheezing sound from deep in his chest. In silence he tore his cloak to ribbons and ripped open his shirt and bared his breast.

And Bathsheba thought: But Solomon is alive!

And then she thought: David can still draw strength from the empty void. The Lord can still take back the old age He has breathed into his body. David does not recognize compliance or defeat. He will fill the women's house with new wives and begin again to beget sons. I am infertile now myself. Before a year is past he may again possess sixty king's sons. I am infertile.

Nathan had now come running in, tearing his hair and howling like a mourner, and sprang towards the King as if to embrace him. And when David pushed him away he threw himself to the floor and banged his head over and over again on the cedarwood boards, crying out incessantly: 'I knew it! I knew it! I knew it!

Mephibosheth too was weeping. He often found weeping

infectious. His cheeks drooped in heavy folds, his lower lip fell forward and tears poured from his eyes. From his nose there ran a fluid that might also have been tears, and he groaned in a ridiculous, whining voice: 'King David's house is lost, a reaper has cut down all the royal sons. What is the nature of God? Who will save us from our enemies in times to come!'

But Bathsheba could not in her heart comprehend what had happened. Absalom had committed a deed the enormity of which far exceeded her expectations. My son lives, she thought, the Son among sons. And she pressed close to the King and whispered it: 'Solomon still lives.' But he did not hear her words, for just at that moment, just as she moved up against him, the servants shouted that another messenger was coming, a messenger who had come on a fresh, unwearied ass.

It was Jonadab.

His face gave no sign of important tidings – no, he seemed to have nothing at all to report.

'Amnon is dead,' he said. 'Absalom had his servants slay him at Gibeon.'

'Yes? And then?'

'Then all the King's sons fled. They fled to Ramah. They will soon be back here in the King's city.'

'Did you see this?'

'Yes. I saw it.'

And they realized that Jonadab was telling the truth. The King and Bathsheba and Nathan and Mephibosheth and all the servants thought: That is just how we might have expected everything to come about.

They did not need to be smitten by sorrow for all the King's sons: they could content themselves with lamenting Amnon.

And Nathan, the prophet of the Lord, said: 'I knew it.'

'And Absalom?'

'He has fled to Geshur, to his mother's father, King Talmai.'

And now David asked calmly and sadly about Amnon: 'Did he suffer greatly?'

'He was extremely drunk. He did not even have time to call out the name of the Lord. Everything took place so fast that he himself must still believe he is alive.'

'However long he had been given,' said David, 'he still would not have called out the name of the Lord.'

Then David sent them all away. With a movement of his hand he indicated that only Bathsheba was to stay with him; he wanted to be alone with the Lord. For that was how it was: in the irreconcilable and the impossible he perceived the true presence of the Lord. When he was forced to grieve and rejoice simultaneously, as he now had to lament Amnon and Absalom and rejoice for the other sons, he felt that God filled both his body and his soul. It seemed to him that God was the fusion of joy and sorrow. And Bathsheba stayed with him, grieved for him, commiserated with him and pronounced him fortunate.

And King David commanded that Absalom should never more set foot in Jerusalem. He had slain Amnon, who might perhaps, after all, have been the one who should have reigned after him. Absalom had done what he himself had not dared to do, that which only the Lord had the right to do.

So Absalom remained in Geshur. His mother's father built a house for him, he took new wives who bore his daughters for him, and Nathan declared that David and Absalom would never meet again among the living.

In the King himself the process of ageing seemed to have halted. In that brief moment when he had believed that all his sons had been slain, a rejuvenating thought had sped through his mind, a stimulating notion about how all those lost sons could be replaced, and he began again to visit the women's house. 'No longer shall they be forced to suffer the ignominy of widowhood,' he said.

Once more he began to devote himself seriously to royal duties in the tabernacle of the Lord, just as if he had suddenly remembered that the Lord did not belong to him alone, but was also God of the people, and that he himself was the priest of priests, the only divine mortal. He let himself be deposed and humbled and then raised again and crowned at the coronation ceremony. He himself put the crown on his own head and the priests affirmed in a solemn chant that all his power flowed like fresh holy water from God, the spring of springs. And the Lord promised him eternal life. And at the new year festivities he performed all the playing of cymbals and drums, all the exaggerated ceremonial dances, all the strewing of dust and ashes, and all the burning of incense that were needed to bear witness to the eternal, God-given distinctions between the empty void and the created world, between evil and good, destruction and resurrection, the realm of death and the land of the living. Yes, he wallowed in this holiness as a bull wallows in newly-threshed corn, and his voice was youthful and strong when he proclaimed to the people that the Lord was again sitting on His throne and had renewed His promises of rain and fertility and flowing honey and victory over all enemies. And he took part himself in the ceremonies of the new moon: from the steps of the palace he greeted the waxing moon which made the corn glisten and infused a beneficial and pleasureable warmth into all living beings.

And Bathsheba admired and praised the garments he wore, and the venerable movements and gestures he practised when they were alone, and the ancient and mysterious words that he committed to memory in a muttered undertone. He was both stately and childishly touching. She gave him advice and instructions to make his performance even more lofty and moving, and she thought: Solomon.

She also assisted him in his judicial office: he condemned and she spared. For many years the majority of the people who sought help or mercy or justice from David had been refused. The Cherethites and Pelethites had stopped them at the gates. But now the King opened his house again to a never-ending stream of defrauders and defrauded, starving widows and fatherless children, women afflicted by witchcraft, merchants in dispute, violated virgins with weeping mothers, herdsmen robbed of their cattle, wives disowned without cause. Bathsheba took great pleasure in the administration of justice. She assimilated easily the age-old laws, which often seemed to become age-old from the very moment the King introduced them. He sat on the little stool with the leather-thonged seat, the stool he had brought with him in his youth from Ziklag. This was the royal throne he held most dear. Bathsheba sat on a pile of cushions at his side, slightly behind him so that she could lean forward and whisper in his ear.

It was in the mornings that the King received the plaintiffs and petitioners and sufferers of injustice. On one occasion he sighed: 'Alas, my countless people.'

'No,' said Bathsheba. 'They are not countless. Just uncounted.

That was the origin of the great census.

Scribe: All my garments smell of myrrh, and aloes and cassia. At his right hand I stand as Queen.

If Absalom is still alive in Geshur when the King dies, he will return here and be anointed as the one who will reign after him. May the King's old age last another generation – yes, may the Lord grant him eternal old age.

My son Solomon has now learned the art of writing. He is his own scribe. What he writes I do not know. He has a thoughtful smile. What sets him apart from other men, the only thing that distinguishes him, is the fact that he is my son.

If I search my heart I find that I know nothing about Solomon. I do not think that anyone will ever really get to know anything about him. He is almost always with me, but I know him not. He is biding his time. That is very clever of him. That is what I know of my son Solomon: he is clever in a mysterious way. He is now fifteen years old.

His father the King has given him a sword. He beats time on it with his little silver knife when Shebaniah plays. He does not want to put the sword to any other use.

Shebaniah, the little boy, is now thirty years old.

Solomon is the one. Even he himself knows that. But it has never been said. It is not even said here. Such things must not be expressed. He who voices it loses the right, through that very utterance, to be the one.

Absalom has often said it about himself.

Absalom. He exists and yet he does not exist. He is biding his time in Geshur. He must be tempted away from there.

While he is absent he is too much present in the King's thoughts.

Even Nathan and Mephibosheth and Joab think that he should come back here. But the King says: 'I cannot tolerate a fratricide in my house.'

Who can prevail upon him to take Absalom back?

Joab.

I, Bathsheba, cannot plead Absalom's cause to the King: he would see through me. He knows that I am constantly thinking: Solomon. He can read the name written on my face.

Sometimes I think: My beloved little son David. I do not know why.

My son Solomon is fat and heavy. He loves sweet wine and figs. That is fare which induces procreation, peacefulness and plumpness.

If only Absalom could come back here to Jerusalem, he would himself bring about his own downfall. He is filled with holiness. But his holiness is not pious and godly. His kind of holiness is like fire, it devours and destroys.

Nathan has said so. We have all said so. Nathan said: 'Yes, what you say about Absalom and holiness is true.'

Joab and the army have long been in camp. They cannot understand this peace that has afflicted them. Guarding peaceful borders is no task for warriors. They say: 'But if Absalom . . .!'

I shall suggest something to Joab. Joab shall speak to the King.

Sometimes I wonder: Can anyone reign after David?

David has given the Lord a city where he can dwell: Jerusalem. The Lord was rootless and homeless before. Do you hear, scribe? That too I have learned!

Yes, previously the Lord was not even settled in His own Being, He had two shapes He had to fill alternately.

At times He was the God of the people, the Almighty, He who revealed Himself in the desert, He who was sometimes a fire, sometimes a pillar of cloud, sometimes a flash of lightning in the sky, He who led His people through fear and danger.

Then He was called Yahweh. Some called Him the Dwelling Place.

At times He was the God of life, the God of heaven and earth, He who created the world, He who breathed His Spirit into our nostrils, He who was in the hearts of men.

Then He was called Shalem. Some called Him Fortune.

But David let God become at one with Himself. He was the son who let God find His own reconciliation. And he said to Him: 'Here in my city canst Thou remain throughout all eternity, here canst Thou let Thy mercy endure from eternity to eternity.'

Now God is the Lord.

David is the son of God.

My house-god is nothing but an ornament. When I anoint him with holy oil it is solely to preserve him. Because I love him.

The one who reigns after David will not be the Son of God but merely the son of David.

All his sons know that to please the King they must ask him: 'What is the nature of the Lord?'

No one asks that question as often as Solomon.

Once, when he was still a little child, he asked in all innocence, 'What is the nature of the Lord today?' And then the King was very angry.

King David is the slave of the Lord.

Joab will have to use cunning; we must find a weakness that can be exploited, just as Joab seeks out the weakest point in the city walls of the enemy. The word enemy here does not signify enemy. If the King cannot be outwitted, he is immutable. That I have learned.

I have told him that he should count his people.

He who rules over a people must know them. The only

possible knowledge about a people is their number. When human beings are counted they lose their individual characteristics and are transformed into a people. A King needs his people, and nothing else.

Solomon has asked me, 'Shall we too be counted?'

No, we shall not be counted.

And I have explained to him: We belong to the house of David. I too belong to the house of David. When I was deserted by Uriah – yes, I have told Solomon about Uriah, sometimes it seems to me that Uriah is also Solomon's father, but a distant and lost father, a remote ancestor – when Uriah abandoned me and King David took me into his care, I belonged at first just to him. But then I was raised up. David's house is a temple of the Lord. Nathan has said so. A royal palace is a body with a spirit of its own, a spirit which we cannot know but which sometimes speaks through our words and our deeds. The King has said so. One cannot belong both to the house of David and to the people. To count us would be to degrade and defile us.

And Solomon smiled. He understood everything.

I give my advice to the King only when he asks for it. He often asks for my advice when I have already given it to him. I stand at his right hand.

Scribe. It was I, King David, who commanded that the people should be counted. The Lord instructed me to have my people counted.

The prophet said to me: 'The Lord will punish you!'

But I replied: 'Why should He punish me? He Himself inspired me with the idea of ascertaining the number of the people!'

'There is knowledge that is reserved for God,' he said. 'There is knowledge that is the Lord Himself. To steal such knowledge is to cut off for oneself a piece of God's flesh.'

But I answered: 'We are made in God's image. We must seek His knowledge in every way. It is our likeness to God that raises us above other living creatures.'

'Do you think that God counts the parts of His creation?'

'Yes,' I said. 'I believe that He is a God of reckoning and that He takes delight in seeing everything multiply.'

'No,' he replied. 'The Lord does not reckon. He rejoices, but He does not reckon.'

'It is fools who hate knowledge,' I said. 'No insight is so wondrous that we are unable to bear it.'

'When human beings eat of the tree of knowledge, they must die,' said the prophet. 'You can count everything else, possessions and cattle and fig trees, but not human beings.'

'I am one,' I said defiantly. 'I and Bathsheba are two. I and Bathsheba and Solomon are three.'

Why I mentioned Solomon's name in particular, I do not know.

'Yes,' said Nathan. 'That is how Belial in his evil way sits and counts us. Counting is part of his evil. It is because of his counting that God has banished him to the underworld and the darkness.'

'It is you who want to dwell in darkness,' I said. 'There is something about you prophets that makes you shun the light. You want us to be shackled by ignorance and superstition.'

'Why do you abuse me so?' he asked indignantly.

'I am not abusing you,' I said. 'But the more knowledge we human beings possess, the more accurate you prophets have to be in your predictions.'

'The Lord has hardened your heart,' he said.

'Time will show which of us two is right,' I said.

'Yes,' he replied menacingly. 'Time and the Lord will reveal the truth.'

I commanded Joab to carry out the counting of the people.

But Joab said: 'The people are holy!'

And he raised his hands aloft and pulled and twisted his hair as he always does when he is confused. 'The people and their increase and their number,' he said. 'It is all holy.'

'Yes,' I said. 'The people are consecrated to God.'

And I composed a song.

They that trust in the Lord shall be as Mount Zion,
which cannot be removed, but abideth for ever.

I sang.

As the mountains are round about Jerusalem,
so the Lord is round about His people from henceforth even for ever.
For the rod of the wicked shall not rest upon the lot of the righteous;
lest the righteous put forth their hands into iniquity.
Do good, O Lord, unto those that be good,
and to them that are upright in their hearts.
As for such as turn aside unto their crooked ways,
the Lord shall lead them forth with the workers of iniquity.

But peace shall be upon Israel.

'If the Lord wishes to multiply the people a thousandfold,' said Joab, 'then you can see it with your own eyes. What pleasure can it give you to have every head counted?'

And we looked at each other without understanding each other. It was never like that in our youth between Joab and me.

'Pleasure?' I said, as if the word were unfamiliar to me. 'Pleasure?'

And I ordered him to go, him and the captains of the army, and they moved off across the Jordan to Gad and thence to Gilead and on to Sidon.

And the people allowed themselves to be counted. Yes, in many places the women gathered too and demanded to be counted. They thought they would cease to exist if they were not counted. My men were often forced to exert harsh measures to disperse these crowds of women.

From Sidon, the Lord led them up to the stronghold of Tyre, from there down through the land of the Asherites, across the plains of Jezreel, through Sharon to Aijalon and to Judah. And the Lord laid his hand upon them and gave their spirits the strength to add up the ever-growing numbers.

I celebrated nine festivals of the new month while the counting lasted.

The Joab returned.

'Eight hundred thousand men that draw sword in Israel. Five hundred thousand men that draw sword in Judah.'

These numbers overwhelmed me. When I heard all those hundreds of thousands, I burst into tears.

The numbers smote me like a blow from the hand of the Almighty.

The heart of man cannot accommodate such quantities of human beings. Mankind is not made thus. The heart is not made thus.

And I realized that I had sinned against the Lord. I had stretched forth my sceptre into the realm of the Lord.

I sacrificed ten ewes, a sufficient guilt offering.

In the morning the prophet came to me. The Lord had sent him.

'Yes,' I said to him. 'I have behaved very foolishly in having my people counted. A ruler who turns human beings into sums of numbers deserves nothing but death. Tell me now my punishment.'

'You shall choose it yourself,' the prophet replied. 'Seven years of famine. Or three months of pursuit at the hands of your enemies as they force you to flee from your kingdom. Or three days of pestilence in your land.'

And I answered: 'I shall choose pestilence. For then at least we shall remain in the hands of the Lord.'

And I added: 'Nothing could be more dreadful than to fall into the hands of man.'

And the angel of pestilence came. He rendered every sum null and void and overturned every number in my census. He cut through like a knife, obliterating every sign that had been inscribed by the assessors. And Joab said: 'What did I say?' And the angel did not stop until the third day, by the threshing place of Araunah. I saw him standing there, his figure tall against the evening sky. It took my people, my countless people, ten days to bury their dead.

I have bought the threshing place of Araunah, I have bought it for fifty shekels of silver. I have built an altar for thank offerings, beneath the foot of the angel, just where he stopped.

Bathsheba avers that my son Solomon has said: 'A temple should be built there to the Lord.' He seems to have the Lord frequently in his thoughts. With me he never speaks of anything but the Lord. It wearies me.

Bathsheba says of the pestilence that afflicted our people: 'I do not understand why the Lord punished you.'

But I reply: 'It was the Lord who inspired me with the idea of having the people counted.

'It was also He who forbade me to do it.

'And it was He who led my men's steps and gave them the strength to keep their figures continuously spread so that they could count every head.'

In that very duality I recognize the Lord. Ambiguity and contradiction are His signs. The idea and the prohibition. Temptation and responsibility. Promise and judgment.

'The irreconcilable is His glory.'

And she asks: 'But why does He punish you?'

'In order to reveal Himself,' I reply. 'If he did not punish me, I would not see Him.'

Absalom is still in Geshur. I have decided: when two years have passed, I shall let him return to Jerusalem. Joab will try to persuade me. Perhaps Bathsheba will too: Absalom was like a son or a brother to her, son or brother, nothing more. They will try to inveigle me. I shall let myself be inveigled.

Scribe: The Lord is round about His people, from henceforth even for ever.

But peace shall be upon Israel.

David had begun to listen to people. In his youth he had been filled with the desire to turn everyone else into listeners. Perhaps he listened now from weariness.

Bathsheba had also constantly forced him to practise the art of listening.

Everything he undertook in his remaining years was the result of listening. His soul seemed to have moved from the outside of his body, from mouth and throat and hands, to the inside, to a previously empty space between his ears.

He was listening now to an old woman from Tekoah. She avoided his eyes – she was dressed in a cloak of black sackcloth which signified mourning or poverty or both. She belonged to a shepherd people from the edge of the desert of Judah.

'I am a widow woman,' she said. 'My two sons hated each other, and one slew the other. And now the people are demanding that the one son, the one who killed his brother, should be stoned.

'They want to extinguish this sole spark of life that would remain after my husband and me.'

'You may go,' said the King, realizing that her petition was a difficult one, that it could not be decided then and there. 'I shall send you my decision in due time.'

'The iniquity weighs upon me,' said the woman. 'I have to bear all this guilt.'

'If anyone accosts you, you must say, "The King has absolved me from my son's guilt." And bring to me anyone who molests you.'

'And if they slay my son?' the woman asked.

'Continuation of the family line is the most important thing of all,' said David. 'Nobody shall hurt a hair of your son's head. Your husband's seed is holy. The spark of life dwells in the seed of man.'

'Shall I continue to protect and preserve my son?'

'Yes,' said David. 'He may indeed have committed fratricide, but he is also holy, since he is the fragile vessel in which your husband's seed is carried forward through time.'

Now the woman was silent for a moment. Then she said: 'Will you permit me, O King, to say a few more words?'

'There are many others waiting on the stairs,' he said. 'You must be brief.'

And the woman from Tekoah said, 'You yourself have a son who has slain his brother. But you have banished him. We must needs die, and when we die we are as water spilled upon the ground, which cannot be gathered up again. But God wants the spark of life to continue to glow even when we are dead and departed. How then can you, who hear everything and see everything and are as wise as an angel of God, be so blind that you do not let your son come back to you?'

And now David understood the meaning of this woman and her sons and her description of her suffering.

'Who has sent you?' he asked. 'Was it Bathsheba? Or the prophet? Or Joab?'

'It was Joab.'

'And your story of the son who slew his brother? Is that a lie?'

'No,' said the woman. 'Not a lie. But a parable.'

'So it was Joab who invented this parable about Absalom?'

'Joab put these words into my mouth, one after another,' the woman from Tekoah replied.

David gave her a dried haunch of kid for her journey, and sent for Joab. Then he commanded Joab to fetch Absalom back home from Geshur. But Absalom was not to come into the King's house, and he would no longer be allowed to practise shooting the bow with Bathsheba, and he was to be kept apart from Solomon. Anyone who has once acquired the taste for the tempting of fratricide can easily relapse. He was to dwell peaceably and quietly in his own house.

So Absalom came back to Jerusalem. Joab brought him. And those who had so cunningly arranged his return had given themselves all this trouble only so that he could bring about his own downfall.

Yes, David had become the most avid listener in the whole kingdom.

In the last few years two advisers had become closer to him than any others, indeed almost as close as Bathsheba: Ahithophel of Giloh, whom Bathsheba had brought to his house, and Hushai of Bethel.

It was these two and Bathsheba who advised him to send back the enormous royal crown of the Ammonites to Rabbah, the crown that no one could wear and which Absalom loved. Hanun's son Shobi had now become king in Rabbah, and for him the crown was holy, whereas in Jerusalem it was merely a bulky monstrosity. 'Nothing,' said Bathsheba, 'is as precious as a King's friendship, and few things can be obtained for so slight a price.'

And so David sent the crown to Rabbah, and thus the peace between his people and the Ammonites was sealed, the peace that Joab had established by the sword.

Ahithophel was Bathsheba's paternal grandfather. She had wanted to have a reminder of her past near her, living flesh that carried her family's seed. He was older even than David; he used to tie his sparse white beard in a double loop, which hid his wrinkled neck, and when he spoke he would close his eyes to show that he was filled with nothing but his thoughts.

Hushai was one of the officials who had followed David since the early years when he had fought Saul for the royal throne. He had a severe limp, one kneecap having been crushed when he

193

fell from his mule in the flight from Saul at Nob. The King sometimes doubted his wisdom, for his utterances were often confused and difficult to interpret, but he could not ignore him because Hushai was one of the few people who regularly met God. These meetings took place in Hushai's dreams, yet they were meetings he perceived with his sight, and he retained the memory of the dreams in his eyes. Hushai was the only person in King David's house who could give a clear and simple answer to the question: 'What is the nature of the Lord?'

'He is like the King. He sits on a leather-covered stool, His belly rests upon his thighs, His face is like that of a wise old bird of prey, and He fills me with fear and joy.'

'But what does He say?'

'He is silent. But I think that He would listen if I could bring myself to say something. But my lips are paralysed when I see Him.'

So King David felt a tender affection for Hushai, a man who could associate with the Lord without being consumed or being transformed into a prophet.

For that was how it was: he listened less and less often to the prophets. Their pronouncements, which always had to be interpreted, their shrill voices and their constant state of agitation gave him no pleasure. No, prophets only made him angry and depressed and sleepless.

Now David said to Ahithophel and Hushai, and also to Bathsheba who was standing at his side, 'I have been tricked into letting my son Absalom, the fratricide, come home to Jerusalem. The woman from Tekoah who persuaded me was sent by Joab. But who had sent Joab?'

He wanted to prove his clear-sightedness to them.

'Absalom is a destroyer and a scourge,' he went on. 'He spreads devastation around him as if he were an angel of pestilence, and if the Lord does not stop him he will annihilate the whole of my house.

'Who can want that? Who has secretly planned his return?

'It is not the Lord.'

And he looked at Hushai: 'No, it is not the Lord.

'If the whole of my house perishes, if Absalom exterminates us all, who will then be next in line for the throne?'

And he answered his own question:

'Mephibosheth.

'It is Mephibosheth who has deceived me. He is the last of Saul's line. It is he who has woven the net and dragged Absalom here. When I descend to the realm of death, he will ascend to the throne.'

He was smiling continuously as he spoke. It was this smile, inappropriate to the time and place, that Solomon used to try to imitate.

But now Bathsheba and her grandfather Ahithophel could no longer control themselves, and burst into loud laughter; even Hushai gave a shrill bleating laugh.

Bathsheba's laugh was one of relief and liberation.

When they had laughed enough, it was she who said: 'Are you blind, my lord King? Are you deaf and blind? Do you not see the days and years consuming and devouring all the people of your house? Do you not see all of us declining and changing?'

And he raised his eyes and looked at her.

And at that moment, for the first time, he looked so deeply into her face that he saw how much it had changed: beauty had given way to wrinkles.

But he said nothing.

And she continued: 'Mephibosheth cannot think out plans any more. His spark of life has been drenched and drowned in wine. His eyes see, but he no longer knows what he sees. It is only with difficulty that he can remember his own name. He cannot form a thought which stretches further than from hand to cup.'

For that was how it was.

And she asked: 'He eats and drinks every day at your table. But can you remember when you last exchanged a word or a thought with him?'

'No,' said the King. 'No, I do not remember.'

And then the King asked no more who could have cast out the net that had brought Absalom home. His eyes were fixed on Bathsheba.

The days, he thought. The years.

But Absalom demanded to see the King. He sent Jonadab and he sent Shebaniah. But his father David refused to talk to them about his son.

And he sent a message to Joab. But Joab did not come. No, he was much too busy: the army had to be trained for the wars that must be imminent, the border strongholds had to be inspected and reinforced, the armourers had to be supervised. Joab had no time at the moment for Absalom. Time enough, time enough.

Thus passed almost two years. And not even Bathsheba dared speak to David about Absalom.

Finally Absalom made his servants set fire to Joab's cornfields, the fields that lay next to his own beyond the brook at Kidron.

Jonadab, who had now transferred his shallow friendship from the dead brother to the living one, had advised him to do it, and Jonadab had been advised by Shebaniah, Shebaniah by Bathsheba.

Then at last Joab came to him.

'Why have you burned my corn?' he asked.

'To force you to come here to my house.'

'If you were not the King's son, I would not have come,' said Joab. 'I would have just let my servants fetch you.'

'I shall pay you tenfold for the corn,' said Absalom. 'Yes, a hundredfold.'

Joab seemed untouched by the passing of the years and days. He looked exactly as Absalom remembered him from his youth. His hair was black and gleaming, his back was not bent and his shoulders had not fallen away.

'You must have a good reason for burning my field,' he said.

'Growing corn is holy. And it is holiest of all now when it is ripening.'

'I must meet the King,' said Absalom. 'You are the only one who can bring us together.'

'I brought you here from Geshur. Was that not enough?'

'As long as his house is closed to me, I do not exist. I cannot do anything. I cannot make any plans or cherish any hopes. My days pass without aim or purpose. I am like a shadow lengthening and fading away.'

'And what can the King do?'

'He can recognize that I exist. He can restore me. Yes, he can create me anew.'

'Create you?'

'Yes, create. That is what fathers can do to sons. Create them. And destroy them.'

And so Joab went to King David. And Bathsheba said, 'Casting a person aside into obscurity in this way while he is still among the living is more cruel than killing him with your own hands. I can imagine no greater affliction than being both alive and non-existent at the same time.'

'Yes,' said King David. 'Perhaps that is so.'

'Man shall live among the living,' said Bathsheba. 'And be dead among the dead.'

'Take him in your arms,' said Ahithophel. 'And bless him!'

'Yes,' said Hushai. 'Bless him!'

David was silent. But then he said, 'Yes, I shall see Absalom. I shall avow to him that he still lives.'

And so Bathsheba sent for Shebaniah to fetch Absalom.

He threw himself to the floor in the doorway, smote his forehead seven times against the threshold, and then crawled towards the King's feet without raising his head, groping his way like a blind man.

And the King bent forward and lifted up his head and kissed him on the right cheek just in front of his ear.

But neither of them had anything to say to the other.

Absalom resumed his place among the living with terrifying speed. On the morning of the first day he sat on his mule at the Gihon gate. And he shouted to everyone who passed by, 'Look, here I stand! I am the King's son and I am not counting you! You, you and you – none of you is being counted! No, when my time comes, not a single person will lose his name and be turned into a number!'

And he stopped all strangers from afar who turned their steps towards the royal palace. He spoke to them in a warm and friendly manner and asked them where they had come from and what their business was. And he gave a detailed account of all the mercy and justice he would have showered upon them if he had been king. Unfortunately, he explained, King David was now much too old and tired, he no longer had strength enough to bother about people. Bathsheba and the Lord were the only living beings for whom he still had room in his shrinking heart. As proof of this he also mentioned himself: 'I am his son, but he denied me. He cut off my remembrance from the earth, he robbed my soul of its spark. Only with difficulty did I manage to save my life.'

And he hired men of his own age – he was now nearly forty – to go round the city speaking well of him and spreading lies and bitter truths about King David. Sometimes he would have himself driven in a four-horse carriage through the gates, and his men would jump down ahead of him and shout 'Make way for Absalom, the Chosen One! His time is almost come, he has vast amounts of work to do, nothing must hold him up or hinder him!'

He wore a gold-embroidered robe which emphasized his

handsome figure, and his shoulder plates were of silver. Sometimes he would stop the carriage and step down to the people, and they would crowd around him so that he could shake them by the hand or embrace them.

And he reminded the people about King David and the horses: when he had conquered King Hadadezer he had severed the tendons of all but a hundred of his horses. He did not understand that horses were holy! And he reminded them about all the foreigners in the service of the King, all the foreign men who guarded him and built his city for him. And he said: 'Look at all the extravagance in his house. Look at Bathsheba, his wife: wherever she goes a hundred maids go with her. Look at her garments of embroidered gold. Look at the palanquins the King has given her and all the slaves who carry her wherever she goes!'

Bathsheba saw him once from her window. Perhaps he took that particular route in order to be seen by her. She saw the carriage on its two mighty copper wheels, drawn by four horses. They were Assyrian horses with plaited manes. And she thought: There may be no future for Absalom, but the horses are unforgettable and invincible – yes, the future belongs to the horses!

The truth was that Absalom had chosen himself. He was a mock king.

But nobody dared tell King David what Absalom was doing. Not Ahithophel nor Hushai nor Joab. And none of the officials and none of the priests. They feared David and they feared Absalom.

It was Bathsheba and Shebaniah who finally told him all about it.

'You must send out your men against him,' said Bathsheba. 'While there is still time.'

'They would kill him,' said David.

'They would stop him. They would take the horses by the bridle and lead him home to his house.'

'I cannot sacrifice my son. A father who sacrifices his son destroys himself.'

'Even if he sacrifices his son for the sake of the whole people?'

'Yes. Even then.'

'You must put a limit on your mercy,' said Bathsheba.

'Mercy?' David responded. 'The most merciful father would probably sacrifice his son. No, it is weariness. A mixture of weariness and a long lifetime of piety and fear of God.'

And Bathsheba was forced to begin again.

'Do you not understand, then, that this is a revolt? Your son is rebelling against you to depose you!'

'And what if he is? Perhaps the people want him. He is young and he is as handsome as an Egyptian idol.'

'You are the Lord's Anointed,' said Bathsheba. 'You remain the Anointed One until you reach the gates of the kingdom of death. Yes, perhaps even beyond them.'

'Saul was also the Lord's Anointed,' David answered. 'But the anointing was capable of little against my youth and strength and desire for victory.' David's lined face was twisted and contorted in the strange smile that Bathsheba could never understand.

Shebaniah stood silently at Bathsheba's side, carrying his lyre under his arm. He never went in to the King without his instrument, his music was ever less frequently required. He seemed to imagine that it was this little lyre that gave him the right to exist.

'You too were anointed as king,' Bathsheba pointed out. 'You were both chosen and anointed.'

'Yes,' said David. 'That was one anointing against another. But my anointing was younger and holier than his.'

'The people do no want any other king than David,' Bathsheba continued stubbornly. 'If only you would go out into the city and show yourself. The coronation and the new year festivities and the new month festivals are not enough: you must speak to the people, you must ride your mule through the streets, you must drive out in your carriage and feed the poor from your own hand!'

Her tone was ardent and persuasive.

'Then they will forget Absalom,' she said. 'He will fade like the moon before the sun!'

'You do not know our people,' said David. 'I know the people as if they were of my own seed.'

'Nobody has the people's love as you do,' said Bathsheba.

'The people cannot feel love. Not the sort of love that binds husbands and wives and fathers and sons and brothers and sisters. No, love is alien to the people. One can arouse the excitement of the people, but never their love.'

And now Bathsheba had no further arguments.

But David turned to Shebaniah.

'Whose side are you on, Shebaniah? In your heart are you my boy or Absalom's?'

Shebaniah seemed at first not to understand the question. His face dropped in amazement and uncertainty, and the King had to repeat it. 'Whose little songster, whose little chirruping bird would you rather be?'

Then Shebaniah's cheeks contracted as if they had suddenly shrunk, his lips were drawn in so hard between his teeth that the blood flowed. He could not utter a single word. He threw himself down and clutched the King's knees as if there he might find the only firm point in a collapsing world. The little bearded middle-aged boy wept so violently that he was no longer in control of his voice: it produced groans and screams, which to Bathsheba sounded frightening and unnatural – gruff and manly, yet at the same time shrill and baby-like.

But David stroked his hair and caressed his cheek with the back of his hand. He thought to himself, Yes, that was what I might have expected, the only possible response to my foolish question.

When Shebaniah had at last calmed down again, David said to Bathsheba, speaking softly and slowly and thoughtfully, 'Do you remember when Absalom was a little boy? He was always alone against his brothers. It was always Absalom and the others.'

Yes, Absalom and the others.

'When they played with their bows, he preferred his sword. And when they fetched their swords, he would leave them in order to play undisturbed with his bow.'

How could Bathsheba remember that? When Absalom was a child, she too was a small child, a very little girl in Giloh!

'Yes,' she replied, 'I can see it extraordinarily clearly in my memory. Sometimes he would inspect his brothers' armies, he could lead them, he would capture imaginary strongholds and conquer make-believe enemies!'

'Yes, it is strange.'

Yes. Strange.

But that same evening, soon after the meal was over and Mephibosheth had been carried to his room – yes, Bathsheba had a litter constructed for him, with carrying poles, a litter on which he could eat and sleep, live and die – Shebaniah went to Jonadab and repeated all that had passed between himself and Bathsheba and the King. It was Bathsheba who had anxiously exhorted him to go to Jonadab. 'He is our only friend, he cannot be left out,' she said. 'It is only right and proper that he should be informed of our little conversation with the King.'

And Jonadab went straight to Absalom.

Thus Absalom realized that he could no longer bide his time. David was not only the most merciful but also the most ruthless man he knew. Now it would be revealed whether the Lord was prepared to make him the Chosen One as he so desperately wanted – indeed, as he unconditionally demanded.

But a deep feeling of peace filled David's mind. That night he slept in Bathsheba's arms with a lock of her hair in his mouth. Everything was about to be fulfilled, in one way or another. The

Lord would direct his life towards its preordained and perfect end. He slept with a smile on his face, and a faint image, a shadowy dream, flashed through his mind, that he was already sleeping in the arms of the Lord.

In Hebron, up in the mountains of Judah, Abraham the ancestral father had built an altar to the Lord. That altar may have been the first the Lord had seen; it was before the cities and the people and the kings had been created. It was built of living stones – that is, stones that God Himself had hewn and left lying on the ground. It had pointed, horn-shaped blocks at the corners. It was situated on the outskirts of the city, in a grove of oak and terebinth trees on the Plain of Mamre.

There, in Hebron, Abraham also lay buried. There too Joshua, the newcomer, had lived. And for seven years David had ruled the kingdom of Judah from Hebron.

Early in the morning Absalom sent a message to all his men: 'We shall go to Hebron!'

Then he called upon David.

'I want to make a sacrifice to the Lord on the Plain of Mamre. I want to present a thank offering to Him for letting me return here to Jerusalem and to my father's house.'

And David let him go. But he thought: Was that really the Lord?

Absalom stopped at the threshing place of Araunah, by the altar that David had built, and counted the men who had followed him: 200. Then he gave them instructions on the ways they should take to Hebron. They were each given a different path, and they were to gather together all the men they met and take them with them to Hebron. It should not prove too difficult, since everyone in the kingdom of Judah knew that the Lord dwelled in Hebron.

When he had gone some little way beyond Giloh, he noticed that a very old man with a beard tied in a double loop across his neck was riding at his side.

'Ahithophel!' he cried. 'What are you doing here?'

'My son's daughter Bathsheba sent me,' Ahithophel replied.

'You are the King's oldest and most trusted adviser next to Hushai,' said Absalom. 'Have you really deserted him?'

'Both you and the King need advisers,' said Ahithophel. 'David kept Hushai. You have got me.'

'And if I turn you away?'

'The advice I can give you is worth more than a thousand men with sword.'

'Everyone knows that you are the King's adviser.'

'Everyone also knows that I was Uriah's friend, Uriah the Hittite whom David had slain. And everyone knows that I am Bathsheba's grandfather, Bathsheba whom he snatched for himself as a thief would steal a lamb.'

'How could I put my trust in you, you who have guided King David for a generation?'

'Advice is not what you think,' said Ahithophel. 'Advice can never be assigned to one single person. Advice is advice. It is independent and incontrovertible – yes, frequently even inhuman.'

'One must be able to believe and rely on one's advisers,' Absalom persisted stubbornly.

'You must not put your trust in me, but in the Lord. But you must listen carefully to everything I may have to say to you. He who accepts advice is wise, and the beginning of wisdom is the fear of the Lord.'

'I have heard that before,' said Absalom.

'Yes,' replied Ahithophel. 'Your father David often says it.'

The people seemed to have been waiting for an uprising for a long time. The people, the men that draw sword, are always waiting for a rebellion to support or put down. Uprisings are like earthquakes and eclipses of the sun: they just come. Thus spoke Ahithophel. Soon Absalom had 7,000 men around him in Hebron, men from Judah, and their number was steadily increasing.

At Abraham's altar Absalom had himself proclaimed king. He himself called out the decisive and conclusive words: 'Behold, the Lord has anointed me to be captain over His inheritance.' He performed the burnt offering and the priests anointed him with holy oil and called down the spirit of the Chosen One upon him, and he commanded horns and trumpets to be sounded.

When David heard that Absalom was now king in Hebron, he put his head in his hands and wept. He could not think of any more fitting or pious action. An army can march from Hebron to Jerusalem in two days, a determined and ambitious army under the command of a new and greedy king can do it in one – the men would be swept along on the tide of eagerness. And the King thought: Tomorrow he will be here. I shall meet him on the palace steps. The Lord has forsaken me.

And he saw before him, as if in a mirror, what had happened when he took Rabbah: the King divesting himself of his raiment and his holy status, Absalom taking up the crown and pressing it to his breast, and King Hanun's conversation with God, the god who had forsaken him.

Thus it would come about: what had been is what shall be, what had already come to pass is what shall come to pass.

The Lord is waiting for Absalom, he thought. I can see Him. He is sitting upon His seat of mercy beneath the cherubs' wings and waiting for him. If I go down to the tabernacle of the Lord I shall just feel like an intruder. The Lord no longer has time for me.

And he thought: Why is He smiling so strangely?
But Bathsheba understood his thoughts.
'He has not forsaken you,' she said.
'Who?'
'The Lord.'

'No,' David replied. 'But He is smiling at me so oddly, and when I invoke His name He turns His face from me.'

'If you stay here, Absalom and his men will take Jerusalem by the sword. They will kill and sack and burn exactly as if they were in an enemy's country. They will do the same as you did in your youth with the cities of the worshippers of false idols. What has been is what shall be.'

'Absalom is not my enemy,' said David. 'He is just the one who should reign after me.'

'The Chosen One?' asked Bathsheba.

'For the moment he is the Chosen One,' said David, and it seemed to her that he wanted to share what he had come to understand: that being chosen is a fleeting and inconstant state – who can catch and hold a breath of wind in his hands?

'You must flee,' said Bathsheba.

'Perhaps your men will have to force you to flee,' she continued. 'Perhaps the Cherethites and Pelethites will have to tie your hands and feet and carry you on your flight. Perhaps you will have to flee, bound and fettered. But flee you must.'

'Has my guard not forsaken me?'

'No, all the foreign men are loyal to you.'

'Your grandfather Ahithophel is with Absalom?' David asked.

'He thought that Absalom too might need an adviser,' Bathsheba replied.

'May the Lord turn all his advice into the most profound folly,' said David, and Bathsheba could detect a note of renewed bitterness in his voice.

'And Hushai?'

'He is in Bethel with his sons. It is time for the almond harvest.'

'Joab?'

'He is summoning your men. The men who are not with Absalom in Hebron.'

'King Absalom,' David corrected her.

'No,' said Bathsheba. 'Absalom the insurgent. Absalom the miscreant. The evildoer.'

'He is my son for all that.'

'Yes. And you must flee from him, he seeks your life.'

And so David decided to leave Jerusalem. They decided to abandon Jerusalem, the city of David, so that Absalom would not slay the people of the city with the blade of the sword.

And Bathsheba rode out of Jerusalem with David at her side, he on the royal ass, she sitting sideways on the pack-saddle of a she-ass. They rode to the east down through the Valley of Kidron, towards the Mount of Olives. The royal household and the servants followed behind, Shebaniah among them, mostly on foot but some riding, and the wives and the concubines who had not yet reached the age when their legs would no longer carry them. And the wretched scribe. Lord! What was there to write now? On each side of the pitiful procession marched the Cherethites and Pelethites and the escort of 600 soldiers from Gath, the city of Goliath, the giant. They bore their shields and weapons aloft as if they were marching out to battle, or as if there were still something to protect and defend. Finally came the men who served in the tabernacle of the Lord; most of them wanted to know nothing of any other king than David. They carried the ark of the covenant: they had not wanted to leave the Lord sitting alone on the seat of mercy in an abandoned city.

In a closed circle to one side of all the others were David's thirty-seven mighty warriors, those who had followed him constantly and who were always ready to obey his orders, those who would not desert him even if he commanded them to do so.

If Uriah had still been alive he would have been one of them. In his place was Hezrai the Carmelite, a valiant bowman. They must always number thirty-seven.

Solomon rode his mule alone and smiling between the mighty warriors and the priests. He had chosen his place in the retinue carefully. The other royal sons, those who had not joined Absalom, were spread out among the people; they were boys and men, just boys and men.

And the fleeing people were everywhere on the slopes of the valley, walking and running and riding and stumbling, men and women and children and old people, those who were just ordinary people and nothing more, those who had nothing holy to defend or lose, those who had only their own lives.

The King had never been a horseman; he swayed in the saddle, hunched and bent over the withers of the ass, his ungainly legs thudding against its flanks. He squinted into the silvery-white light. He did not turn round to survey the exodus. He had never been one to look back. Bathsheba looked both backward and forward – that was the kind of person she was. No, David did not even see that she was riding at his side, but he felt it, as he always felt her nearness. His heart was aware that some mysterious and spiritual substance flowed forth from her, an aura or a sound or light or energy, and that it was this unseen emanation that held him upright on his ass.

'But you chose to follow me,' he said suddenly, as if they had been in the middle of a conversation.

'I have never had any choice,' said Bathsheba.

'My heart would like to think: She chose to follow me.'

But she did not wish to speak of his heart.

'Mephibosheth,' she said. 'I sometimes think of him with envy. To live, and yet not to be among the living. To be among the living and yet not to live. To consist just of hunger, thirst and weariness, and to be given food and drink and sleep in abundance.'

'I have given him all the love I could,' said the King.

'Yes,' said Bathsheba.

'Is he still in my house?'

'He is asleep. Shebaniah tried to wake him, but could not. He will wake up for the evening meal.'

And David thought: The evening meal.

'Absalom does not know which vessels are holy,' he said. 'He does not know the prayer which has to be said over the bread.

He has no knowledge of how the wine must be purified and blessed. Can he even see whether there is still blood in the meat?'

She understood his thoughts – he should have taught Absalom.

'Does knowledge not come from being chosen?' she asked.

'He is not chosen. He has merely chosen himself. He was chosen in his mother's womb to be the kind of man who chooses himself.'

'Can the Lord not choose him now, retrospectively?'

'The Lord never does anything retrospectively,' said David. 'He does everything before its due time is come. Yes, He has already done everything from the beginning.'

'Even this?'

'Yes. Even this.'

They rode side by side conversing. It was a happy moment.

She held the reins loosely in her right hand, sitting very upright, with the upper part of her body facing forward. Her bow and quiver hung from the pommel. Indeed, that was all she had brought with her: her bow and her arrows.

Not even her house-god.

'No,' she said. 'The one who is chosen never has any choice.'

But he was still thinking about everything that was already determined from the beginning of time.

'The nations and the peoples and the cities that have been laid waste,' he said. 'They are destroyed because they are chosen for destruction. All the devastation I have seen and caused and with the Lord's help been able to forget. It sometimes seems incomprehensible to me that the world can still exist.'

'The Lord has only just created it,' she said.

And suddenly she realized that he was reliving in his imagination what he had performed and submitted himself to at the new year festival: the deposing and humiliation of the King and his descent to the realm of death, that venerable and absurd pageant which always ended with his resurrection and rein-statement on the throne, that heart-rending and trumpet-blasting ceremony in which the King was alternately the created and the creator, in which every word and movement, all the derobement and derision, elevation and ovation were prescribed in the priests' holy books, perhaps even by the Lord Himself.

She had asked many times whether a queen should not also be humiliated and restored in the same way, but he had replied that this representation of life and death and new life could only be performed by the priests and the King and the Lord. And she thought: He will soon say, 'Let the floods clap their hands: let the hills be joyful together before the Lord; for he cometh to judge the earth!'

'Let the floods clap their hands,' said David, 'let the hills be joyful together before the Lord; for He cometh to judge the earth!'

'Whom would you have chosen?' she asked. 'Whom would you have chosen if Absalom had not done this?'

But he did not reply. He had entrenched himself behind the wall of his thoughts: With righteousness shall He judge the world, and the people with equity. The Lord reigneth.

When they reached Beth Hammerhak, where the priests used to empty the jars of blood from the sacrificial animals, they stopped.

Then David saw that Zadok, the high priest, and the other priests had carried the ark of the Lord with them.

He commanded them to return to Jerusalem at once: the Lord was an old God now, who had grown accustomed to a settled habitation. If His grace and mercy followed David beyond Kidron they would, perhaps, finally meet again on Mount Zion. 'I am going to the land of the Ammonites,' he said to the Lord. The priests should watch and listen around King Absalom – 'Absalom the King,' he said – they should inform him of everything of importance and value that they might hear of see or understand. Yes, they should be scouts and spies in their own city, and their secret messengers would always be able to reach him at the ferry beyond Gilgal.

And Bathsheba explained to the Levites: 'We have King David. Jerusalem, the abandoned city, has greater need of the ark of the Lord than we have!'

Then David and the whole of his retinue set up camp for the night on the eastern side of Kidron, on the slopes of the Mount of Olives.

In the evening Absalom and the men of Judah, those who had heard him proclaim himself king, came to Jerusalem.

The empty palace seemed suddenly overwhelmingly large to him. They found Mephibosheth there and that was all. He was about to wake up, if waking is the right word, and Absalom commanded that wine be brought to him, and a portion of the young bull he had sacrificed, part of the haunch of the thank offering.

And Absalom opened up his slain brother Amnon's wine store for his men, the wine store that had remained locked and bolted ever since the day Amnon had gone out to his last sheep-shearing. Many of the men became ill and even polluted the forecourt in front of the tabernacle of the Lord; they were the ones who had drunk of the deep red, almost brown, wine. Others thought the wine the noblest drink they had ever tasted; they were the ones who drank the golden, honey-sweetened wine.

Now he was King, and he sent for Ahithophel. 'Counsellor,' he said, 'what must I do first?'

'Go in to the King's concubines.'

'Have they not fled with the King?'

'Ten concubines have been left. They have cloth bandages bearing King David's sign around their wrists. He has left them for the one who will reign after him.'

'A sign?'

'Yes, a sign from one king to another.'

'I already have my own wives,' Absalom argued. 'They await me in my house.'

'They are not king's wives. There is nothing princely or godly about them. They are just concubines for your pleasure – they bear your daughters for you.'

For that was how it was: only daughters and dead sons were born to Absalom.

And so a tent of camel-hair mats was erected on the palace roof. No building of stones or bricks can ever be as holy as a tent. It was set at the edge of the roof so that it was easily visible to all the men in the courtyard. Its flaps were also turned towards the people.

Then the concubines were carried up there. They were carried on Mephibosheth's litter which Ahithophel appropriated for the purpose. Mephibosheth had to lie on the floor on his cloak. One after another the concubines were carried up to Absalom so that all the people could see him go in to them in the tent and lie with them. Many of them were sore afflicted with aches and pains and frailty of old age. Their wailing and whimpering could be heard by the people in the courtyard below. He carried out the first of these holy and unavoidable duties quickly and in an almost devotional spirit: it was an Ammonite woman who had been his own wet-nurse before David took her as his concubine. By the third he began to feel a nauseous satiation – yes, it was as if he had drunk brown, over-mature wine. He would not have been able to fulfil the last of these duties, the eighth, ninth and tenth, had his soul not been filled with the knowledge that this was an act of ordination, a sacrifice that the Lord expected of him.

And later, when night descended on Jerusalem, Ahithophel said: 'After this, no turning back is possible, no reconciliation between you and the King is imaginable. With this act you have carved an ineradicable notch in the staff of time, a deep cut between the heretofore and the hereafter.'

'It seems to me rather that I have broken the staff of time clean in two,' said Absalom.

For he realized that Ahithophel's counsel might have been not just questionable but also fateful. Advice is advice, it is uncommitted and incontestable, often, indeed, inhuman.

He went out in the darkness to David's well, accompanied by some of his men. He leaned against the side of the well; all was still and quiet in Jerusalem. And he passed water into the well.

The women's well, he thought to himself.

And the men who saw him did the same. They thought it was a holy ritual that had to be performed on the first night when a new king had taken Zion. Yes, they filled the well half full.

And at daybreak, when the time came for the women to meet at the well, the few women who were left in the city, the rumour spread that a miracle had occurred at the well: steam was issuing from it, a spring had arisen at the bottom of it.

And they said: 'That is the nature of King Absalom.'

Then the women fetched pitchers on long ropes. They all wanted to carry home some of the holy water to their houses. But when they pulled up their pitchers and saw the colour of the liquid and smelled its odour and realized what kind of water it was, they said: 'That is the nature of King Absalom.'

After this David's well was never again holy.

A tent was also erected for Bathsheba and David. It stood on a ledge in the Valley of Kidron on the side towards the Mount of Olives, and was made from the untreated hides of four asses that had broken their legs on the steep slopes of the river valley.

At nightfall Hushai arrived there, the second of David's two foremost advisers. The King met him in front of the tent. Hushai had come on a mule, and now when he had to stand on his feet, his limp was worse than usual.

'Is the almond harvest over?' King David asked.

'Yes,' replied Hushai. 'The almond harvest has all been gathered in.'

'Was it a good one?'

'It was a richer harvest than it could ever have been under any other king.'

Hushai had torn his cloak to shreds and rubbed oil and ashes in his hair. The sight in one of his eyes had been dimmed since his youth, when a drop of quicklime had splashed into it; over the other the eyelid hung paralysed, and from time to time he lifted the heavy flaccid fold of skin with the thumb and forefinger of his right hand. Then he could see.

But he maintained that he could see the Lord even from behind his lowered eyelid.

He looked at David now, waiting for an answer to a question he had not expressed.

But David did not respond. Bathsheba did so instead. She had come out from inside the tent, and sat crouched beneath the open tent flap.

'No,' she said. 'He has no need of any advice.'

'I will not forsake you,' said Hushai. 'To forsake you would be like forsaking the Lord.'

'You cannot do him a greater favour than to forsake him,' said Bathsheba.

'Truly forsake?'

'Yes. Forsake.'

Hushai suddenly began to weep. He wept bitterly and desperately. David had never seen him weep before – indeed, he had not believed that this contorted face could be contorted even more. But when the King raised his hand in a gesture of blessing and solace to accompany the warm and loving words he was about to address to him, Bathsheba stopped him.

'Your advice has always pleased the King,' she said. 'But it was only advice, nothing more.'

And the only thing David managed to say was, 'Yes, Hushai, your advice has always been pleasing to me.'

'Advice is advice,' Bathsheba continued. 'It is only images and words strewn at our feet; we make our way over them without slowing our steps or changing our direction. It is not inevitable or imperative.'

'What, then, is inevitable or imperative?' Hushai asked, controlling his tears.

'We do not know that until we have carried out the inevitable to which we have been compelled,' said Bathsheba.

But David said: 'The Lord commands.'

'I saw the Lord last night in my dream,' said Hushai. 'He was walking in the Valley of Kidron. He went to Beth Hammerhak, and there He rested, and then He went back to Jerusalem.'

'Yes,' said David. 'That is what He did.'

That was how it was: the Lord had undertaken a short journey. Now He was home again. They considered this in silence.

'And I?' said Hushai at last.

'You too shall go back to Jerusalem,' said Bathsheba.

'To Jerusalem?'

'Yes. Jerusalem.'

'Where Absalom in now king?'

'Yes, Absalom and his hosts have marched into Jerusalem.'

'Shall I go to Absalom?'

He turned to David; he wanted David himself to answer his questions. But the King only sighed and raised his empty palms towards him in a gesture that meant, I have no further instructions to give, I have enough to do to answer my own questions.

'What advice shall I give him?'

'You shall be generous to him with your advice,' said Bathsheba. 'Advice is advice. The more you can give him, the better. Ahithophel is already with him. Your advice will be balanced against Ahithophel's.'

'Shall I then serve King Absalom?'

'Yes, him and none other shall you serve.'

And she added: 'If the King had a thousand counsellors, he would send them all to Absalom. Then his fall would be inevitable.'

And King David said: 'Ultimately God brings all advice to nought.'

And that same night Hushai rode to Jerusalem. His mule found its own way, and he was well received by Absalom, who was overjoyed at now having the two wisest of King David's counsellors in his service. And Hushai lifted his paralysed eyelid with his thumb and forefinger and opened his eye and looked at him and said: 'Long live the King. Long live the King.'

The people covered the ground in Bathsheba's and David's tent with their cloaks. They lay there now, they lay exactly as they would have done if they had still been in the palace.

Outside in the dark his people, that remnant of the people, were resting. Everything was as silent as that night long ago in the Valley of Rephaim when he and Uriah and the other men had heard the Lord's footsteps in the tops of the mulberry trees. It was the time of the year when even the birds are silent.

The untreated asses' skins filled the air with the dank and heavy stench of blood. It was an odour he knew well and liked: it had always permeated the tabernacle of the Lord, particularly in the holy of holies. Even Bathsheba felt stangely at home with this smell and by his side. She had always thought that King David smelled of blood.

The holy of holies, thought David, raising his head higher on her breasts so that he could put his lips to the skin beneath her ear. He lay at her left side. He had entwined his left hand with hers and placed it between her thighs. The holy of holies.

'If only he had not been my son,' he said.

'Yes.'

'Then my humiliation would not have been so great. Then this would have been just one incident among all the others.

'A son,' he reflected. 'One should be able to take him by the ears and lift him up from the ground and teach him.'

He spoke slowly, in a whisper, a gulf of silence between every link in the chain of his thoughts.

'But if he had not been my son, then that profound, almost

incomprehensible significance would have been missing – the Lord lifting me by my ears and teaching me.'

'What profound significance?' asked Bathsheba, understanding his words but not his meaning.

'The father who is lifted aside for the sake of his son. The father who goes into obscurity so that the son shall shine all the more brightly.'

'Absalom?'

'Yes. Perhaps Absalom.'

And he continued: 'The Lord has the father cast out for the sake of the son. It is the son in man that He wants to promote, the successor rather than the predecessor.'

And Bathsheba said: 'Do you really think that He has cast you out?'

'He has pushed me aside. As one lays aside a broken pot. As one puts away a bow when it has become too soft.'

And he went on: 'My sons repay my love with hatred. Perhaps it must be so. Perhaps it is right and fitting. If it were not so, there would be no balance in the world.'

'Love?' said Bathsheba.

Yes. Love.

'Do you know what love is?' she asked. She spoke quickly as if to disguise the burning seriousness in her question.

He was silent for a long time.

'Yes,' he said at last. 'I know.'

For it was true: now that his love was powerless, now that he could no longer unite a household or a people or build cities with its help, now he knew what love was.

And Bathsheba understood what he had meant to say: he knew as much as man always knows when he claims to have knowledge of something of which he is only dimly aware.

But she did not want to make him search for words for what he knew. His beard was tickling her throat; when he spoke, his breath wafted over her face – she had thought for some time that it was becoming increasingly like Mephibosheth's. His left hand lay heavy and limp against her groin, his stomach rested against her thighs and hips and waist.

No, instead of forcing him to struggle for words, she tried herself to express something of what ought to be said.

'To be side by side, neither above nor below.

'To put one's soul in one's hand without fear, and hold it out.

'To inflict this exquisite pain on one another unceasingly.

'Not to be able to do without.

'To give oneself up as Mephibosheth gave himself up to wine.'

His left leg had gone numb and stiff; he moved it laboriously and laid it across her thighs.

'Yes,' he said. 'That is the nature of the Lord.'

And she thought: My poor son David, he cannot express himself more clearly and simply than that. And she drew her knees together so that his heavy, and doubtless aching, leg would lie more gently and comfortably on her.

And softly and tentatively he repeated what she had said: 'Not to be able to do without.'

They were alone. Perhaps they had never before been so alone. They both felt as if at that very moment they were celebrating a holy festival together. It would have been a desecration to have seen them or heard them.

And they were both aware that their thoughts and discourse on love merged and blended with the stench of blood from the asses' skins.

He could not understand how he could ever have lived without Bathsheba. When he thought about his youth, that was what surprised him most: she had not been there. He freed his hand from hers and let it grope its way blindly over her body. If she had not been infertile he could have begotten a son with her.

'Bathsheba,' he said, and he prolonged the separate sounds in her name so that it sounded like a psalm, yes, like a song of praise in the tabernacle of the Lord.

And she waited a moment before asking her question:

223

'Whom would you have chosen? Whom would you have chosen if Absalom had not done this?'

And he knew that he had no choice, he could not bear to lose her, he could not allow himself to make the slightest movement of his lips which she might misunderstand. No price was too high: to be forced to do without her would be like being forced to do without the Lord.

'Solomon!' he cried. 'Your son Solomon!'

'Can you swear before God that you would choose Solomon?'

'Yes!' he said. 'Yes! Solomon!'

And he swore the oath, he held out his soul there in the darkness and promised that it was Solomon who was the Chosen One, Solomon and no other, his was the kingdom, the power and the glory. Had it not been for Absalom.

And just at that moment, just as he swore the oath, Bathsheba realized that they were not alone. A faint sound from the other side of the tent flap indicated that someone was standing there, someone who hardly dared breathe for excitement and compassion and involvement. She jerked herself free from the King, jumped up from the bed of folded cloaks and rushed out to see who the listener and intruder could be.

It was Shebaniah.

The young boy, Shebaniah. Before they left Jerusalem that morning she had seen the first white hairs in his beard.

'Shebaniah!' she cried. 'How long have you been standing there behind the tent flap?'

'I have been standing here the whole time!' said Shebaniah, his voice trembling with fervour and involvement. 'I heard it all!'

And she told him to make himself a bed in front of the tent. She wanted him once more to watch over her sleep.

When morning came, before any of the others had awakened, while the King was still sleeping as if not only the almond harvest but all time had come to an end, and the people were lying about on the ground hunched up as if in their mother's wombs, she took her bow and her arrows and went out to Shebaniah and woke him.

And she led him a little way to the north, to the edge of the brook. The sun would soon be rising over the top of the Mount of Olives.

'I have often wondered,' she said as they walked, 'what your name means, Shebaniah.'

'It does not mean anything.'

'Has it no meaning at all?'

'No. My father said to me, "You must yourself ensure that your name acquires a meaning. Your life and your actions will give your name its meaning."'

And she asked him, 'What do you know about the nature of involvement?'

He replied almost immediately, just as if he had been preparing himself all his life to answer this one question.

'Our very existence comes from involvement. By involving ourselves in the lives of others we create ourselves. Without involvement with others we would not exist.'

It was an answer Bathsheba had not expected. She had thought that he would immediately hear the threatening, even censorious tone of her question.

'First the Lord created human beings,' said Bathsheba. 'But from human beings He created the people. Just as he breathed His spirit into human beings, so He has breathed involvement into the people.'

And she continued: 'But even involvement has its limits. No one steps over those limits unpunished.'

Then Shebaniah suddenly understood what he had done, what transgression of involvement he had been guilty of. And he saw himself and his whole short life as a fluttering bird glimpsed in a shaft of sunlight between the trees, saw that he himself consisted of nothing but guilt and stolen property, that his life had been an unbroken chain of guilt, and he thought, this too is possible, involvement is as uncertain as the wind, involvement is the only thing there is, it besets me behind and before.

Bathsheba lifted her bow, she made him turn away from her, and she aimed just below the shoulder blade. That was the first and only time in her life that she used her bow to serious purpose. Thus she gave a meaning to his name: Shebaniah, the pierced.

She had expected the King to ask about Shebaniah when he awoke. But he did not.

No, that was strange: he asked about Solomon. And Solomon came to the tent and helped to comb his hair and smear him with oil and rub him clean. And all he said was, 'Yes, Solomon, you, too, are my son. Yes, you also are my seed.'

But in Jerusalem Ahithophel continued to press his advice on Absalom.

'Twelve thousand of your men are healthy: those that drank of the golden, honey-sweetened wine. Send them after the fleeing King now. He is dispirited and exhausted; his people will scatter. Before the evening the King could be slain and you can adorn your table with his head . . . yes, before the evening meal you could be holding the severed head in your hands!'

But the counsel Ahithophel had given him concerning the ten concubines had made Absalom cautious and suspicious. He also wanted to hear the advice of Hushai, the one who often saw God.

And Hushai exhorted caution. That was the way he always was. He wanted to pass on to others the caution with which he himself had been imbued since birth. 'Your father and his men are powerful in their wrath,' he said. 'They are like a bear robbed of her cubs. They are formidable warriors, they never rest, and will not let themselves be taken by surprise.'

And Absalom thought again of Ahithophel's abominable advice about the concubines. Ahithophel seemed inclined to exaggeration and rashness, not to say recklessness. Hushai on the other hand really pondered the difficulties, behind those closed eyelids of his.

And he decided to follow Hushai's advice: he would wait, he would summon all the men that could be found in what was now his kingdom, and then, in due time, he would meet David on the battlefield and destroy him.

But Ahithophel could not bear to have his counsel rejected. He invoked the name of the Lord and of Bathsheba. After all, she was his son's daughter. 'If only she were here!' he screamed, not realizing how objectionable and undesirable her presence had come to be for Absalom. He was beside himself with anger and resentment at Absalom's preference for Hushai's advice. Hushai raised his eyelid and scrutinized him sympathetically. He could see that Ahithophel's rage was divinely inspired, but nevertheless supported his King. 'Yes, bide your time, gather an army together, one that is mighty enough to annihilate all David's people. Do not let your heart rush you into anything.'

But when Ahithophel had calmed down again, he took his mule and rode home to Giloh. He forsook Absalom, he even cursed him; and when he arrived home he divided his inheritance among his sons and then hanged himself from a beam in front of his house altar. He hanged himself in the sight of the Lord. And Hushai spread the rumour that he had hanged himself by a loop of his own beard.

From Kidron, Bathsheba and David and Joab and Solomon and the people moved on across the Mount of Olives towards the Valley of the Jordan.

David no longer sat so hunched on his mule. From time to time he even exchanged words with those around them, simple words of comfort and encouragement, and when they met men and women standing with their heads bowed in sorrow at the side of their path, he raised his hands in greeting, signifying: This is merely an exodus. After the exodus there follows the return, yes, the resurrection.

And when others mocked and reviled him and scoffed at him because he was now dethroned, when some even threw stones at him and cast dust, he simply said, 'Let them alone, they know not what they do. It is the Lord speaking through their mouths. No one can be raised who has not first been humbled.'

On the eastern slopes of the Mount of Olives, on the road to

Jericho, they met Mephibosheth's servant Ziba with two asses, laden with bread, bottles of wine and bunches of raisins. And David asked where he was going.

'To Jerusalem,' Ziba replied. 'My lord Mephibosheth must have asses to ride on and wine to drink. He expects justice from King Absalom – after all, King Saul was his grandfather.'

And before Bathsheba could say a single word in Mephibosheth's defence, David decreed that all his property should be taken from him and given to his servants.

Yes, he was, in truth, on the way to recovery from his vacillation and despair.

They stopped at Mahanaim, by the River of Jabbok, where Jacob, the father of the people, had seen God's hosts of angels. There they were awaited.

Bathsheba had sent word to King Shobi in Rabbah – she had said she would never be able to forget the delightful city of Rabbah – and to Mephibosheth's stepfather Machir, the one who had taken pity on Mephibosheth before David had, and to Barzillai, the merchant who owned the whole of his native city of Rogelim – yes, he owned everything: the houses, the animals, the people. She had sent a message to them: King David and his household had need of food and tents and beds and wine, and also, in the longer term, men, men with swords and spears and bows.

That was all now ready and waiting for them at Mahanaim: bread and beans and honey and meat – Barzillai had had a flock of sheep driven there from Rogelim – and wine and butter and cheese, cheeses which surpassed the royal crown of the Ammonites in size. And men too: 1,000 men from Gilead, the region around Rogelim; 3,000 from the land of Ammon, 5,000 men from Mahanaim and the rest of the land of Gad; and men were streaming in the whole time from every direction. The city of Mahanaim could not hold them all. David and Joab made the majority of them set up camp at the ford where Jacob had wrestled with one of the sons of God and vanquished him, before their people had even existed.

After two days Joab was able to make a final count of his army: six full hands of thousands.

And the spirit of battle was awakened in David. He gave out orders and advice to the men, he inspected their weapons and garments, he had them practise with bow and sling and sword. Suddenly he was able to run again and perform dances with the javelin, and swing himself up on his mule with a single leap. The thought of going out to battle once more seemed to wipe out many of the years that normally weighed him down and bent him double. Wherever he went, Bathsheba and Solomon went with him. And he said to them: 'The spirit of God is with me again.'

But when the message came that Absalom and all his men had forgathered in the Wood of Ephraim, beyond the Jordan on the borders of the lands of Ammon and Moab, Bathsheba said to David: 'You are no longer a warrior. If only you could see yourself: your belly is too heavy, your arms have lost their flesh, your eyes have receded into your head, your shoulders have sunk towards your midriff.' She said this lovingly and yet with mockery, mockingly and yet with love. 'No, what you still have is the fact that you are chosen and holy, and that is what the battle is about, but it must not be put at risk in the battle.'

And she asked Joab and the people 'Should he really risk his life?'

'No, no! He must stay here in Mahanaim!'

And his mighty warriors said: 'If the battle goes against us, then he must be carried out of the city. Then he shall take the place of the ark, yes, the place of the Lord. Then he will be worth more than 10,000 men!'

So when the men marched out, Bathsheba and David and Solomon stood at the gate of the city. And to every captain and to every section of the army David said the same thing: 'Deal gently with my son Absalom, let him come to no harm. He has not fully understood what he has done – he is still a child.' And when the last man had gone by, when nobody could hear him any more, he shouted: 'For know that I love him!'

The battle lasted two days and one night. Twenty thousand men were slaughtered. The earth between the trees, mostly oak, tamarisk and terebinth trees, was covered in blood and men and mutilated bodies. The wood is no bigger than a good runner can run round between morning offering and the noon offering.

By the evening of the second day Absalom would see that he had lost too many men, that this was a battle that could be neither won nor lost. But he did not want to flee. No, he would not be a fugitive king as David had been. He decided to ride to Mahanaim and surrender himself to his father's mercy – yes, each could surrender himself to the other's mercy.

He turned his mule to the north, towards Ramoth, which was a city where the people of Gad let murderers go free. He had previously seen a well on that road, and his mule was thirsty. And he came to a rose thicket, a dense rose thicket beneath two oak trees, and he thought to himself: I shall cut my way through the thicket with my sword. But his mule took fright at the thorns and from his movements as he hacked around him with his sword, and it kicked violently with its back hooves and reared up.

Just then two of Joab's men arrived at the thicket, and they looked at one another, Absalom and the two men. Absalom sheathed his sword and tried to free the bow that was hanging over his shoulder. The quiver of arrows hung in front of him, and he could easily reach it with his left hand. But at that very moment a sharp rose thorn pricked the mule under the eye, and in a frenzy of fear it gave a jerk of its body which threw Absalom up into the boughs of one of the oak trees; his hair became entangled in the branches, the hair that weighed more when it was clipped than a new-born lamb, so that he was caught and left hanging between heaven and earth. And the mule ran off. He tried again to draw his sword – with his sword he could hack off the branches that held him fast, or his long thick hair – but he was not able to: his hanging and kicking took up all his strength. The bough bent under his weight so that the tips of his toes kept touching the ground and gave him the support he needed to prevent his neck from breaking. The two men observed him for a while, and then hurried off to Joab.

And Joab asked: 'Did you kill him?'

'No,' said the men. 'We did not kill him. The King said "Let Absalom not come to any harm, he is still only a child".'

But Joab said: 'A child! He has already lived a man's lifetime!'

And he rode out to the rose thicket and the oak tree where Absalom was hanging.

He was no longer struggling with his sword; he was not dead, but his body was weak with exhaustion. His face was scratched to pieces as if a raging woman had clawed him bloody with her nails. When he saw Joab he knew at once what was going to happen. He did not appeal for mercy – no, he did not have the strength to appeal for mercy. All he managed to force out from between his lacerated lips was this: 'What is the nature of the Lord?'

Joab did not reply at once. No one had ever put such a question to him. He thought Absalom was really asking him; he did not realize that Absalom just wanted to say to himself: Man's life is absurd. The Lord should never have created us!

No, Joab answered his question at last: 'The Lord is weighty,' he said. 'Our God is the weightiest in the whole universe. He weighs you down so that your neck will soon break. He is weight itself.'

For that was what Joab had seen of God: His weightiness. He had seen stones drop, men fall, walls collapse, asses and camels sink under enormous burdens, kingdoms come crashing down. Everything had been unremittingly cast down to the ground by the weight of God.

Absalom tried to force his face into a smile, but the cramp of exhaustion prevented him, and Joab thrust his spear through him three times and ordered the men who had followed him, ten young men who were always close to him, to cut him down and finish the slaughter.

Then Joab let trumpets be sounded so that all the people would hear that the battle was over. And he sent two runners with a message to King David: they were to tell him the truth – that his must be the victory, that he would doubtless again be king in Jerusalem, and that most of his enemies must be dead.

And he had Absalom buried beneath a great mound of stones there in the Wood of Ephraim. There is a grave of Absalom in the valley of Jehoshaphat, but that is not the one.

David saw the messenger running towards the city, but his sight was no longer sharp enough to discern individual features, and he asked: 'Who is it?'

The watchman standing beside him replied, 'He is running with his arms hanging low, leaning forward and stepping high. It is like the running of Ahimaaz, the son of the high priest.'

'He would not run so eagerly if he did not bear good tidings,' said the King.

And Ahimaaz threw himself down panting at the King's feet.

'Blessed be the Lord . . .' he puffed.

'Yes,' said David, 'blessed be the Lord.'

'Your God, who has delivered up . . .' Ahimaaz went on, 'the men who lifted . . . their weapons against you.'

And the King cried: 'Let us rejoice! Glory be to the Lord!'

Then he asked, 'Is my little son Absalom safe?'

'I saw a great gathering of people,' Ahimaaz panted. 'They

were collecting stones for a mound. What that signified, I do not know.'

At that moment the second messenger arrived, an Ethiopian, who was a weaker runner than Ahimaaz. And David asked him too: 'Is my boy Absalom safe?'

And the Ethiopian replied: 'May all your enemies go the same way as that young man, down to the realm of death!'

Then King David was afflicted with a weight of sorrow that surprised even himself. He faltered, but stayed upright with the support of Bathsheba's arm, and began to groan and lament like an abandoned child. 'Absalom, my son,' he wailed over and over again, 'Absalom, my little son, my son, my son Absalom, would God that I had died for you, why did I myself not meet death in your stead?' And Bathsheba and Solomon supported him and led him up the steps to the watchmen's room over the gate, and he did not cease from his weeping and lamentations until his eyes ran dry and his voice became hoarse and finally failed.

There was great confusion among the people. Some mourned with the King, others rejoiced with him. They found it hard to know how they should behave, some thinking that he had ordered there to be neither joy nor sorrow, others that he had commanded both. He had indeed cried out: 'Let us rejoice!' but had also bitterly lamented Absalom's death. The people's ultimate conclusion was that there was a free choice between mourning and jubilation, a state of freedom which for most of them was hard to bear, indeed almost intolerable.

But Bathsheba was with David in the watchman's room. She had a bed of sheepskin prepared for him and sent for wine and unleavened mourning bread of barley and raisins, and she burned spices to that the air was filled with the heavy aroma of mourning, and when he had fallen asleep, she instructed Solomon to watch over him. If he awoke and asked for her, he was to say that she had fallen asleep exhausted in the Captain's quarters behind the watchmen's room.

Then she went to Joab, and made him repeat three times his story of how Absalom had met his death. She wanted to know every word that had been spoken and every gesture made, and cried uncontrollably the whole time, beating herself repeatedly upon the hips. 'He was the only one!' she said. 'He was the only one! Oh, had I been there to answer his question about the Lord!' And Joab felt great emotion when he saw how deeply she shared the King's sorrow. But when she rushed at him with outstretched fingers and tore at his face and eyes with her nails he could understand her no longer. He grasped her round the wrists, and let her scream and weep until she was exhausted before letting go of her. But she did not beg his forgiveness; she seemed to think that nothing could have been more right and proper than if she had scratched his face raw and bloody and clawed out his eyes.

And she cut off a lock of her hair, which was now as much white as ebony, and sent it with one of the young men who followed Joab. It was to be buried in the cairn with Absalom.

Jonadab, the son of David's brother and friend to all, had also been killed in the Wood of Ephraim. His name was listed among all the others. Somebody had slain him and only discovered afterwards who he was. But nobody asked after him, nobody made an offering for his sake. No one asked on whose side he had been when he had fallen – perhaps he did not even know himself.

Joab went to the King; he sat and looked upon him as he slept, he looked at his wrinkled face, which even in sleep was expressionless and unfathomable. Joab stroked his hand over his own cheeks and forehead and was surprised to feel how smooth his own skin still was. The King is only five years older than I, he thought, but the carefree nature of war has preserved me from old age.

When the King finally awoke, he said to him: 'No, Bathsheba is not here.'

'Where is she?'

'She is preparing a grave offering for Absalom.'

'On my behalf too?'

'Yes, for you too.'

The King became calm again, and Joab continued: 'You have shamed this day the faces of all your servants, who this very day have saved your life and Bathsheba's and Solomon's and the lives of all your other sons and daughters – with the exception of Absalom – and the lives of your wives and concubines.'

'I am indifferent to them,' said David, without specifying which of them he meant.

'You seem to love your enemies and hate your friends,' said Joab. 'All we others are nothing to you, we are mere breaths of wind which you do not notice. We can see that if Absalom had lived and all we others were buried beneath the cairn it would have pleased you well.'

'Do you think that he coveted her?' said David, his voice uncertain, as if he would rather not have his question answered.

'Who?'

'Bathsheba.'

Joab thought long and hard now: he must provide an answer more cunning than true.

'Yes,' he said at last. 'He coveted her.'

David seemed to have expected that answer, indeed even wished for it. His face was calmer as he declared: 'I have never said what you assert.'

'If that is so,' Joab continued, 'if it is not your view that we are all useless and our actions vain, then you must arise from your bed, put your sorrow behind you and go out to the people and speak comfortingly to your servants. Otherwise not a single one will stay with you tonight!'

'Yes,' said David. 'I am coming.'

'If you do not come,' Joab added, 'then you must expect misfortune greater than all the evil that has befallen you from your youth till now.'

But although he followed Joab, he said to him, speaking with a

heavy sigh so that Joab could not doubt his seriousness, 'The
King is dead. Yes, the King is truly dead.'

But the people had already dispersed. Their perplexity had
driven them to return to their various tents.

Only when David had been waiting in his room above the city
gate of Mahanaim for three days did the representatives of all
the tribes of Israel come to him again, though no one came from
the tribe of Judah, the people who had followed Absalom. And
Bathsheba and Solomon and Barzillai, the merchant of Rogelim, stood by him the whole time, distributing gifts to the people,
cheeses and raisin cakes and copper jewellery, and they spoke in
the King's stead. He himself did nothing, except to sit there
silent and sombre, and perhaps even absent in his heart, just like
the Lord on the seat of mercy in Jerusalem.

'The King,' they said, 'saved us out of the hand of our
enemies. And now he has fled out of the land because of
Absalom. But Absalom, whom we anointed over us, is dead in
battle. He is buried beneath a mound of stones. Is it not time to
take the King back to his city?'

And they sent the priests with a message to the people of
Judah that one of their men, perhaps Amasa, who had led the
army under Absalom, could be commander of the army
instead of Joab if they were willing to swear allegiance to
David again as their king. Joab was now old, they said, and
should devote his remaining energy to his properties and his
wives.

And finally David spoke. 'Yes,' she said, 'Amasa shall be the
captain of my army. I will succeed Absalom, his captain shall be
my captain, and I will forsake Joab, the man who slew my
innocent little son.'

Then the tribe of Judah also entreated David to return to
Jerusalem. And as a gift of reconciliation they sent Bathsheba
Absalom's Assyrian horses and the two-wheeled carriage that
had been left in Jerusalem. Absalom had wanted to save the

237

carriage and the horses for the great coronation ceremony in the forecourt of the tabernacle of the Lord.

And so they went back to Jerusalem. Bathsheba's carriage went shamelessly, even presumptuously, in front. She herself declared that it was only appropriate and sensible, because the carriage and its four horses might come to harm in the throng behind the King. Beside her rode Solomon on a mule; in front of him on the saddle he had Shebaniah's lyre which his mother the Queen had given him. The King himself rode on the royal ass, the one anointed by Nathan as royal, which had borne him for more than twenty years through celebrations and mourning ceremonies and now, too, through this dethronement and renewed accession, this resurrection.

At the River Jordan they were met by a great multitude from the tribe of Judah, and by Mephibosheth. Nobody had shaved him or cut his hair or washed him since the day the King had departed, but nor had anyone given him wine to drink, nothing more than the cup of welcome for Absalom, and so he was able to sit upright in a palanquin between two asses. He let out ear-splitting cries of joy when he saw David coming. He thirsted for mercy as a wine-bibber for wine; he would die of thirst if he could not drink forgiveness from the King's hand. In truth, he explained, in truth David had been deceived by his servant, Ziba. At the time of David's meeting with Ziba on the road to Jericho, he himself had been in a dreadful and delightful sleep that had lasted three years. That sleep had been the reason he had stayed in Jerusalem. If he had only been awake he would have raised his sword in the King's defence. No, he had not been able to send messages or orders in any way. But he wanted to forget all this now – yes, he would forget everything, the properties he had lost and his wasted life, he would enter into a sleep of forgetfulness like a suckling child if only the King would return to his own table.

And David commanded that half of Mephibosheth's former

possessions should be returned to him. And he thought: Imaginary possessions.

Everywhere they passed, the people cheered them and greeted them with veneration and love. Many wept uncontrollably in their love. Those who had mocked them and thrown gravel and stones at them on their departure now strewed palm leaves in their path. And the servants asked the King: 'What shall we do with these people who at one moment mock and throw stones and curse you and at the next strew palm leaves and bless you and weep for love?' But King David just smiled that strangely tense, taut smile that nowadays almost always covered and distorted his features, and made dismissive gestures with his hands, which meant: They are merely carrying out their duties as the people: fickleness is God-given, that is the nature of the people breathed into them by the Lord. I call down God's mercy upon them, that is all.

In Jerusalem they were met by another of the King's sons who had decided to be the one who would reign after him: Adonijah, born, when David had reigned in Hebron, to Haggith, one of the ten concubines left behind. He had moved into Absalom's house and taken over his wives and daughters. Yes, he had taken over everything that Absalom had owned and had been and had done; he was the new Absalom, with the sole difference that he would bring everything to a successful conclusion.

Scribe: My house-god was waiting for me – no one had stolen him, no one had desecrated him. I have anointed him with oil, that is all. But he was waiting for me.

He is not divine. But he is holy.

The divine is the sphere of the Lord. The holy is that of mankind. I do not know.

It seems to me as if we made only a short journey to Mahanaim. And yet we have both lost and won a kingdom.

David seems no longer to notice the immense difference between losing and winning.

He is most frequently to be found in the tabernacle of the Lord. 'I am a priest in the manner of Melchizedek,' he says. Melchizedek was both priest and king here in Jerusalem before David came. Perhaps he was also the Lord Himself, I do not know. His name is one of the names of the Almighty: he is also called the King of Righteousness. The temple servants carry him; his palanquin is like the Ark of the Lord, and he sits beneath the wings of the cherubim. Yes, I am speaking of King David.

I have received emissaries from the Kings of Achmetha, Chittim and Salah. I have been given spices, ewes with lambs, and a palanquin borne by six servants.

I told the emissary from Achmetha that horses are the most beautiful things I know.

The King's son Adonijah has tried to do the same as Absalom. But poor Adonijah, he can never be more than a pale imitation. Absalom had holiness and strength, Adonijah only has his greed. Adonijah is as Mephibosheth would be if Mephibosheth thirsted for power.

Some of the priests and Joab gave him their support. The priests think that the King has involved himself too deeply in what should be priestly concerns. They want to keep the Lord for themselves. Joab wanted to become commander of the army again, and Adonijah had made him that promise.

Adonijah had himself proclaimed king at the fountain of Enrogel: he proclaimed himself king. What has come to pass is what shall come to pass. He had told his servants to ask my advice beforehand. And I had said, 'Yes, do what you please. All things stay as they are unless someone sets them in motion. Ultimately King David must decide who is the one who will reign after him. Go on out to Enrogel and proclaim yourself king. Then at least something will happen!

The fountain of Enrogel is situated where the King's orchards end in the Valley of Hinnom. That is where kings were crowned until David came here.

Before Joab and Adonijah went up to Enrogel, Joab slew Amasa, the Commander of the army. He slew him with his own sword. Amasa was going to fetch men from Judah to put down an uprising among the Benjaminites, as I had commanded. He was due back in Jerusalem within three days, but he tarried for four. Joab went to meet him, saying to David, 'Amasa has failed you.' And Joab embraced Amasa by simultaneously grasping his beard and slitting open his belly with his sword so that his intestines spilled out on to the ground. The cruelty of men to one another is incomprehensible. A short, sharp thrust slanting upwards from below.

And after Adonijah had sounded the trumpet, and after he had chosen himself and when he thought that he was king, I went to David. Nathan was with me. He has come back here; I summoned him for this very purpose. Nathan has said to me: 'Yes, you are the one who shall reign after him.'

And I went in to David and said: 'Do you still remember the

promise you made me that Solomon would be the one who would reign after you?'

'Yes.' said David. 'I remember.'

'Now, behold, Adonijah reigns,' I said. 'He has become king and you do not know.'

'I am the one who is king,' said David.

'Adonijah has sounded the trumpet and sent for all the King's sons. He has slain fat cattle and sheep for the coronation feast. The priests and Joab are with him.'

At that moment Nathan came in; he had been standing at the door. I had said to him, 'Come when I mention Joab's name.'

The King's face had darkened now. I said, 'Nathan the prophet is here.'

And David said, 'Nathan the prophet.'

'My lord, O King,' said Nathan, 'have you said Adonijah is the one who shall reign after you? Everywhere in the city I hear the cry "God save King Adonijah!" And at Enrogel there are preparations for a coronation feast to which neither I nor Bathsheba nor Solomon have been invited. Has this thing been done by you, my lord King?'

And David said, 'Call Bathsheba to me!'

And I said, 'I am still here.'

'I have promised and sworn you an oath,' he said. 'I remember it: it was a night filled with the terrible odour of blood, and we lay alone, overpowered by love, in a tent of asses' skins. I promised then that Solomon would be the one who would reign after me. It was the night you slew Shebaniah. I shall never forget it.'

'You knew that?' I exclaimed.

'How could I not know it?' he replied. 'You had no choice. He only had himself to blame, that young boy.'

'Shebaniah?' said Nathan. Nathan knew nothing.

'Yes,' I said. 'Shebaniah.'

'I believed then that all my promises were mere breaths of air,' said the King. 'I thought that I could make any promises at all. That was why I swore the oath.'

'Yes,' I said. 'I shall never forget it.'

'But the Lord took me in His arms and lifted me up again on to the throne. Thus He transformed all my breaths of air into tempests and my oaths into mountains.'

'Yes,' I said. 'Mountains.'

'And so Solomon is the one who shall reign after me, he shall sit upon my throne and he shall ride the royal mule, and Zadok the high priest and Nathan the prophet shall anoint him king over Israel.'

And we all said, 'Amen.'

And Solomon was anointed, and he rode on the King's mule, and the cry went up, 'God save King Solomon,' all over Jerusalem. The people piped with pipes and strewed palm leaves on his path. And Adonijah was in great fear – no, he was never even a show-king – and he rode at once to the tabernacle of the Lord and ran in to the altar and caught hold of the horns of the altar, for then no one could slay him.

And I said to Solomon, 'You have nothing to fear from him, let him go, promise him on your oath that you will not slay him.' And Solomon gave him his oath, and Adonijah went home in peace to his house, which was Absalom's house.

Now David sent for Solomon and told him which men he must have put to the sword. 'I shall soon go the way of all the earth,' he said to Solomon. 'Be strong, therefore, and show yourself a man. First and foremost Joab, who has wallowed in blood all his life – he slew Amasa, the Commander of the army, and he slew my beloved little son Absalom. Let not his hoary head go down to the grave in peace. Moreover, you must slay the men who mocked and cursed me when Absalom in his duplicity cast me from the throne, the ones who later blessed me and wept with love when I returned: make sure you bring down their hoary heads to the grave with blood.'

Solomon is to have all this carried out when the King is dead.

May the King have eternal life, may he soon die!

He has stopped having the great evening meals. Mephi-bosheth lies sunk in a deep sleep; if he wakes at any time there is always a servant ready with a cup of wine.

Since the King stopped having the evening meals, he has become thinner and thinner. He only eats a little of the sacrificial meat in the tabernacle of the Lord. He sucks on little pieces of the roasted meat. His limbs are shrinking, the bones in his body are projecting through the skin; even his stomach has shrunk, and he had lost his teeth.

Solomon practises on his lyre every day. King David likes to hear him play. King David can no longer sing, yet he does sing. His vocal cords, which resemble the horn on a sacrifical altar, used to vibrate before in a wondrous way when he sang. He was like a turtle-dove. Now they merely quiver and produce a strangely cracked, bleating sound. He gets smaller and smaller. Soon, scribe, you will no longer be able to capture him in your little signs.

Joab still wanders around in the house. He knows that he is doomed to die. He makes sacrifices every day in the tabernacle of the Lord. He feels the terrible weight of the Lord upon him. He has become stooped, his legs bent and stumbling; God has begun to press him down towards the earth. Now he knows the nature of God.

Joab gives me figs every day. He owns a fig orchard at the foot of Mount Carmel. He knows that I love figs above all other food. He brings them to me as if they were an offering that might benefit him in some way, early figs and autumn figs and fig cakes. It is figs that are making my body heavier and increasingly venerable.

The ten concubines who did not accompany us on our journey to Mahanaim, and with whom Absalom lay in holy madness, have been locked in the women's house on the King's orders. No one can come out or go in; food is put through a hole in the door for them. They are to live as widows, he says. I have said. They are mourning for Absalom.

244

Food is pushed through to them every day, but perhaps they are now all dead.

Sometimes the King asks: 'Where is Shaphan? I want him to play for me. Shaphan the little boy?'

Then Solomon goes in and plays for him, and the King says: 'Do not forget to practise, Shaphan! Music shall flow from your right hand like a blend of holy oil and the trilling of birds!'

Now King David was stricken with frost in his body, to his very bones. It was in the month of *zif*, when to everyone else the heat seemed unbearable. He could get no sleep; he became more and more like a solitary bird on a rooftop.

They covered him over with layer upon layer of sheepskins, skins that had been displayed before the face of the Lord, and yet still he shook and shivered incessantly from cold.

And wine, wine which had in Mephibosheth produced an over-abundance of warmth and sleep, he could not swallow – it merely trickled out from the corners of his mouth.

And Bathsheba said: 'Woman is the warmest of all God's creatures. Let us find him a woman who is in her warmest years.'

For this she knew: both kings and gods had been awakened to renewed life, had even arisen from the dead in the shimmering heat exuded by youth.

It was Abishag from Shunem they found. Solomon found her. He called her the Shunammite after the city where he found her. It was said of her that withered trees she touched bore fruit within ten days, and that infertile asses became pregnant at once if she slapped their hind quarters. It was for these reasons that Solomon asked to see her. Babylonian merchants thought her real name was Ishtar. She had once been taken out into the desert and red-blossomed oleanders had grown up in her footprints.

When Solomon saw her, he realized at once that she was the one who could cure the King. If the frost in his body could

246

withstand Abishag the Shunammite, then it was incurable. The sun had burned her dark brown: she had once been the guardian of a vineyard. Her teeth resembled a flock of newly-washed ewes, her hair was long and gleaming black, and her breasts were firm and pointed.

And Abishag from Shunem went to the King's bed. She crept in beneath the pile of sheepskins, and those who had stood nearest said they heard her whisper Tamar's name. When her fingers brushed against a fig cake that had been laid on one of the festering sores on the King's neck, there sprang forth from the cake a fig branch with magnificent leaves.

She remained there for twenty-eight days, the length of time she was clean.

But not once did he have carnal knowledge of her. No, when he felt her with his withered hands he could not even distinguish the parts of her body one from another. He no longer knew for sure what was breast and stomach and pudenda, and he no longer remembered how the various parts of the body were to be used – the frost had turned his fingers blind.

And when Abishag the Shunammite rose from the bed on the twenty-eighth day, King David had still not ceased shaking with cold. But the skin on the side of Abishag's body that had lain against the King had become wrinkled and dried up.

Then Bathsheba commanded them all to leave the King's room. And she took off her cloak and slipped into his bed.

Quite soon his trembling abated, the terrible iciness retreated from his body. She lay at his left side, and he pressed himself against her like a new-born lamb against a ewe: he nestled into her warmth as if he were a little babe.

As if this warmth were the one truly godly experience of his entire life.

She could feel how shrivelled he was: his knees and pelvic bones and elbows cut into her flesh as if they were deer antlers. She lifted his head carefully on to her arm, and she felt his breath on the lobe of her ear.

And for the first time in a very long while she heard his voice.

'Bathsheba,' he said.

'Yes,' she replied, very gently and carefully in order not to frighten him.

'Holiness no longer helps me,' he said, panting for breath.

'Has it ever helped you?' she asked.

'I do not know,' he said. And then, after a pause, 'What is holy?'

'The incomprehensible and the uncertain are all that is holy,' she said.

Then he asked – and he asked as if he had perhaps been mistaken all his life – 'How is uncertainty holy?'

'By the very fact that we know it exists,' she replied, 'and that we recognize that it is incomprehensible and uncertain.'

'I have always sought holiness in the Lord,' he said.

'Yes,' she said. 'And sometimes you have found it.'

Then he lay silent for a long time. He let himself be permeated by the incomprehensible warmth which she radiated.

But finally he asked – and his voice had now become such a low whisper that she could catch his words only with difficulty – he asked, as if groping for words and almost fearful that she would not have any answer: 'What is the nature of the Lord?'

And she answered at once from within her warmth and certainty, 'He is like me. He is exactly like me.'

She felt him relax in her arms: his legs and joints seemed to soften and his breathing became calm as if he were about to fall asleep.

But then she heard him quietly, almost inaudibly, repeating her words to himself, as if he were trying to interpret their mystery and to understand fully their unfathomable significance.

'He is like you,' he said. 'Yes, He is like you.'

And there was a distinct note of bliss in his almost soundless whisper.

Then they lay in silence together. She heard his breathing becoming weaker and slower. He sucked on a lock of her hair which she raised to his mouth with her right hand; from time to time his lips made a feeble supping sound like a sleepy babe at the breast.

But then, long after she thought him to be sleeping, when in fact she was already sure that he had fallen asleep for ever, he spoke, loud and clear, and she could feel the vibration of his throat against the skin of her shoulder, that tremor which she had so often seen and heard but never before felt: 'You are perfection, Bathsheba. Your perfection is your greatest flaw.'

Those were King David's last words.

King David was buried in Jerusalem. Bathsheba had his last words written down by the scribe. It was a psalm, one of the longest psalms he had ever composed, and the priests sang it in the tabernacle of the Lord.

David's son Solomon was now king. But he was still very young and had no desire to rule the kingdom. He sat every day with his builders and his scribes, constantly engaged in planning what he would do when he reached maturity and in old age.

Mephibosheth died too. He died only seven days after the King. There is a grave of Mephibosheth in Lo-Debar in Gilead, but that is not the one.

And Bathsheba ruled the kingdom for seven years. During her time the army was equipped with horses and chariots from Erech of Shinar: 4,000 horses.